ASLAN

ASLAN

RUNNING JOY

Kristin Kaldahl

CrossLink Publishing

CrossLink Publishing
1601 Mt. Rushmore Rd, STE 3288
Rapid City, SD 57701

Ordering Information:
Quantity sales. Special discounts are available on quantity purchases by corporations, associations, and others. For details, contact the "Special Sales Department" at the address above.

Aslan/Kaldahl —1st ed.

ISBN 978-1-63357-329-1

Library of Congress Control Number: 2020938493

First edition: 10 9 8 7 6 5 4 3 2 1

This is a work of fiction. Names, places, and events are either the product of the author's imagination or used in a fictitious manner. Any resemblance to actual persons, living or dead, or actual events is purely coincidental

Cover photos by Steve Bull, Sirius Photography

To my mom, who always believed.

Contents

Acknowledgments

Running Joy is inundated with firsts. It's my first book of any stripe, the first work of fiction I wrote as an adult, my first agented book, and my first published book. All those firsts point to one fact—I am a total noob to the publishing world. I had to learn it all, from soup to nuts, to get this book to print. Yet this education didn't happen in a vacuum. I had tons of help along the way, and I'd like to thank those who encouraged me, pointed me in right directions, critiqued my manuscript, shopped my book to publishers, and worked diligently to create the final product.

First, thanks to my beta readers Gayle McNish, Kathleen Snow, Caryn Hoang, Gail Storm, Joyce Kaldahl, and others for your honest and yet encouraging critiques that helped transform my reeking rough draft into something publishable. Bravery comes in many forms, and agreeing to read a new author's novel is one of them. I'd also like to thank my editors Robin Patchen, Jacquelyn Carberry, Lauren Smulski, and Heather Beck for your amazing talent and skill. I don't know how editors are able to give harsh critique and yet leave the author feeling upbeat about themselves, but you ladies have that ability in spades.

I would also like to thank my superhero agent, Stephanie Hansen of Metamorphosis Literary, for her dedication to *Running Joy*. I am so glad I signed with you, Stephanie!! This would not have happened without your drive and wisdom.

Of course, I would like to thank CrossLink Publishing and the kind Rick Bates for taking a chance on an unknown author and a tiny sheltie.

I want also to thank my encouragers: my mom, Joyce Kaldahl, who told me I could do anything; my brother Rev. Paul Kaldahl;

my sister-in-law who shares my name, Kristin Kaldahl; my aunt Mary Miller; my best friend, Danette Sharp; Erin Taylor Young, who gave me excellent advice when I needed it most; my agility students and friends, who are all well-loved; and my extended family. I am blessed with a large support system, and I appreciate each and every one of you!

And moving to my canine support system, I want to thank my dogs, current and past: Aslan, Aenon, Asher, Jericho, Laika, Razz, and Ruffis. Each one led me into new worlds in canine training and behavior and unselfishly offered their boundless love while doing so. What precious gifts they are. I'd especially like to thank Aslan, who walks beside me in spirit every day and never leaves my heart. I miss you, little man.

And most importantly, I thank God whose hand was in every step of this journey and all journeys I take, as always.

CHAPTER 1

Whickery Gone

May: Six Weeks Old

The butt end. The butt end was the last thing she would see of her beautiful, spirited Whickery. Why did that somehow feel like payback?

Krissy leaned against the dirty white post-and-rail fence, her thin arms resting on the top rail as Whickery's thick chestnut tail cleared the back of the horse trailer. Two dust-covered stable hands dressed in the usual cowboy hats and boots closed the trailer's door, locking away the mare and all the dreams she represented. One of the men slapped an open palm against the closed door—as if that somehow tested its integrity—and the two climbed into the cab of their battered baby-blue pickup. The engine sputtered to life, and the truck with its attached one-horse trailer crunched a dirge across the gravel drive as it pulled Whickery away from the stables.

Krissy's eyes burned. She blinked hard, refusing tears. No way would she show weakness in front of Mom. Besides, tears would be a distortion of the truth. She wouldn't be crying because Whickery had been sold. If tears came, they would come because deep inside—where even she didn't like to snoop around much—she was glad. And that felt very, very wrong.

The trailer turned west onto the highway and disappeared. And with that, Whickery was gone. There would be no more trips to the decaying stables at the edge of the suburbs. No more acting as if she enjoyed riding round and round the sandy, boring, and way-too-small horse arena. No more hot days grooming an animal weighing a thousand pounds.

No more pretending she wasn't afraid of her own horse.

Mom put her arm over Krissy's shoulders. "I'm sorry, honey. I know this is hard." Krissy pushed off the fence and stomped toward the car. Keys rattled as Mom hoisted her purse and followed.

After sliding into the passenger seat of the silver Avalon, Krissy slammed the door shut. Mom would figure her anger was prompted by grief over losing Whickery. That was okay. That made sense. But the truth? The truth festered in fear caused by her own abnormal and inescapable body.

Posture stiff, Mom lowered herself into the car and after starting it, drove away from the stables—for the last time. Krissy didn't look back. She knew what the rows of stalls with their peeling white paint and beautiful equine occupants looked like. It had seemed like a princess's castle when her parents took her there for the first time to meet her new horse. A year later, the stables had lost their royal luster. Now, she saw it for what it truly was—two rows of deteriorating horse stalls with a miniscule outdoor arena. She was glad to see the last of it.

After a couple minutes driving southeast on the Northwest Expressway, the suburbs of Oklahoma City began to crowd the scenery. Soon, they passed strip malls with familiar storefronts: Kohl's, Walmart, PetSmart, Target. These big-box stores were packed cheek to jowl beside multiple car dealerships, their latest models sparkling in the early summer sun.

Mom broke the tense silence. "We didn't want to do this. If I had my way, you'd still have her, but your dad and I agree with your doctor. If you fell off Whickery the wrong way, you could damage your new kidney. Then where would we be?"

Krissy stared out the passenger window, teeth clenched against suppressed anger—and guilt.

"I know owning a horse was your dream since you first rode Molly. How old were you?"

Krissy said nothing, wanting to forget the whole owning-a-horse thing had ever happened.

Mom answered for her. "Six, I think. I'm so very sorry this had to happen, but there's no other option."

It was a rare show of sympathy from Mom, but Krissy refused to respond. Sympathy from others had annoyed her more than anything else all through her dialysis treatments and subsequent kidney transplant. Why that enraged her so much, she couldn't say, but call her *brave* or a *trooper*, and she'd be gone—if not physically, then at least emotionally.

She fiddled with her seat belt, trying to get it to lie without pressure over her lower abdomen and the pink scar from her transplant surgery hidden beneath her shorts. As the car turned onto Rockwell Avenue, the old Warr Acres Cemetery appeared out of nowhere. Messing with her seat belt, Krissy almost missed it. She gasped a shallow, hasty breath just before reaching the first corner of the graveyard.

Her eyes widened as the car in front of them slowed for no apparent reason. An irrational dread gripped her; she hadn't inhaled enough air to make it to the cemetery entrance at this speed. Moments later her lungs began to burn. She fought against the desire to push on the Avalon's dash in a useless attempt to make the traffic move faster so the car could reach the cemetery's entrance. Only then could she release the small gulp of air and take a deep, refreshing breath.

Krissy's face was hot and her cheeks puffed out as they finally crept by the gates. Gasping as if surfacing from a dive, she filled her lungs with the car's chilled air. Judging the distance to the end of the cemetery, she did a quick accounting of the car's speed and her oxygen inventory and determined that this time she could make it on one breath.

Years ago, her father had taught her this game. "Everyone, take a deep breath," he'd say as they approached a graveyard in the family car. Krissy and her older brother, Peter, would gasp in air. The rules were firm: you held your breath until you passed the cemetery, with one exception—you could breathe at any entrance. This entrance rule meant it was usually a breeze to make it past most graveyards, unless you forgot and didn't get a lungful of air before you reached its border. The consequences of the game were, however, harsh. If you breathed anywhere alongside a cemetery other than the entrances, you'd be the next person buried there.

It was a pretty gruesome game to play with little kids, and at fourteen she should be too old for such superstition. Yet, with her history, what if? If a person could cheat death, shouldn't they try? Determined, she held her breath to the border of the cemetery where Mom, used to the game and ignoring Krissy's gasps, changed lanes and passed the loitering car that had caused all the breathing drama in the first place. Exhaling, Krissy left the dead behind.

The uncomfortable silence with Mom, who'd surrendered to Krissy's lack of communication, continued until the car rolled into the driveway of their home, a two-story red-brick colonial. The garage door opener began its grinding work, and the summer sun disappeared as the comparative dark of their clean multi-car garage swallowed the Avalon.

Krissy closed the car door and sulked into the house, making a beeline for the fridge. The kitchen's cheery yellow-and-cranberry wallpaper clashed brutally with her vicious mood. Peter sat at the granite-topped kitchen table, wrapping overgrip tape around the handle of his tennis racket. He glanced up at Mom, who walked in behind Krissy, and their brief visual exchange must have tipped him off because he went straight back to work without saying a word. This nonverbal communication heightened Krissy's temper as she yanked a Diet Coke from the fridge and turned her back on her family and the irksome kitchen. She marched through the dining room, wheeled toward the staircase, and climbed to the bedrooms above.

After reaching her room, she slammed her door, creating a loud, satisfying crack. The Diet Coke whispered its familiar hiss as she opened it, and, leaning against the door, she looked around.

Hers was the smallest room in the house. Decorated in a puerile purple she'd chosen as a seven-year-old, it felt dated and held many of the usual trappings of a kid—a dresser, a nightstand, a bed that was made up only because it was a requirement for her weekly allowance, and a desk crowned with an old computer. In the corner stood a painted bookshelf filled not with books, but with her Breyer model horse collection. The glossy plastic representations of equine perfection were frozen in various poses. She'd spent hours as a child playing with those miniature toy horses, dreaming of the intense and special bond she might someday develop with a real horse.

She'd been so naive—even stupid. Because of those delusions, Whickery had been sold. A living, breathing animal had been in her care, and she'd failed her.

Krissy pulled her eyes away from the Breyer collection and tried to avoid glancing at the multiple horse posters tacked over the purple-striped wallpaper. After placing the bottle of Diet Coke on the nightstand, she threw herself on her bed and rolled to give her back to the bedroom horses.

In this position, she faced the small corner devoted to her other passion. Well, her *only* passion, now that horses weren't her thing. She propped her head on her elbow and examined the magazine and computer-printed photos of collies and shelties. The collies stood tall and regal with their long flowing coats, but the shelties ran, flying over white jumps and weaving through white poles.

Horses and dogs. It had always been horses and dogs.

Unable to look anywhere in her room where one or the other wasn't staring accusations at her, she lay back on her pillow and shut her eyes. Whickery appeared in her mind, the trailer's door locking her away. Krissy opened her eyes, banishing the image. She closed her eyes once more, fighting to recall a happier memory. For a moment, she relaxed as she daydreamed about the pond near Grandma's house on a warm summer's day.

Suddenly, the pond was gone, and Whickery's left front hoof weighed heavily in her right hand, while her left held a metal hoof pick. In agonizing slow motion, the sharp pick carved through the accumulated debris pressed into the hoof. It crunched as it ground its way, and she smelled the sour manure, mud, and keratin released from the hoof's crevice. Her mind screamed in horror as the pick hung up on a small piece of gravel and slipped. It plowed into her right wrist, half an inch below the artery just beneath her skin that had been surgically lifted for dialysis.

Krissy's eyes snapped open, her stomach lurching. Although safe in her bed, she clutched her right wrist with her left hand. With her left palm, she could feel the buzzing rhythm of the right wrist's artery racing. She hadn't realized she'd been breathing hard until that comforting beat, which proved all was well with the vein, calmed her, and her panting breaths slowed.

That day in the barn seven months ago had been petrifying. The surgically raised artery in her wrist was called a *fistula*. Before her transplant, nurses had inserted needles into the large veins created by the fistula to pull her blood into a dialysis machine, which filtered toxins from her blood, taking the place of her failed kidneys. Injure the fistula badly enough, and she could have ruptured the artery and bled to death. Even a lesser injury could have prevented her from being hooked to the dialysis machine, meaning more procedures, more needles, and more pain. A lot more pain.

After the pick had slipped, she'd dropped Whickery's hoof and pressed her right wrist against her ear to listen for the healthy whooshing sound of the blood in the fistula. Except for the cold wind whipping through the barn's corridor, silence reigned.

Leaving Whickery tied, she'd frantically run to the tack room, closed the door to block the wind's obscuring howl, and raised her wrist to her ear to try to hear again. Unaccustomed tears sprang to her eyes, and panic raised bile to her throat. For several seconds, there was no sound. Shifting her wrist back and forth by her ear, she tried to find the vital *whoosh*. Then, a faint, rhythmic rushing sound vibrated in the hush. At that point, adrenaline had sent her heartbeat racing, making the *whoosh, whoosh, whoosh* gallop. She'd inhaled deep breaths, trying to control both her heartrate and her tears.

For ten minutes, she'd sat alone in the dark tack room, left hand on her wrist, making sure the steady vibration remained and examining the fistula's scar for any signs of bruising or injury.

She'd survived, but the whole thing had rocked her. And the truth she'd been denying began to scream. She was afraid. Afraid of Whickery's size, of her hooves, of being crushed, of hurting herself, of losing her fistula, of more pain. More hospitals. More dialysis.

Now, as she lay in the bed holding her wrist in memory, a shiver ran along her spine.

Her tongue stuck to the roof of her tacky mouth. She reached for the pop and took a few gulps. Rolling to her right side, Krissy placed her wrist under the pillow and listened to the soothing *whoosh, whoosh, whoosh*. Eyes closed to the room filled with horses and dogs, her heartbeat relaxed, and the Diet Coke leaned precariously in the loosened grip of her left hand. Minutes later, she slept.

She dreamed of maddened horses being herded by snarling shelties.

CHAPTER 2

Lonely Hearts

June: Nine Weeks Old

A bright yellow tennis ball blurred toward Krissy's head. She staggered to the left and swung at the neon missile. Her racket gave a muffled thud as she connected, and the ball wobbled across the net for a tepid bounce on the other side of the court. Krissy's best friend, Violet, sprinted to intercept the languid arc of the ball. With a feminine grunt, she smacked it back into Krissy's side of the court.

Angling toward the far corner, it landed inbounds. Krissy's brain yelled for her to run, but her body responded with two tottering half-hops. Both hands gripped the racket as she swatted with wild hope at the passing ball, but she missed by a foot. Her eyes narrowed at the fleeing ball, and she pursed her lips. She hated the way her body betrayed her.

"Sorry!" Violet yelled, a heavy Central-Oklahoman drawl shading her words. "I didn't mean for that to go in the corner."

Sympathy. Krissy's fingernails bit into her racket's handle. She tried to keep anger out of her voice, but it sounded sharp regardless. "Hey. No. It's how the game is played. Don't make it easier for me."

With a slight frown, Violet pushed a few strands of damp hair away from her creased forehead, and she turned towards a lanky German shepherd lounging under the shade of the half-wall running along the west side of the court. "Heidi, fetch." Violet pointed at the now-motionless ball nestled in a pile of leaves by the fence line. The dog stood and loped across the court with graceful strides. Like any good ball girl, she picked up the yellow ball and returned it, along with a bit of slobber, to Violet.

Dribbling the ball a few times, Violet tested its ability to bounce after the wet retrieve before lifting her racket to prepare for her next serve.

"Wait. That was the win," Krissy called. "It was forty-fifteen. You took that point and the game."

"Good. I need a break." Violet's arms went limp, and she trudged to join Heidi, who'd returned to rest in the shade offered by the half-wall. Krissy walked to her gym bag and grabbed her water bottle before plopping down next to the dog. Guzzling cool water, she watched the air distortions caused by waves of heat shimmering off the concrete court.

"I'm finished." Violet leaned her head against the wall. "It's too hot."

They'd played only three games, but Krissy's legs were leaden, and sweat rolled down her spine. Even ball girl Heidi lay panting, looking with disinterest at something rustling in a tree on the far side of the court.

Violet's arm rested like a wet noodle across the big dog's back. While her brother's name was listed as owner on the one-year-old German shepherd's registration papers, the dog's heart belonged to Violet. Heidi was the girl's constant companion, and together they made a stunning pair. Violet's flawless fair skin and shoulder-length honey-blond hair created a beautiful contrast to the shepherd's black and dark brown tones.

A quick stab of jealousy twisted Krissy's stomach, and she forced it down. After letting Whickery go, she'd lost her right to have a human/animal bond like Violet and Heidi shared. Plus, Violet had been her best friend since first grade and had stuck with her all throughout Krissy's illness. If anyone deserved a dog's loyalty, it was equally loyal Violet.

"Yeah. I'm beginning to think this wasn't such a hot idea." Krissy grinned at her unintended pun. "It must be ninety-five degrees out here. We should head home."

In spite of her own suggestion, Krissy didn't move. Home lay a half-mile away—an interminable distance to walk in this heat. She was wiping sweat from her face with the sleeve of her T-shirt when Violet sat upright, staring in the direction of the parking lot next to the lone tennis court.

"I think that's Peter's car." She grabbed her gear and rose off the ground and into the sun. Sweat stung Krissy's eyes, causing her to squint at the familiar bright red Mustang pulling into a tree-shaded parking space. Her sixteen-year-old brother had gotten his license almost a year ago, and a few months later, his 'Tang. The car was his prized possession, and—in his own vernacular—he treated it "like a high-class woman," as if he knew anything about high-class women.

Before Krissy could gather her stuff, Violet had clipped on Heidi's leash and headed toward the lot, a newfound vigor in her stride. Krissy slogged behind. As usual, Grove Park—called Beer Can Alley by the local kids—was deserted. A small pocket park with a playground, a tennis court, and a tree-covered, sticker-in-fested hill, few people knew of its existence hidden in the middle of a subdivision, making the court a good place to play tennis in private. Krissy liked tennis but hated it when people could see her play.

The Mustang's engine purred as the girls approached, and the tinted front window lowered to reveal Krissy's brother sitting in the driver's seat, his tanned left arm resting on the steering wheel. With a shy smile, Violet took a step toward the car to peer inside. All of Krissy's friends thought Peter was movie-star handsome. Some girls at school had nicknamed him "Superman," because they thought he resembled the superhero with his thick dark-brown hair, angular face, and strong chin. She'd even had two or three girls befriend her with the singular intention of getting closer to him, but since friends were a rare commodity, she didn't care how she acquired them, and riding her brother's popularity coattails worked as well as any other method.

"Hey, Violet," said a smooth male voice from farther in the car. "Do y'all have the court?" Lowering her head a tad, Krissy could see Evan smirking within the car's dark, cool interior. Violet's shy smile turned to a grin.

Another good-looking sixteen-year-old, Evan was Peter's best friend. As he bent forward to see past Peter, the torrent of air from the car's AC vents mussed his long blond hair, giving him an alluring boyish quality. Drawn in by his charm, Krissy edged closer. As she did, she caught her reflection in the closed tinted rear window and breathed an inaudible gasp. She turned her head and took a hasty step to the side, making her image disappear.

Violet shifted her weight to one leg and leaned closer. "We're done," she said, looking past Peter to Evan. Her grin never faded, and her accent thickened. "It's really hot. We're thinking of heading home." As she said this, she reached in and maneuvered the driver's louvered vent to blow cool air on her face.

"It's not that hot," Evan said, exiting the car. "You two should stay, so we can play doubles. Peter and Lil' Sis against you and me."

Krissy's eyes went wide. No way could she play in front of Evan. Ever. She'd die of embarrassment.

"I'm not playing doubles with Krissy. That wouldn't even be fair." Peter shut off the engine. "I need serious singles practice for tryouts."

The car's air no longer blowing, Violet straightened as Evan sauntered over to lean on the car near Krissy. "You'd have the opportunity to protect a full doubles court with her as a partner. It'd be much harder than singles play." His tone changed to baby talk. "And how could you not want to play with Lil' Baby Sis?"

His hand darted toward Krissy's face, and he pinched her round cheek.

"Ow. Quit that." She slapped his hand away and rubbed her cheek, which burned with humiliation.

Evan dug in his shorts pocket and pulled out a cigarette and lighter. With a mocking grin, he continued the baby talk. "Oochie, koochie. Your cheeks are so round and babyish lately. I just want to pinch them."

"Leave her alone." Peter opened the door, causing Violet to take a few steps back. "And I'm not playing doubles."

Evan lit the cigarette, took a deep drag, and exhaled an immature smoke stream. Eyeing Violet, he said, "Stay and watch us play."

Her grin widened. "That'd be fun, but I think we'll head home. Heidi's getting hot." Her soft, shy voice held something Krissy struggled to interpret. A tantalizing coyness, perhaps? Since her kidneys had failed, Krissy had most definitely lost a step or twenty when it came to guys. She'd been so focused on staying alive, she hadn't noticed her friends had moved beyond the "eww-it's-a-boy" stage to this just-shy-of-seductive flirtation.

Evan glanced at the German shepherd, then snorted and reached toward Krissy's face again. She ducked the pinch and backed away, scowling. "Leave me alone!"

"I'm just teasing." He winked at Violet.

"Knock it off, Evan," Peter said, opening the car's trunk to grab his racket.

"I hope y'all make the tennis team." Violet still spoke in that soft tone seeded with a tinge of—something. She joined Krissy, who'd retreated from Evan's menacing fingers. "It's real hot out, though. Don't overheat."

"Too late for that." Evan's eyebrows lifted to emphasize his smarmy joke.

Scrunching her face like she'd smelled something rotten, Krissy turned and walked across the asphalt, headed toward home. She'd received her kidney four months earlier, and the transplant meds had changed her face from thin to round. The new fullness made her cheeks look pudgy, although the rest of her was skinny. Evan was right. She did look like a baby.

Pushing her sweaty dishwater-blond hair away from her face, she frowned and glanced back at him. He leaned against the Mustang, staring at Violet, half of his mouth turned up in a bad-boy sneer—like a Nordic Elvis.

* * *

Fifteen minutes later, Violet and Krissy inched along Thirty-fifth Street, passing an endless succession of 1960s-era ranch-style homes fronted by matching Bermuda grass yards and the occasional tree or flower bed. The summer sun beat on their shoulders and reflected off the light gray road.

"How are you doing after having to sell Whickery and all? I'm so bummed about that." Tucking her racket under one arm, Violet tipped some water from her bottle into her cupped palm and rubbed it on her bare arms. "She was such a cool horse. I'm gonna miss riding her."

"It's no biggie. I'm doing fine. I'm adjusting." This was true in one way, and not in another. When would the guilty ache over rehoming Whickery go away?

A comfortable silence fell, grown out of years of friendship.

The water bottle dangling from Krissy's fingertips swung with each step. A few swallows remained, but it'd be lukewarm, if not hot, at this point. Even so, water of any temperature would offer a bit of relief from the heat. She contemplated which would bring more comfort—drinking it or having it evaporate on her sweat-slicked skin. She glanced back. Poor Heidi's tongue lolled out of her mouth as she trailed behind, claws scraping the concrete with each dragging step. Good thing they'd turned the corner for home.

"You should get a dog." Violet broke the quiet.

Krissy cocked her head. "That came out of the blue. Why?"

"Ruffis is a great dog, but your parents got him before you were born. He's too old to go on walks like this with us anymore. Plus, he's not all yours. Since you lost Whickery, you should get one of those little collies you have on your wall. What are they called?"

"Shelties. Shetland sheepdogs. But I don't think I should be jumping from one animal to another. The horse thing wasn't so successful in the end." Krissy rubbed the back of her sweaty neck as guilt gripped her gut once more. Even Violet didn't know of her secret relief over the sale of her horse. Krissy hoped Whickery was comfortable in her new home.

Another silence fell between them, amplifying the sound of Heidi's scuffing nails. Krissy did love shelties. They were "drivey," medium-sized herding dogs with energy to spare. Beautiful with their long patrician noses, almond-shaped eyes, tipped furry ears, and long coats, they resembled rough collies in miniature, although they were their own breed.

"You could train it to do that obstacle course thing. You know, the one where the dogs run with their owners and go over jumps, through tubes, and on those ramps?"

"Agility?" Krissy asked. "Yeah, maybe. You've got to be an athlete to do that, though."

While researching the breed, Krissy had come across videos of shelties competing in agility, and she'd shown a few to Violet. Shelties, with their innate speed and intelligence, excelled at the demanding sport. When her dreams of competing in horse events had disintegrated, she had instead imagined running a sheltie on an agility course. But each time she thought of it, her stomach soured. It was the same kind of dream she'd envisioned with a horse—and look where that had gotten her. She couldn't let herself fall into that trap again.

"True that," Violet agreed. "But you could bring the pup on walks like we do with Heidi. We could go hiking and stuff." Her expression turned mischievous as she added, "Now's the time to do it. Your parents are all sad you had to sell Whickery, so they'll probably be much more willing to get you a dog to replace her. If you wait, you know they'll start getting firm on the no-dog-but-Ruffis thing again."

"You may be right."

Krissy stared into the middle distance. She'd bombed as a horse owner. Could she do better with a dog? What if she failed again? Yet, this might be her only chance to get her own puppy. Her only chance to try agility. Could someone like her even do agility?

She frowned at Heidi. "I'll think about it," she said.

* * *

He circled the blue roller, crouched, sniffed. It didn't move. The smell of the lady wafted from it, but mixed with her odor, he detected animal. A low, fierce growl rumbled in his chest. His muscles bunched in anticipation. It remained motionless—frozen in fear. But for how long?

Concerned his opportunity for victory might be slipping away, he bellowed his savage war cry and attacked, surging forward in a rush of violence and fury. His jaws closed on it, and it squeaked in terror. Its death wail drew the attention of his fellow warriors, who came near, sensing the kill. One of them, his gray-furred sister, mistook him for the enemy in her dash to join the battle and bit him on the ear. He yelped in pain, causing him to drop the tiny ball-enemy, and he spun to pounce on his gray sister. The blue ball rolled on the floor of the puppy exercise pen, forgotten.

Gray Sister fled, running around the edges of the wire, tripping over scattered toys and Shy Sister. His eyes locked on her gray-and-white tail, and, mouth wide, he lunged to seize the waggling appendage. Just as he reached the spot where the tail had been, two hands lifted Gray Sister to freedom, and his jaws snapped air.

Halting, he gazed up. The lady had pulled Gray Sister from the pen as two humans—a male and a female—entered the room. He'd never seen them before, but that didn't matter. He'd seen this scenario. He yipped, calling to Gray Sister. The female human took her from the hands of the lady, and, holding Sister at arm's length, sang high-pitched noises at her. Sister wagged her unbloodied tail in response.

This was bad. Very bad. He yipped again.

The male human heard him and came over. Brows furrowed, the man stared at him and Shy Sister, the only two left in the wire enclosure. Shy Sister took several steps back, tail down. The human reached in and plucked her up, too.

No! Not both. His yip turned into a short howl. No one, not even his siblings, seemed to hear.

Moments passed while the humans babbled in singsong voices at his sisters, and the word *puppy* was said over and over. He knew that word. When the lady said it, he and his brother and sisters had always come running. It usually meant food, play, toys, pets, or other good things, but this time, the word scared him.

It was happening again. His sister with the funny-colored eyes had been picked up by strange humans and taken away. His brown brother had been stolen by strange humans, too. Now, two more strangers held his remaining siblings, and fear clawed at his heart. What if they took both of his sisters? What if he was left alone?

He nosed the air, hoping to catch the reassuring scent of his mother. A whiff of her odor touched his nostrils, but it was faint and old. She wasn't nearby to comfort him with her warm body and creamy milk. He yipped.

The male set Shy Sister back in the enclosure. She appeared unharmed. He marched to the edge of the pen and glared up at the human who'd taken Shy Sister. The man knelt by the pen, pointed a finger at him, said something, and frowned. The female human holding Gray Sister glanced his way, wrinkled her nose, and shook her head. Her gaze returned to Gray Sister, and the woman smiled.

That settled it. Gray Sister would never return to the puppy pen.

Soon, the strangers rose, and, carrying Sister, left the room. He cried and yipped as she went, but no one noticed. Shy Sister slunk up and sat next to him, head bowed.

It was just them now. None of the thieving strangers had ever picked him up and made singsong noises at him. Shy Sister, though—she'd been sung to several times. What if more strangers came, sang, and took her away, too?

The thought made his chest hurt, and he wailed.

CHAPTER 3

Road Trip

July: Twelve Weeks Old

S oft classical music from the car radio played in Krissy's one ear while a large raucous crowd cheered in her other. In the backseat gripping Mom's phone, Krissy watched a video of a man and his dog celebrating the end of their run at the Agility World Championships. She glanced up from the screen to see trees whizzing by as their car headed south on Interstate 35. About thirty minutes before, they'd driven through the Arbuckle Mountains, so they had to be nearing Ardmore and Lake Murray.

She pulled out the earplug. "How much longer?" she asked yet again.

Dad's voice remained steady. "We're almost to the exit."

After returning the plug to her ear, Krissy searched for another agility video.

It'd taken her a few weeks to muster the courage to ask her parents about getting a puppy, not because she was afraid they'd say no, but because she wasn't sure she deserved another animal. As Violet had predicted, her parents had agreed to a sheltie puppy, most likely from the guilt they felt over having to sell Whickery.

After that, she'd given her whole heart to the quest to find the right sheltie. Websites, articles, blogs, forums, social media—she'd researched them all. She'd learned how to find a reputable breeder, what to look for in a sheltie, and what to look for in a performance pup, and she'd discovered a breeder with a performance sheltie for sale right here in Oklahoma.

But now, in excitement and dread, she tapped her foot in a staccato rhythm on the car's floor.

The video of the agility competition she'd just watched should have been enough of a warning. The handlers were so fast. They'd dart to a jump, slide, bend over, and throw their arms out to cue the dog. Then they'd spin and tear off at breakneck speed in the opposite direction. They were incredible athletes.

She was not. Her battle with kidney disease and the complications of dialysis had left her young body broken. While she could do a weird sort of trotty thing, she could no longer run full-out. Her bones just refused to move when her brain said to go.

Yet, here she was, once again, dreaming. Dreaming and wanting something beyond her physical and emotional abilities, asking her parents to support her even though she doubted herself. She'd talked her parents into getting Whickery and wound up terrified of the big animal. While a little sheltie wouldn't hurt her, could she train and handle it? What if she got a beautiful agility puppy and ruined it with poor training, or worse, become so afraid of failure that she did nothing, leaving the pup to waste its potential by sleeping its days away on the living room floor? She wasn't athletic enough for the sport of dog agility. It was insane for her to get a puppy bred for performance aspirations. She was going to let another animal down, not to mention her parents, her friends.

Herself.

Krissy tossed the phone aside, letting it bounce on the backseat.

In the front seat, Mom closed the book she'd been reading. "Well this is exciting. We're getting a new family member!"

Krissy's parents were in their early forties. Mom, thin and always dressed like she was headed to a society ladies' luncheon, had gone gray young but was now light brown with red highlights. Dad, on the other hand, was proof that opposites attract. Although lanky—almost scrawny, really—as a young man, age had caught up with him. A paunch hung past his belt, and his light-brown hair had somewhat receded. He cared nothing about his appearance, and on weekends came downstairs with such eye-poppingly mismatched clothes that Mom would order him straight back upstairs to change. During the week, she laid his suits out for him, afraid to leave him to his own fashion choices. "A doctor should look like a doctor, not a circus clown," she'd say.

"What's the breeder's first name again?" Mom asked.

"Linda," Dad answered as Krissy opened her mouth to reply. "We were lucky to find this little fella. She's been holding him back as a performance prospect, hoping someone wanting to compete in dog sports would find him. She said she was about to sell him as a regular pet because she couldn't find the right performance home for him."

"I hope he's pretty," Mom said, "and doesn't pee in the house."

Of course, all pups peed in the house before they were properly trained, but Krissy didn't say this. No one was more house-proud than Mom, and if Krissy pointed out the obvious, this puppy trip might end puppyless.

Dad's Ford Edge exited the interstate and turned east toward Lake Murray and the community of homes surrounding it.

He navigated the tree-lined road, heading farther east and a bit north until they turned onto a longish drive leading to a modest two-level Cape Cod in need of a fresh coat of paint. The lake lay to the east through the trees, but it held no interest for Krissy. She was captivated by the occupants of the large fenced yard bordering the drive. There, more shelties than she could count barked and ran along the fence parallel to the car as it rolled to a stop in front of the house.

As she got out, she searched for a young pup among the loud pack, but there were only adults. Flashes of sable, black, tan, blue, and white blurred as the dogs cavorted and barked with a mixture of excitement and alarm.

"You must be the Johnsons!" A voice behind them yelled to be heard over the barking shelties.

Krissy turned. A tall bosomy woman in her fifties with short toffee-brown hair held the home's front door open in greeting. "Ignore them. They love to welcome everyone. I'm Linda, owner of Lynndeson Shelties. The pup you're interested in is inside. Those are several of his aunts, uncles, cousins, in-laws, and outlaws." She smiled and waved for them to enter.

They huddled in the home's cramped entryway before Linda ushered them into the larger open-concept kitchen and living room. An empty puppy play pen sat forlornly in one corner. Tan ceramic tile covered all the visible floors, including the adjoining den and a hall leading to the bedrooms. Good choice. Carpet would be a disaster with teeny, piddling puppies running around. The place didn't have that old pet-pee stink, either, which was a positive sign.

Linda motioned for them to sit on a well-used brown suede sofa as she went into the den. A rattle of what must have been the door to a metal wire dog crate caused Krissy's heart to pound, and butterflies beat a discordant rhythm in her stomach. She might be about to meet her new puppy—a fluffy, beautiful, fifteen-year commitment of love. She reviewed her recent research in her mind. When looking for a potential performance prospect, you wanted an active, fearless pup. The pup should be eager to seek out new people and places, playful, and bold.

Bold. That summed it up.

Krissy held her breath as a tiny brown puppy walked through the doorway into the living area. Her pounding heart jumped into her throat and promptly turned to stone before plummeting to her belly.

There, blinking watery, unfocused eyes, stood the ugliest sheltie puppy ever.

"Here he is." Linda followed the pup into the room, a proud smile on her round face. "Feel free to get on the floor, play with him, pet him. I'm here to answer any questions you may have."

Krissy slipped off the sofa and sat cross-legged on the hard tile. She was numb. And she wasn't the only Johnson who was surprised.

"Is this a sheltie?" Mom asked.

Linda's tone changed from cheery to politely defensive. "Yes. His mom and dad are here on site. I told your husband you could meet them today."

"He's just so...petite." Mom hesitated. "And he seems maybe a bit less furry than the picture I saw of him."

"This is the exact same dog in the photo I sent," Linda said. "He's a small sheltie puppy, which is often quite valued by agility competitors, and he's in excellent health, a beautiful boy."

Krissy clapped her hands and called to the pup in a high-pitched voice. He hadn't moved since entering the room and glanced from person to person, perhaps confused over the escalating, sharp discussion. Drawn to the higher, playful voice, he wobbled over to her, and she scooped him onto her lap.

No doubt, he looked little like the sheltie pups in the pictures she'd seen online. Her research had uncovered breeder websites with photo after photo of adorable, fluffy sheltie puppies. And if she closed one eye and squinted, there might be a resemblance between the photo the breeder had sent and this pup, but it was hard to reckon that image with the dog sitting motionless in her lap.

"He just woke from a nap, so he's a bit sleepy," Linda said. "Most of the time, he's tearing around here with the other shelties."

The pup was homely. His thin coat was a dull, tannish, splotchy brown. His bloated belly made him look obese, yet stick-thin legs poked out from his round body. He sort of resembled a long-nosed, tiny spotted pig on stilts. His ears tipped at their ends as a sheltie's should, but they lacked the surrounding cloud of hair that was normal to the breed, making them appear bare and large. He gazed up at her with big round brown eyes. Sheltie eyes were supposed to be almond-shaped.

To make matters worse, this pup was mellow. He just sat in her lap. Not active. Not playful.

Not bold.

Gritting her teeth, Krissy squelched a strong desire to run. This was all wrong.

"Hi there," she said, forcing a warm tone. The puppy stared at her without interest and then waddled away, sniffing the floor.

This was disastrous. He was not the potential performance dog she'd envisioned at all. "Is he always this quiet?" She almost whispered the question, afraid to further insult the breeder.

"No. Usually he's bounding around here. Like I said, he just woke from a nap." Linda frowned at the pup.

Krissy's parents sat side by side on the sofa, looking almost as bewildered as she felt.

Dad bent forward, eyes narrowing as he watched the puppy. "What makes him a performance prospect?"

"Well, he's the most outgoing of the litter—climbing over things, the first one to check out a noise, a new person, or a new toy. I just knew he'd be the perfect fit for a performance home."

"I know some of his littermates have found homes, but have you sold all of them?" Krissy asked, hoping there were other puppy options.

"We had two litters at the same time. All found pet homes, except this guy. I wanted someone who would do obedience or agility with him. I try to have all of my pups placed by ten weeks, but I've been holding on to this guy, waiting for the right owner."

Krissy looked at her parents' faces. Dad wore a bemused expression as he stared at the pup, who sniffed the legs of the kitchen table with indifference. Mom glanced around the room, clutching her purse as if she were about to bolt.

A sudden fear gripped Krissy. She could see her parents were less than impressed with the pup. She'd shared some of her research with them, and they knew they were seeking a bold, confident, outgoing puppy. This guy was, well, milquetoast. And kind of a fat brown-spotted milquetoast at that.

But maybe if she got a dog that was milquetoast, nobody would expect success. If she failed, if the puppy never did agility, it might not be her fault.

Krissy swallowed hard. Ignoring her instincts and all her research, she said, in a voice much more pleading and desiring than she felt, "Can I have him?"

* * *

An hour later, Krissy squatted on a curb at the edge of a McDonald's parking lot. The new pup sniffed dirt in the gutter with disinterest.

This had been a mistake.

Mom weaved through the cars, a coffee in her hand, and sat on the curb next to her.

"Dad'll be out with the food in a minute." She watched the puppy. "He's a cutie, isn't he?"

Krissy nodded. Was it a lie to nod? Was he so ugly that he could, in some sort of weirdly opposite way, be considered cute?

In her best take-charge tone, Mom said, "He's your responsibility now, Krissy. I mean it. You have to do the potty training, the feeding, the grooming, the playing, and everything else. Dad and I didn't get him to be a family dog. He's your dog, and you'd better not shirk your duty."

"I won't," Krissy said. "We've gone over this a million times."

"He isn't exactly what I had in mind when you described what a performance puppy should act like. It's only a few miles back to the breeder's house. We can return him, if you're not sure."

Krissy wanted to nod. She wanted to say she'd made yet another mistake, but how could she admit that? She'd begged for a horse and failed, and now she'd begged for the wrong puppy. Yet, what if this was her one chance? She couldn't return him. "I think he's tired," she said, cringing inside. Was that a lie, too? How would she know?

"He's your only shot at this agility stuff," Mom said. "We aren't getting another puppy if he doesn't work out."

"He'll be fine."

"I hope so. He's a nice dog. He deserves a home that suits his personality." Mom looked up as Dad walked toward them with two bags of hamburgers and fries. "You have a deal with us. You keep your part by being responsible for him, and we'll pay for his needs. Understand?"

Krissy nodded.

"Dinner's served." Dad waved one bag-laden hand toward the car.

Food. Krissy wouldn't be able to eat a bite.

CHAPTER 4

Art, Angst, and an Anteater

July: Fourteen Weeks Old

T he petite sheltie pup was surrounded. A rainbow-colored bone made of knotted rope. A bright-orange vinyl squeaky ball. A small stuffed squirrel. A red rubber ring covered with little nubs designed to clean puppy teeth. Krissy squeezed her hands into fists in hopeful expectation as the pup nosed the fluffy gray squirrel, but rather than pick it up to play, he meandered away from the toys. His tiny, buff-colored head dipped into the lush grass as he roamed without purpose, sniffing the dirt. She unclenched her hands, and her shoulders sagged.

The back door banged as Peter came into the yard. The pup raised his head at the noise but wasn't startled. Holding his ground, he watched with detached interest as Peter plopped next to Krissy on the tattered quilt spread across the soft turf and crossed his legs.

"Any name yet for the runt nobody wanted?" he asked.

"Nothing's screaming at me," she said. "I can't find something that fits. And, while he was the last in his litter to find a home, we don't know it was because nobody wanted him. And he's not a runt."

"How about Pig? Or Twig for those scrawny legs? Or Puny? Runt?" Peter grinned at his ridiculous suggestions. "Maybe Toad?

That works because he'll probably grow up to be handsome. You know, like the ugly toad that got kissed by the princess and then turned into a beautiful swan?"

She shut her eyes to think. Peter was always mixing metaphors. Sometimes he came up with hilarious mistakes, but more often than not, it just hurt her head as she tried to sort the missing metaphor pieces. "Which is it? Ugly duckling turned swan, or toad turned prince?"

"Either one, though ugly duckling works. He's fine-boned and bird-brained. You could call him Duck."

Krissy snorted. "He needs a real name, not a joke. A name that fits him."

"Those names all fit him. They're perfect fits, in fact."

Krissy glared at him. "He needs a name that will point to his future. To the grand dog he'll grow up to be."

"He's just an animal."

She knew Peter didn't mean that. He loved dogs. Over a year ago, when her kidneys failed and she had to be hospitalized, Peter had been home alone for days while their parents looked after her. During that time, Ruffis, the family's collie, had gotten sick. Deathly sick. He couldn't walk and was unable to eat or drink. Their parents didn't have the time to take him to the vet, so Peter had somehow balanced the big dog on his bike and pedaled the mile to the animal hospital. There, the vet discovered the cause of Ruffis's dizziness—a tick had embedded itself deep within the collie's ear. The vet removed the tick, and Ruffis recovered. He might've died if Peter hadn't taken him in.

A month or so later, at a family meeting at the dialysis unit, the social worker had invited Peter to attend a support group for siblings of kids with kidney disease. "Sometimes, the brothers and sisters of children on dialysis feel isolated," she'd said. "The parents get busy with the sick child, and the other children can feel shoved aside. We have a support group for siblings, if you'd like, Peter. You might find you're not as alone as you think."

Peter had declined, saying he never felt lonely. Then he'd smiled and added, "Ruffis is always there."

Krissy hated how her kidney failure had affected everyone. Things were so different now. She rubbed her hands over her face as if she could scrub her memories clean.

Peter watched the little pup sniff and nibble a fallen leaf. The puppy's fur was so thin that his skin showed through the mottled brown coat. "Why don't you name him Spot? Shelties aren't supposed to have spots, are they? I've never seen a spotted one."

"He's a sable merle," she said. "The merle is a gene that takes the sable color and mottles it up. It gives his coat brown and tan splotches. They're like spots, but cooler."

She hoped she'd made it sound like being sable merle was a special thing. In fact, according to his breeder, sable merles were snubbed in the confirmation ring because their brown tones tended to have a washed-out quality instead of the desired richer sable hues of other shelties. Krissy could see that muted coloring in her pup's coat, which had an overall mousy brown look in spite of some cocoa-tinted spots.

"Spot." Peter said it with finality. "I'm gonna call him Spot."

The pup waddled within an arm's length of Peter, who reached out to pet his chubby body. Stiffening, the pup allowed Peter to scratch him behind the ears without cowering, yet it was obvious he wasn't enjoying the touch.

"He acts like he's doing me a big favor to let me pet him. Like he's saying, 'Okay. I know you want to pet me, so you can. But I don't like it.' He's like a piggy prince holding out his ring to be kissed. 'You may kiss the royal hand. It annoys me, but I deign permission because I know you want to.'"

Krissy smiled. Watching the pup interact with Peter, she had to agree. The dog did have the look of snobbish royalty allowing his lessers to bend and grovel at his feet.

"I've changed my mind," he said. "I'm gonna call him Prince. The name game is done."

Krissy mimicked a snooty, royal accent. "But I so abhor the name Prince."

"*Abhor*?" Peter laughed. "You've either inherited Mom's wicked vocabulary, or you have read too many of those old-fashioned books. *Abhor*?"

He stood, his grin not fading. "Be good, Prince," he said. "You're an odd little guy, but you'll need a bit of oddness to be Krissy's dog."

Peter headed back to the house. As he opened the door to go inside, the family's old collie, Ruffis, slipped into the backyard. Krissy crawled forward and gathered the pup, who had wandered several feet away, onto the old quilt.

In appearance, Ruffis was the pup's opposite. Large for a collie, he had a thick, gorgeous coat the color of ripe wheat. A wide white ring of long fur wreathed his neck and flowed down his chest, becoming short on his lightly feathered forelegs. White also graced his rear legs like anklets and tipped his long, plumed tail. A soft summer breeze made his coat ripple like the field of wheat it resembled.

He was majestic.

Except for his nose. His long, tapered nose, covered with short golden hairs, hooked down unnaturally at the tip, causing his top jaw to bend and his lower jaw to jut forward in a pronounced, unappealing underbite. It looked like an anteater's head on a collie's body.

At eleven years old, white sprinkled his malformed muzzle, and arthritic joints made his gait rigid. However, his eyes remained clear and overflowed with love whenever he gazed at his humans.

All his life, Ruffis had reigned as king over the large, manicured backyard with its stockade fence and mature trees defending the creek in the back. When he was young, he'd been given the choice to stay outside at night or come into the house, which was warm or cool, depending on the season. He'd chosen to remain outside, where he'd prowl his dark yard, protecting his family. After he'd made it obvious he didn't want to spend his nights inside, Mom had bought him an insulated dog house. Even that luxury he'd ignored in favor of his starlight rounds.

This protective nature had been exacerbated by the arrival of the diminutive pup. When Krissy had first introduced him to Ruffis, the old collie looked questioningly at her, lifted his lip at the intruder—showing a few old tarnished teeth—and walked away in disgust. She'd never seen Ruffis lift his lip at anyone, so she hovered over the pup whenever the big dog came around, just in case.

Throwing the sheltie the stink eye, the collie stepped stiff-legged in a wide arc around the little menace on the quilt.

The pup crawled into Krissy's lap and curled into a tight ball. She frowned at him. When she'd studied what to look for in a performance dog, all of the articles and blogs said the puppy should be active, playful, full of life, and have a desire—or drive—to play with toys. So far, her pup was a slug. He played little, with or without toys, and often wore a studious expression, as if he were researching the world to write a scientific paper on his discoveries. If he were a human, he'd be a lonely professor, maybe like Mr. Chips in the old movie *Goodbye, Mr. Chips.*

"Chips." She said it aloud, sounding out the potential name. No. It wasn't right for a high-drive agility dog.

She pushed him out of her lap, determined to get the pup's real personality—the one with drive, athleticism, and love of life—activated through yet another attempt at a rousing game of tug. Holding the rope toy by one tousled end, she shook the other end in his face, making cheery and what she hoped were playful comments.

"Get it, boy. Puppy, puppy, puppy. Come on, you can grab it. Let's tug like agility dogs are supposed to. Puppy, puppy, puppy."

He stared with cross-eyed annoyance at the toy shaking in his face. Like a maniacal bird, she chirped in high-pitched tones until he turned his back on her and waddled over to re-sniff the half-chewed leaf.

Ruffis had finished his first sentry round in the yard and stood like a statue on the patio. He raised his malformed nose and scented the breeze. His ears pricked, and with a start, he tore along the lengthy north stockade fence to the far back of the yard. The pup, drawn by the older dog's sudden motion, scampered after the collie. Krissy, wanting to keep the pup nearby, jumped up and gave chase.

Although only three and a half months old, the pup's bird legs stretched forward, eating ground as he pulled away from her. Her brain screamed to her legs for more speed, faster rhythm. Instead, she hobbled in a weird trot, and after a few seconds, stopped.

How on earth could she ever do agility if her baby pup was already so much faster than she was? She'd never be able to run. Dialysis had made sure of that. Granted, her transplant worked great, and it was heaven to be free of dialysis. The doctors had pronounced her fit as a fiddle for now, and she looked fine when she walked. But when she attempted to run, things just wouldn't work.

And that, they said, couldn't be fixed.

The videos of the handlers at the agility World Championships flashed in her mind—athletes spinning and sprinting at full speed.

Her chest constricted, making it painful to fill her lungs. She wanted to run with her dog like that. The teams looked so amazing, like ballet with a dog. Like art. She longed to be one of the painters out there on the agility course, showing the skill, the bond, the beauty of a clean run.

Standing there, watching her pup chase the older collie, she fought back tears. She didn't want to settle for second best, for second choices all her life. She didn't want to settle for broken and slow and sick. She wanted to be fast and healthy and normal. She wanted to believe she could have that someday. And perhaps, somehow, like the athletes in the YouTube videos, she could create art on an agility course, too.

The pup neared the back fence and slowed. As usual, his nose fell into the grass, sniffing. Her head fell, too. "If wishes were horses, then beggars would ride."

Krissy dropped the toy in her hand and returned to the quilt. After flopping down, she rolled onto her back and stared at the cloudless blue sky. The sun dipped lower in the west. Soon Mom would call her in for dinner. Conversation around the table would turn to the new pup, and she'd have to say how wonderful he was, how great he was going to be at agility. Once again, she would put on a mask and pretend to her family that all was wonderful when it came to an animal in her care. Shifting to one side, she squinted at her puppy, who had returned to tasting grass near the quilt, and shut her eyes.

* * *

The pup stared at a tiny black ant climbing over a clod of soil between the blades of grass. Although its pace was slow, the ant's motion transfixed him. He tracked the bug, mesmerized, before glancing up at the great golden collie prowling by the fence bordering the large backyard. It was so quiet here compared to his real home. There were many dogs at his real home. All were furry like the collie, but they were smaller and barked a lot. And they smelled like family—moist fur, musky, familiar. The giant collie had a musky odor, too, but he also smelled of non-family scents, like that sudsy shampoo stuff and his humans.

The pup had tried to play with the old dog, but each time he neared, the collie raised his lip and made a low growl. The pup had learned what that noise meant at his real home. One of the old shelties had once been chewing a stick, enjoying its bark and pulp. Wondering if it was as tasty as it appeared, he'd approached to investigate. The older dog had lifted his top lip and made a similar low rumble. He'd never heard that sound coming from another dog, so unaware of the warning, he'd continued to bound up to the older dog. When he was close to the stick, the old dog lunged toward him and nipped his shoulder. Fearing for his life, he'd turned and run away, yipping. He didn't stop his flight until he realized the older dog hadn't given chase and had returned to chew his stick with contentment.

It was a good lesson. At this place that wasn't home, the old collie also snarled and growled when he got too close. He never pushed that boundary, not wanting a repeat nip from this larger, scarier creature.

Sitting on his haunches, he studied the collie and the sleeping girl-human. His stomach made growling noises similar to the collie's snarl, but he knew these noises only meant he was hungry. He loved food. Almost all food. He ached for his mother's warm, creamy milk and his siblings' squeaks of delight as they sucked her full nipples to get the sweet meal. He missed his mother. She'd smelled of milk and that musky family odor all the dogs at home had.

The grand collie walked toward the back door to the house, giving him a long, hard stare. He lowered his eyes in an instinctual gesture of submission as the collie passed.

On the ground, the ant struggled through the grass. Not wanting the collie to hear and thus know his weakness, he whispered an almost inaudible whine to the oblivious ant. He desperately, deeply longed for home.

CHAPTER 5

The First Step

July: Fifteen Weeks Old

K rissy held the pup close as she entered the dog training school. Several metal chairs formed a circle in a large open room, a few taken by humans who grasped leashes attached to puppies. She'd expected the scene to be serene and peaceful—cute puppies with big expressive eyes sitting straight and unmoving next to their owners. This, though, was chaos. The pups lunged on the ends of their leashes and barked at each other as they strained to ambush their new, furry classmates. The owners issued unheeded commands in rapid succession, all at the same time: "No! Come here! Heel. Sit. Sit. No! Sit." The resulting mayhem created a scene more like a cafeteria food fight—minus the food—than an obedience class.

A heavyset woman with bushy, gray-streaked black hair and wearing a roomy purple T-shirt stood in the center of the circle of chairs, talking to one of the other dog owners, who tried to listen while simultaneously keeping her tan cocker spaniel pup from peeing on the leg of a nearby chair. Dad gave Krissy's shoulder a gentle push, guiding her farther into the large training room of Positive Pup Dog Training School.

It had been the "positive" part of the school's name that prompted Krissy to ask her parents to enroll her new pup in class here. From what she'd read, agility dogs needed to be trained using positive methods, which meant the dog learned by getting rewarded for good behavior instead of punished for bad behavior. She wasn't sure how that worked, but lots of online articles had said agility dogs trained with positive methods ran faster and in general did better than those trained with punishment.

A blogger and agility instructor from Maine had put it this way: "Agility is a game. It's a game of speed. If a dog is asked to play a game where she is punished for each mistake, she will slow down to ensure a minimum of errors and thus avoid the associated punishment. This negates agility's purpose—fun and speed." It kind of made sense, so Krissy had researched each training school in the Oklahoma City area, making a list of those that employed positive methods. Then she narrowed the list to those nearby. Now, here she was with her pup, starting their first training class on their way to the agility ring. Well, maybe to the ring. Probably not, in fact, but at least it would look like she'd tried.

Positive Pup was located in a run-down strip mall with a crumbling parking lot and a bare, rusty pole—the sole survivor of a sign that had once advertised the mall's shops. Once inside the school, the feel of delayed maintenance continued with a water-stained ceiling and chipped, age-yellowed linoleum tiles on the floor.

It didn't feel positive at all.

Krissy chose a chair in the nearest corner of the room next to some leashes displayed for sale. She sat, grasping the pup. Dad pulled a chair out of the circle and set it next to two metal dog crates by the door, one empty and one occupied by a beautiful red-merle Australian shepherd. With a snap, he opened a newspaper and hid behind it, the signal clear.

She was on her own.

A black-and-tan wire-haired terrier mix puppy stormed through the door, pulling on its leash and dragging in a disheveled middle-aged man. With a look around the room, Krissy sized up the other pups in her class. Aside from the tan cocker and the terrier mix, there was a golden retriever puppy with big floppy ears and curious eyes who romped in circles. What looked to be an Akita mix with a thick reddish coat played tug with his own leash, ignoring the scolding of his owner, a thin, older woman. A teeny-tiny, cream-hued Chihuahua puppy cowered behind her owner's legs, her color blending with the tile floor as a large bouncing ball of blond fluff surged on her leash trying to reach the scared Chihuahua. Was the mop of hair a bearded collie? The fluffball's owner, a heavyset man with curly salt-and-pepper black hair and a sheen of moisture glistening on his round face, gave a hearty laugh at his pup's inept attempts to pounce on the teensy dog.

The door swung open again, sending a small clump of black dog hair floating across the floor on a gust of warm evening air. This time, a thin, athletic young woman walked in followed by a stubby gray short-haired hound mix with long Snoopy ears.

"You must be Krissy." She jumped at the words and turned to see the woman in the purple shirt, who wore a small smile, sit in a neighboring chair. The woman's soft voice twanged with a heavy, non-Okie, southern-belle accent. "I have only one teenager enrolled in this class, so I'm assuming that'll be you. I'm Shelly, your instructor."

"Um. Yes. I'm Krissy, and this is my puppy." Krissy stared at a crack in a floor tile to avoid eye contact. She hated eye contact.

"Welcome, Krissy, and . . .What's your pup's name?"

Heat flushed Krissy's face. She supposed all the other puppies had names. What if a name was a requirement for taking puppy class? She'd owned him for three weeks, and he'd already learned to come running whenever Mom called, "Come, Puny Puppy!" Her family's creative joke names had worsened in the absence of a real one.

"I haven't named him yet," Krissy said. "Right now, we're calling him Puny Puppy, except for my brother, who calls him

Prince. I don't like either name, though." She wiggled one sneak-ered foot and stared at the small nameless wonder in her arms.

"Naming a new dog is important," Shelly said. "You want to give him a name he can grow into, not a silly one. For instance, I had one student who named her puppy *Stupid*. The name led the owner into a mindset that her dog was dumb. He wasn't, but calling her dog *Stupid* all the time made her think so. Choose a good, solid name, but do choose soon. Tonight, we'll be teaching our puppies to respond to us when their names are called. You can use *Puppy* for now."

Shelly continued, her tone instructive yet full of southern hos-pitality, "Also, I see you've been holding your pup since you got here. With small dogs like yours, owners tend to carry them ev-erywhere. But he's a dog, not a doll. Unless there's a good reason to carry him, keep him on the ground. It'll build his confidence. Make him feel like a big dog."

Shelly patted Krissy on the shoulder and left to meet the other newcomers. Krissy placed her little sheltie on the ground, and he waddled over to sniff a poof of white fur under the empty chair next to them. He was brave, exploring the new environment. She, on the other hand, wanted to find a large fur poof to hide under.

Taking the brave cue from him, she lifted her eyes and glanced around the room. As far as she could tell, no one had heard the instructor's reprimand, and that was good. But two mistakes? This wasn't the start she'd hoped for. Her pup had no name—a necessity for one of tonight's lessons—and she wasn't supposed to carry him.

Shelly moved to the middle of the circle. "Welcome, every-one, to puppy class! I'm Shelly, your instructor. Tonight, we're going to begin your training journey with your new puppies. It looks like we have some wonderful dogs here. Let's go around the room and introduce yourselves. Tell me your dog's name and age and what you hope to get out of puppy class."

* * *

Near the end of class as Krissy watched the puppies play, she couldn't help but grin. They were the cutest clowns ever. Shelly had said that puppy playtime riled the pups up, keeping them from focusing, so playtime was the last activity of the night.

The pups cavorted and pranced around the room, all except for the beardie named Honey. She didn't just cavort—she'd bolt across the room and then screech to a halt, which caused her to slide on the linoleum and slam into a wall or a chair, or, in one case, some hapless human's legs. After regaining her large hairy paws under her, she'd tear off in the other direction. Honey repeated this slide, slam, and run game over and over. In contrast, Puny Puppy sniffed the terrier-mix and then trotted a few steps more to sniff a human's shoe. He'd played for a second with the cocker, though. That had to be a good sign.

So far, class hadn't gone as Krissy had hoped. Trying to get the pup to focus on her instead of the activity in the room had been difficult, but the hardest part was how far behind they were. Almost all of the other puppies already knew how to sit on command. Tonight, she and Puny Puppy had trained sit for the first time. He did it, sort of, but only when lured with a treat.

And when it came to the Name Game lesson, she'd been a total failure. Not having a name made the whole exercise useless. Calling him Puppy and then pressing a clicker the moment he looked into her eyes was dumb. Not the clicker part, but the *Puppy* part. Why train him to respond to a name he would never have?

Her pup had done well with loose-leash walking, but only high-drive dogs struggled with that. Her pup never left her side while they'd walked in circles around the room. With independent drive so necessary for agility, excelling at this behavior seemed more like a negative than a positive.

At least loading the clicker was something they could do. It taught the pup that the click-click sound made by the small hand-held device meant he'd get a treat. "The idea is to teach the puppy that the click equals a treat," Shelly had said. "Then, whenever the dog does the behavior you're asking for, you click at just the right time, and the pup knows, 'That's what Mom wants me to do, and a treat is coming!' This is not voodoo. It's science. It's proven learning theory."

Shelly had demonstrated the clicker with her red-merle Aussie, Cally. Cally *rocked*. Her intense focus and her immediate and happy responses to Shelly's commands were flawless. Krissy couldn't take her eyes off them as the two worked together as a team. Yet, they were more than a team. They worked as one, not two, and definitely not two different species.

The rectangular clicker in Krissy's pocket pressed against her right hip as she watched the pups play. The big fluff ball that was Honey the beardie had all of the pups corralled in a corner of the room while she barked and bounced back and forth to keep her charges locked in place.

Shelly said, "This is a good example of herding behavior. Honey is already displaying a great talent for herding." With care, she took Honey aside for a moment to let the other pups escape. Let loose, Honey again ran and slid into objects, a huge puppy grin on her face.

Honey's owner, Mike, guffawed. She careened off one owner's legs and turned in an out-of-control gallop, straight for the runty sheltie. Before Krissy could react, the beardie's sturdy body slammed into the smaller pup, throwing Puny Puppy to the floor.

Her heart leaped at the collision, and she stepped forward to lift him to safety.

"He's fine." Shelly held out her hand, stopping Krissy. "Leave him be." She was right. The sheltie pup rose and trotted over to inspect a dark spot on the floor—probably a dirt clod. For the rest of the play period, he spent most of his time nosing the other pups, although he did play chase for a few seconds once or twice.

Shelly called a halt to playtime, and the owners attempted to get their charges under control. As the class had yet to learn the come command, the pups were almost impossible to gather, and, of course, Honey ran pell-mell around the room well after all of the other pups were back on lead.

Once Honey had been cornered—literally—by three people, Shelly released the class. "That's a wrap. You all did amazingly well tonight. See you next week."

Krissy sat for a moment as her pup watched the other students gather their things. It'd been only the first class, and there was so much to train. Good thing it was summer, but where would she find the time when school started?

Start. That was the word. It was a start. They'd taken the first step down Training Puny Puppy Lane. Only God knew how far this road would go. It might go for miles—or one block.

* * *

Krissy watched as the street lights of the city blurred past. The pup slept in her lap in the back seat of the Edge. She blinked, forcing her dry eyes to stay open. Puny Puppy hadn't been the star of class. Other than Shelly's encouragement, there had been no compliments on their training at all. People had said things to her like "he's so cute" or "oh, he's so tiny," but they were just being nice because she was the youngest. In all honesty, there were no other compliments to offer.

Smoothing the pup's fur, she revisited her list of potential names for him. They were written in a spiral notebook at home, but she had them memorized. Levi, because it sounded cool; Sirius, after the dog star; Titan, because he wasn't. Even the old-fashioned Fido, which was short for fidelity, was on the list. Fidelity was a good characteristic for a pup, and Puny Puppy had showed great loyalty by staying with her during the loose-leash walking exercise. Then again, it may have been fear keeping him by her legs.

Head wobbling with exhaustion, the pup leaned against her stomach, and his liquid brown eyes, much too large for a sheltie's, gazed into hers.

Aslan.

The name crashed into her from nowhere. Aslan, the lion in C. S. Lewis's *Narnia* series. Giant, honorable, and fierce, Aslan was the Christ figure, the Lion of Judah.

The little guy sitting in her lap lacked any resemblance to a lion except in his buff color. His minute size, bird-like legs, and thin coat raged against the name.

It wasn't a fit. Not at all.

So why was it so perfect?

"I've got his name!" Sounding triumphant, she leaned toward Dad in the front seat. "I'm gonna call him *Aslan*."

CHAPTER 6

Sunk

August: Eighteen Weeks Old

A slan's nose told him he'd smelled them before, but this one looked nothing like the others he'd seen in the big yard. He took a hesitant step forward, stretching his neck to get closer to the squirming brown stick that wasn't at all like a stick. He sniffed again. Yep. It was another one of those worms he'd found all sun-dried and dead on the patio. He'd nibbled one once and had immediately spat it out. It had tasted of dirt, which, while not a bad flavor, didn't seem like food. This one, all moist and slimy, smelled a bit more appetizing.

The girl stabbed it with a metal wire, and the worm wriggled in protest. The wire was tied to a thin, almost invisible rope, which was attached to a big stick with something he didn't understand on the bottom end. What he liked best about the whole stick toy was the plastic ball that hung on the rope a ways above the worm. He wanted the girl to throw the ball for him. While he didn't much like fetching balls, they were good to sniff and chew, and this one looked small enough for him to give it a good gnawing. Fascinated, he watched as the girl put a hand on the contraption at the end of the toy and flicked the stick back. Then, with explosive force, she whipped it forward. The rope sailed over the lake, making a whirring noise as it went. After a silent splash, the worm disappeared under the water. The only thing visible was the floating, two-toned plastic ball bobbing temptingly. Aslan wanted to run and sniff it, but as a little puppy, he'd learned lakes weren't solid. They were water, easily penetrated by a puppy's paws, and he hated getting his paws wet.

Humans intrigued him. They were always doing odd, puzzling things. He spent most of his days following them around the big house and big yard, studying their interesting activities. This, though, was a mind-boggler.

The older human everyone called *Dad* struggled to untangle the rope on his stick, while the boy's rope, worm, and plastic ball were already in the water. The boy rested in a chair that had appeared from a simple cloth bag. Aslan didn't know what the boy was called. He'd seen him react to *Tiger, Peter*, and *Booie*. This didn't make sense, as everyone else was named something. The girl was called *Krissy*, and the older female in the family was *Mom*. Aslan knew his name was *Aslan* because the girl gave him treats for looking at her or coming to her when she said his name. He liked that game. He liked treats. They were much better than the dried-worm sticks on the patio.

The girl laid a towel on the end of the great wooden walking path, which led a long way out over the water. He sighed in contentment and stretched out on the soft cloth. It felt good to be off the sunbaked path, which was hot on his paws. He was the happiest he'd been since leaving his real home, and he breathed in the comforting smell of lake. Why didn't they come to this place more often?

The day had started as usual with the occupants of the big house waking and performing their normal morning activities. Things had changed when the girl had called him to her, clipped on his leash, and led him to the car. He spent a while in the back seat with the girl. It was the longest car trip he'd taken since leaving his home—the place where all the other shelties lived—and it had both worried and stirred him. Was he going somewhere else?

Then, a beautiful longing had filled him. Was he going home at last?

He'd scented his destination before he'd even got out of the car. Lake. That mossy lake smell had made his heart sing, and the hope that he'd returned home soared. With anticipation he'd hopped out of the back seat, the lake visible in the near distance. He'd nosed the air, hoping to catch the musky family smell he so missed. But, while he caught many familiar smells—damp vegetation, wet soil, chemicals from the car, and more—he hadn't scented the other shelties. He'd scanned the area and saw only unfamiliar surroundings. Even the lake smell wasn't quite right.

Sticks, boxes, and bags were removed from the back of the car, and the girl had led him along a path to the lake. On the way, he'd stepped off the worn trail into the tallest grass he could find. There, feeling a bit wild, he'd peed. Not because he had to but because this place smelled like his.

* * *

He must have fallen asleep on the soft towel, warmed by the summer sun, because he startled when the boy lurched upright. In a blink, the boy went from half-dozing like himself to standing, muscles flexed, maneuvering the line in the water. The boy flicked the pole up, and the two-toned- ball dipped below the water's surface.

Aslan didn't even realize the boy had stood, until he found himself at the edge of the wooden walking path. Tense with anticipation, he mimicked the behavior of the humans. Dad spoke in animated and encouraging tones to the boy, pointing to the stick and then out to the place where the plastic ball had been. The girl leaned forward and stared with wide eyes at the water where the rope disappeared.

Then, the boy raised the pole high, and the most peculiar creature Aslan had ever seen was hoisted from the water. It was silvery and sort of flat. The thing flipped its body, its head almost meeting its tail, and then inverted its shape again. Back and forth the lake beast contorted itself as the boy lifted the animal with the rope and stick. Even when it became captured by the boy's almost-grown hand, the animal continued flopping around. It smelled wonderful—like lake personified.

Aslan couldn't take the excitement, and he joined the humans in voicing his thrill at the animal's sudden and spectacular arrival. This was the best human game he'd seen to date.

Dad bent down at the edge of the wooden walkway and pulled a wire cage from the water. The mystifying animal was placed into it, and the cage disappeared back into the lake. The humans returned to their seating arrangements: Dad on one end sitting in one of those bag chairs; the boy (Tiger, Peter, Booie?) in the middle; and Aslan and Krissy on the cloth. The girl talked to him in quiet tones, signaling it was time to stop celebrating the capture of the shiny creature.

He settled back on the towel and pondered the whys of the game as the boy attached another worm onto his wire. Then the boy snapped his wrist once more, causing the stick to fly back, and then, like his sister had done, he shot the stick forward.

As the worm and wire whizzed past his face, they snagged the corner of the plastic shield that covered the boy's eyes and yanked it off. The eyewear sailed with the worm out over the lake, the smooth plastic reflecting the glare of the sun as it flew. With an ominous splash, the worm and the eye cover hit the water and disappeared from view.

The boy gasped. Dad glared at the boy, mouth agape. Krissy covered her mouth with one hand and stared at the water where the worm and the eye shield had sunk below the surface. The mood changed from exultation over the arrival of the silver, flopping animal to utter despair. And...was that *fear* Aslan smelled coming from the boy?

* * *

Krissy stared in shock at the spot where Peter's glasses had descended. For a few stunned seconds, no one spoke or moved. Then Peter stood and, jaw clenched, reeled in his line. An eternity passed before the hook emerged, slipping far too silently from the water. Not even the worm remained.

"Your mom's going to kill you," Dad said in a menacing tone that held more weight for its quiet, slow delivery. "Your brand-new glasses. Gone. And you could have taken your eye out with that cast."

Peter glared at the water, marking the area where the glasses had disappeared. "I'll swim out for them." He bent to remove his sneakers.

"You'll do no such thing," Dad said. "You can't see two feet in front of your face in this lake."

Krissy gazed into the water. It was indeed murky, and the brown-green tentacles of one of the lake's infamous algae trees perilously waved inches beneath the surface near where the glasses had fallen. Although a small lake with pretty treed shores, this part was rumored to be deep.

Peter had gotten his glasses that week. He really liked them, and this attachment may have been bolstered by the oohs and aahs of his many female admirers. When Violet saw him wearing them, she'd whispered in Krissy's ear, "Your brother looks like Clark Kent." It made sense. Clark Kent was Superman's nerdy alter ego, after all.

Perhaps that was why he'd gotten that particular pair, or maybe Mom had talked him into them. Probably the latter because after returning home with the new glasses, Mom had told Dad at dinner, "They were more than I wanted to pay, but they fit his face as if they were custom-made."

But now, Clark Kent's expensive new glasses were lost under the waves.

Dad's voice lost its soft, menacing tone and amplified. "Your new glasses. Those made my wallet scream. Come on, Peter. Can't you take care of your things?"

"It was an accident." Peter's volume matched Dad's. "It's pretty obvious I don't have the skill to hook my glasses on purpose. I've been looking forward to spending time fishing with you. Why would I ruin it?" When Dad's expression didn't waver, Peter added, "I can swim for them. It can't be too deep there."

"No!" Dad almost yelled. "They're gone. You might as well have thrown the cash into the lake. What if you'd hooked Krissy? Or the puppy? I could be removing a bloody hook from someone right now. Hooks are dangerous. I've told you to be careful a hundred times."

Peter stared in desperation at the spot where the glasses had sunk as if waiting for them to swim back to the surface. Krissy bowed her head but said nothing. It would be stupid to say anything with the tension between Peter and Dad so thick. She didn't want to become a shrapnel victim in today's bomb. Dad was under a lot of stress at work, and he'd become even more touchy since she'd gotten sick. A sour taste filled her mouth, and she swallowed against the guilt. She hadn't caused her kidneys to fail. It wasn't her fault. But sometimes it felt like it was, and she couldn't do a thing about it. Because of her, family fights had increased in number and intensity, and every once in a while, Dad exploded.

Although only four months old, Aslan must have sensed the tension, too, because he stood still, head swiveling from father to son in bewilderment.

Dad continued, "You'll need to take responsibility for this and tell your Mom. She'll be madder than a hornet."

While Dad spoke, Peter picked up his fishing pole, removed the bobber, and cast the empty hook toward the spot where the glasses had sunk. He muttered an anguished prayer as he cast, "Please, Lord. Please hook them."

Dad gave a sardonic laugh at the futile cast. "What do you think you're doing, Peter? There's no way you're going to hook those glasses. No way. Look out there. It's a *lake*!"

"Everything okay here?" Krissy jumped and turned, startled by a deep male voice to her right. A rowboat plowed the water in silence, coming their way. Two older men dressed in fishing gear sat on the boat's benches.

"We're fine," Dad said, his voice filled with disgust and controlled anger.

"You okay, son?" the man asked Peter. Dad's face reddened from anger—or maybe it was embarrassment.

Peter slumped as he reeled in the empty line. "I lost my glasses in the lake." His voice sounded tight and odd. Was he trying not to cry?

"That happens," the man said, but he made no move to leave.

Peter repositioned his pole, and, in spite of the presence of the men, prayed aloud, "God, please help me find them. Please."

He cast again. The hook hit the water several feet to the right of where the glasses had gone down.

Struggling for a calmer tone, Dad said, "Come on, Peter. Stop this. They're gone. Reel it in, bait it, and let's keep fishing."

Peter continued to pray under his breath, but he obeyed Dad, reeling in his line. As the hook rose from the water, there, dangling precariously, were the expensive brown-rimmed Clark Kent glasses.

CHAPTER 7

Feeding Emotions

August: Nineteen Weeks Old

K rissy sat pigeon-toed and slouched in one of the metal chairs at Positive Pups with Aslan at her feet. He stared at the left front pocket of her jeans hoping for a treat. He was right. There were a few treat bits stowed deep inside. The other students filed out of the building, chatting with each other and cajoling their puppies through the door. Dad had gone to cool the car down in the hundred-degree heat.

Earlier, Shelly had asked her to stay after class, but Krissy couldn't figure out what she'd done wrong. Aslan had performed his sits and drops well. His loose-leash walking had been perfect, although he'd always been good at that. He'd also rocked the Name Game, and they'd made progress on focused attention, which involved training him to keep his eyes on her during heightening degrees of distraction. He was doing fine, even if he lacked the sharp precision and enthusiasm of some of the other teams.

As the last student left the school, Shelly took a chair next to her. Sitting this close, Krissy could see laugh lines crinkling from the corners of Shelly's brown eyes.

"I understand you want to compete in agility." Her southern-belle Georgian drawl made the statement sound like a question.

Krissy's shoulders relaxed. This was a discussion about their next step in training. She wasn't in trouble after all. "I'd like to try, anyway."

"That's fantastic," Shelly said. "Agility is such a fun dog sport. Aslan is a smart guy and a willing worker. You're getting the science of training down, too. All of his behaviors look nice. But I'm a bit worried about one thing." Shelly petted Aslan's silky head and stared into his eyes a moment before continuing.

"Agility is a game of speed. The dog who completes all of the obstacles the fastest and in the right order wins. This means the dogs have to *love* to work. The best ones live for their sport. Aslan works well, but he doesn't seem to love training. I want you to have the best success possible, and you build the love for training at this beginning level—right here in puppy class. The foundations are where your dog learns that training isn't something he *has* to do, but something he *lives* to do." Shelly smiled at Krissy.

"Dogs learn this from their human teammates, so Aslan will learn the joy of training when you give him joy during training. But right now, you're so serious about it all, and I'm curious. Are you having any fun?"

It was such an unexpected question. Was she having fun?

Krissy hadn't thought about training being fun. It was a means to an end—a way to get to agility competitions. They'd be fun. Competing like a normal person would be fun. Training was the work it took to get there.

Before she could answer, Shelly continued. "Do you look forward to training time? I can see you practice with him. But is it a chore, or something you love to do each day?"

Krissy wrinkled her nose. "I guess sort of a chore. Like homework. I know it's good for both of us, and it's the only way to get where we want to go."

"Do you *want* to do agility?" Shelly asked. "Don't get me wrong. There will be days, and plenty of them, when training is a chore. But there should be more days when training is fun—even exhilarating. Agility takes a lot of work—much, much more than people realize. If you aren't dedicated and in love with the idea of training, the long haul between training and competition will eat you up. There are other dog sports that require less training that may interest you, too."

"No." The single word held more emphasis than Krissy had intended. "I want to do agility." The determination in her own voice surprised her.

"Great," Shelly said. "Then we need to talk about two things. These are skills good trainers employ right from the get-go. First, feed your dog the right emotion. Second, understand that what happens at home bleeds into the ring."

Huh? Krissy stared at her, confused.

"Aslan seems like serious little guy," Shelly said. "He studies things. Mulls them over. You, Krissy, train in the same serious manner—like it's homework, not a game. If you take this serious training style into agility, you may have some success, but he won't be as fast or as good as he would if you had taught him that training is a blast, a joy."

Krissy looked at Aslan, who still stared with longing at her pocket, waiting for her to dip into it and pull out a treat. "How do I make him different than he is? He was a serious puppy when we got him from the breeder. I worried about it, in fact. I worried he wasn't a good agility prospect."

Had she really said that aloud to another human? So thrown by her admission, she almost missed Shelly's reply.

"He's already treat-motivated." Shelly waved at Aslan. "Look at him. He wants to work for food. You use his desire for food, and then you feed him something else. You feed him your joy— your enthusiasm—as you train. Over time, this may not only transform his love of training but his personality as well. So, even if you have to fake it and become an actor during training, you make it fun. When you're having fun, you laugh, you talk in a happy voice, you smile, you play. Bring all of this into each training session. I'll teach you how."

Acting. Krissy had acted like everything was fun with her horse when it wasn't. Acting she could do.

Shelly continued, "The next thing often overlooked by trainers is that life at home bleeds into training, so if his daily life has stresses, he'll bring those into training just like you would. You have to learn to control his environment and feed him the right emotions outside of training too."

"I can't control everything." Krissy sounded whiny even to her own ears. "I can't make the world perfect."

Like the fight between Dad and Peter over the glasses. She couldn't stop the escalating family arguments. Shoot, she often fought in them herself. How was she supposed to control that?

"No one can, but you can do things to help ease those stresses for him. Let's say you're on a walk along a street, and a car backfires right by you. Aslan panics and pulls on the leash. How you respond to that stress will help him deal with loud noises better going forward. So, feed him happy emotions. Say something like, 'Ha! That was funny! Did you see me jump, too? Ha ha!' If you have a treat, feel free to give it to him. Let him know you aren't afraid. Feed him your happiness, and he'll be happier too."

Krissy nodded but then shook her head. "What if there's an argument in front of him? I can't fix that by laughing. I mean, people get mad, even me."

"Good point. Like you said, we can't control everything. But we can do other things, such as put the dog outside if you know an argument is brewing, or, if you're not involved, take Aslan outside and play games with him. If he sees an argument or family stress, it's okay. You can try your best to mitigate the consequences, but you can't control it all. Forgive yourself if he sees or becomes involved in something super stressful. All a good trainer can do is work to keep her dog safe and happy whenever possible. Does this make sense?"

Krissy stared at the tile floor, unseeing. "Yeah. It does."

It made too much sense. Dad's temper flares. Peter's moodiness. Mom's strictness. Even Krissy's own tantrums. They'd all gotten worse since her kidneys failed. This advice didn't just apply to dogs. Maybe she could use it on her family, as well. Feed them happiness. Feed them peace. If she acted happier, acted normal, wouldn't the family go back to normal, too? It had all gone wacko with her. Maybe it could all be returned to normal with her, too?

She could start by practicing the principle on her dog. This was something she'd need to ponder later.

"Good!" Shelly said. "I know your Dad's waiting, but I told him this would take a few minutes. Let's go over your first lesson on how to feed Aslan the emotions he needs."

* * *

Sweat trickled over Krissy's temple, and she wiped it away with the back of her hand. The high-summer locusts rattled in the backyard trees, their noise so strident it was hard to think. Even with the sun dipping well to the west, the heat of the day refused to surrender.

Aslan trotted ahead of her to the middle of the large yard, nose to the ground. After class yesterday, Shelly had said training shouldn't feel like a chore, but it did. For Aslan's sake, though, she'd play the actor, and pretend it was a fun game. The true losers were those who never tried, right?

Her hand slid into her pocket to finger the clicker and treats, and at her movement, Aslan lifted his head. He darted back and barked.

At five months old, he'd entered the gangly puppy stage. His legs were long—at least in comparison to the rest of him—but they remained bird-boned. The fine puppy fur was disappearing, and the guard hairs of his overcoat were growing in. His nose was sharper than a normal sheltie's, and his head was domed—a fault in the conformation ring where looks matter. However, his ears, currently alert, were perfectly tipped. And his eyes were his most striking feature by far. Round and dark brown, they'd become more expressive as he aged, although their shape was unorthodox for a sheltie. Right now, they studied her in an attempt to figure out how to make the gumball machine—i.e. her—dispense the desired treats.

She plastered on a smile, pushed her palm toward the ground, and commanded, "Drop." With slow deliberation, he lowered himself to the ground.

"Good dog." For the first time, those words echoed in her ears, and she heard how flat they sounded. No thrill. No play. No joy.

No fun.

She placed the treat between his paws as he lay in the sphinx position and, smiling, released him with an "Okay." The smile was fake, but it was a start.

This time, she tried to put more fun into her voice, making it higher pitched, more immediate. "Drop!" She grinned while she said it. It was still a command, but one given with enthusiasm. In her attempt to be more fun, she bounced once as she lowered her hand, palm down—the hand signal for drop. He looked confused, studied her hand, but then, inch by inch, lowered himself to the ground.

"Good dog! You're bringing it!" She almost yelled in her pretend falsetto excitement and hopped on her toes. Again, she dispensed the treat between his forelegs, released him, and repeated verbal praise like Shelly had taught her. "That was *tres* cool, buddy! Awesome job! Good drop!"

After Krissy repeated this more entertaining form of the command several times, Aslan's speed in reaching the drop position increased. Now, he sank to the ground rather than thinking about it and descending like a lazy cottonwood puff on an updraft.

She hadn't expected to see results so quickly, but he enjoyed this happy new training regime. Eager to see if it would transfer to their other behaviors, she retrieved the clicker from her pocket and got to work.

* * *

By the end of their twenty-minute training session, Aslan's eyes shone brightly, and his tail wagged, happy with her newfound but pretend enthusiasm. All of his behaviors were a bit sharper than before, except his stay, which had gotten worse. Maybe her animation made it harder for him to stay in one position for more than a few seconds? She jotted a mental note to ask Shelly about that.

Pocketing her clicker, Krissy started to head inside but found she didn't want to quit yet. She diverted her path to the shed to retrieve a ball, the rope toy, and the old quilt. Maybe after this fun training session, there'd be a miracle, and Aslan would want to play.

She laid the quilt on the grass. Its musty, antique smell floated in the air as she sat cross-legged on it with the toys. Shelly had demonstrated how to drag a tug toy to interest Aslan in play instead of sticking it in his face and wiggling it. "He's a herding dog," Shelly had said. "He's bred to chase things. Use his natural instincts to engage him."

Krissy called him to her, and he trotted, tail up, to inspect the familiar quilt and toys. Speaking in a bright, playful tone, she dragged the rope toy on the ground away from him, wiggling it. This time—for the first time ever—he followed it. She let him reach it, where she rewarded him with praise. A few treats were left in her pocket, so she gave him one.

Repeating the process, Krissy soon had him chasing the rope with his little puppy tail held high like a flag. Once, he even pounced on it. The back of her neck tingled with the flush of success. At last, she'd gotten her serious puppy to play with her!

A puppy bark split the air as he chased the moving rope. What would it be like to run this little dog on an agility course? Could he learn to love training?

Or was this just another impossible dream, like her horsey pipe dreams?

She dropped the toy on the quilt. The pup grabbed it and chewed its stringy tassels. His scrawny front legs wrapped around the rope to hold it in place, and he gave the toy an unconvincing treble growl.

How could she and this gangly, serious pup bond? Shelly and her Cally had had such a beautiful relationship. There had to be a way to nurture something that deep.

She wanted that bond. She wanted that beauty. But how?

CHAPTER 8

The Stars

September: Twenty-Three Weeks Old

"To solve this equation with addition, you first have to cancel out one of the variables by adding the two equations together."

Krissy should have nodded off ten minutes ago. She was so comfortable with her head propped up by her elbow—balanced just right—but her exasperation with the slow progression of the minute hand around the face of the clock had kept her awake. The clock hung above her teacher's head as he wrote algebraic insanity on the white board.

"To find y," he droned, "simply put thirty-three back into x in the original equation."

As the minute hand drifted closer to 3:10, she lifted her head, blinked several times, and straightened her books. In seconds, the school bell would ring, and she wanted to be the first out the door. There was so much to do before tonight's last puppy class.

"Then you put your answer in the form of the ordered pair," her teacher finished, setting down the dry-erase maker and turning to face the class. "Please turn in your assignment on Friday. There are two bonus questions this week. I recommend you complete them."

The bell rang. With a jump, Krissy grabbed her things and bolted for the door. She streamed into the hallway, joining the flood of teenagers looking for a quick escape from the tedious day.

After sliding to a stop in front of her locker, she spun the combination lock with deft fingers, opened the door, loaded her backpack with the appropriate books for the evening's home-work, and snatched her flute case. With a flick of her wrist, she slammed the locker and hurried to the freedom of the large park-ing lot, which was absorbing the flow of teenagers either seeking their cars or begging rides home.

She didn't stop her awkward trot until she reached her broth-er's red Mustang. Panting, she carefully placed her backpack and flute on the car's hood and scanned the ever-growing mass of teens. Sounds of both greetings and goodbyes shot across the lot as everyone fled to find what adventures they could in the re-mains of the afternoon.

It wasn't the afternoon's adventures she was anxious to be-gin—it was the evening's. Tonight, Shelly would be administer-ing the S.T.A.R. Puppy Test at their last class, and Violet was coming to the house this afternoon to help Krissy refresh Aslan's behaviors. Then Krissy had homework and dinner before Dad would chauffeur her to Positive Pups for the first real test of their training.

Krissy heard someone call her name. She lifted her hand above her eyes to cut the sun's glare, and Violet came into focus, Jessica in tow. Each girl lugged a large black bass clarinet case. Though they were only freshmen, both girls were incredibly skilled clari-net players, so they'd been given the choice to continue playing the alto clarinet or take up the bass version, an invitation usually reserved for the best sophomore clarinetists. They'd both chosen the bass instrument.

"This thing weighs a ton." Violet dumped her case on the ground when she reached the Mustang. Rubbing her arm, she asked, "Have you seen Evan?"

"Shaw? No. He might be with Peter, so he could show up soon."

"He's our ride," Jessica said in her sassy Okie accent. "We're gonna go practice at Violet's house. There's no way I'm walking home carrying this monstrosity." She pointed at her instrument case, which was now also resting on the hot blacktop.

Krissy looked up in surprise at Violet, who was eyeing the school's exit. "I thought we were going to train for Aslan's S.T.A.R. Puppy test?"

"Oh yeah. Shoot." Violet rubbed a finger over a brow, smoothing it. "I can't believe I forgot. Um, let me think—can we do that after we practice? I can come over after dinner. Jessica's brother is planning on picking her up when he gets off work."

"Or Evan can take me home when we're done," Jessica said.

"Evan? You're practicing with Evan?" Krissy asked, shocked.

"Yeah. And it was his idea." Violet grinned.

"We're hanging with the cool kids." Jessica flipped her red hair in mock snootiness.

"He's Peter's friend," Krissy said with an eye roll. "And while I'll admit he's hot, he's not that cool."

"Oh, he's cool," Violet said. "I can't believe he wants to practice with us! Anyway, I can be over to your house after dinner."

"I'll be leaving for class then," Krissy said.

"I'm sorry." Violet seemed sincere, but her apology did nothing to dampen Krissy's disappointment. "I promise to help the next time, though. Will that be okay?"

It wasn't. There would never be another puppy test, and she'd counted on this afternoon's training to prep. Sure, it was hot-but-not-so-cool Evan, but to be forgotten hurt.

She pasted on a small smile and lied. "That'll work. You can help us train some other time."

"There he is. Evan!" Jessica waved, bouncing on her toes, smile wide. He saw the girls and motioned them toward his car.

"I'll call you later." Violet heaved her instrument case.

The girls lugged their stuff to Evan's car. As neighbors, Violet and Krissy had been friends since first grade. When they'd advanced to middle school, Violet had met Jessica through band, and they'd formed a fast friendship, too. Soon, all three girls were friends. Jessica, with her long auburn hair, green eyes, and a girl-next-door attitude, was well-liked by girls and attracted boys like coons to trash cans. Violet and Krissy found themselves propelled into Jessica's circle of band friends—a level of popularity Krissy had never known.

Things had gone well until Krissy went into kidney failure in eighth grade. When she'd started dialysis, she'd become breathless and had found it difficult to make her flute produce a decent tone. The clear timbre she'd once created began to sound airy. Over the next few months, she sank from second-chair flute to eighth, and there were only nine flute players in band. Because of her inability to produce a consistent tone, Mr. Phillips, the middle school band director, eventually dropped her from regular band to what he called "Advanced Band." It was a ludicrous name designed to make kids feel better about being demoted to the junior varsity of middle school musicians, but it fooled no one. *Advanced,* her foot.

Violet had thrown a fit. After the names for regular band and "Advanced Band" were posted, Krissy had sat numb in the eighth-chair flutist seat, putting her flute away and fighting tears, when a loud crash came from Mr. Phillip's office. Violet yelled—really yelled—about "unfair" and "stupid." To this day, Mr. Phillips's desk sported a deep dent in the front right corner where Violet had kicked it in. Yet she was never punished for that dent. Krissy figured it was because Mr. Phillips knew it had been wrong to allow a kid on dialysis to drift away from her friends in that way. The dent had been a show of fierce loyalty.

Krissy quit band altogether rather than join Advanced Band. The flute had lost its charm. But after her kidney transplant six months ago, she'd regained her ability to produce a clear tone, and upon completing private flute lessons over the summer, the high school band director, a far more reasonable teacher, allowed her to rejoin the band. She was overjoyed to be back with her friends after a year of watching from the outside, although it didn't feel quite like old times. Her year's absence had left a gulf in those relationships.

Except for Violet. She was *that* kind of friend, loyal to a fault. Krissy forgave Violet for forgetting their afternoon plans. How could she not? Violet just wanted to make everyone happy, and sometimes, it split her in too many directions. Yet, the sting of being overlooked remained.

"Ready to blow this bug in a rug?" Peter strode up, pressing a button on his key remote to unlock the 'Tang. Two girls glanced his way as he passed, giggling and whispering with their heads together. A goofy grin spread across his face, too, but it wasn't because of the girls. He'd intentionally created that mixed metaphor and was waiting for a snide correction from Krissy about his annoying comparisons.

She wanted to do just that and lash out at him with the leftover emotions from being snubbed, but she controlled herself. After seeing Aslan's success with her "feeding the right emotion," she'd decided to employ Shelly's technique on her family. Maybe it could heal the rift brought about by her illness. If she were happier and easier to live with, tensions in the house might dissolve. Everyone would realize she was fine, and they'd all go back to normal.

It was time to test the theory. She swallowed a critical retort and peered through the heat waves rising off the asphalt as Violet and Jessica muscled their instrument cases into the trunk of Evan's green Impala. Turning to Peter, she flashed him a smile she hoped didn't look fake. All this forgiving of friends and "feeding happiness" stuff was hard. "Yep. I've got a boatload of stuff to do this afternoon."

* * *

Mike's voice boomed, telling the class yet another story from Honey's growing list of humorous exploits. "And then, ignoring the dead cricket, she pounced on her dish, sending dog food flying all over the kitchen. It took us an hour to find all the kibbles. They were under the fridge, lodged under the cabinets, on the kitchen chairs. All over."

Classmates laughed as Honey's furry face and mischievous light-hazel eyes scanned her audience, absorbing the attention. Krissy grinned, too. Honey's zeal for, well, everything, was contagious. No wonder Mike adored her. His laugh joined the others as he looked with pride at his dog.

Shelly waved the pair toward their chairs. "Well, it's a good thing her leash walking is better than her dinner habits, or you'd have failed that part of the puppy test. Good job, Mike and Honey!" Shelly surveyed the other students. "Who wants to try next? How about Abby and Jeeves? Are you guys ready?"

Krissy's shoulders relaxed. Abby and Jeeves were a good choice for the second team to attempt the first task of the S.T.A.R. puppy program. They would give her another chance to observe how Shelly ran the test.

The gray mixed-breed pup and his owner plodded to the front of the class. Abby, a thin woman in her early twenties, looked as anxious as Krissy felt.

"Do you have any questions?" Shelly asked.

"No, but I'm a bit nervous," Abby said.

"No need to be. No one dies or gets hurt if you fail to earn the S.T.A.R. puppy certificate. Besides, it's meant to be fun, and I know Jeeves has got this down pat. Give it a try."

Really, this step in tonight's testing was simple. Each team would go to the center of the class and stand behind a line drawn in chalk on the floor. Then the handler and pup would walk straight to a line drawn fifteen steps away. The puppy had to walk the distance on their leash without the owner pulling her along. Because the test was designed for young puppies, owners could use their voice, hand signals, and even food lures to encourage their dogs to walk with them. Mike and Honey performed it without a food lure, but Krissy had treats in her pocket in case Aslan needed a little help.

Abby patted her leg and called to Jeeves. He looked at her, and they crossed the start line. The tension in the class was palpable, and even the puppies stopped their constant activity to watch the pair work. Jeeves trotted in perfect position by Abby's side, gazing into her face with complete trust. As they crossed the finish line, the tension transformed into cheers and claps.

"Fantastic!" Shelly said. "Great job, Abby and Jeeves!"

As the pair sat, she asked, "How about Krissy and Aslan next?"

Krissy licked her lips and rose, calling Aslan to follow. Like a falling rock, his nose went straight to the ground to sniff. Panic rippled through her. They often struggled with this nose-to-the-ground thing, and if he wouldn't move with her, they'd be sunk. No one wanted to be the team that failed puppy class. Worse, if he couldn't perform these simple behaviors, how could they hope to do agility with its extreme skills?

She walked to the start line, pulling on the leash to force Aslan to follow.

"Talk to him like we've trained," Shelly said. "And don't forget, you can use food to lure him if needed."

Krissy nodded, but neither Mike nor Abby had used treats. Krissy didn't want to use that crutch if she didn't have to, though she did take Shelly's advice to speak with her happy voice.

"Aslan! Watch me, buddy!" she said in her fake falsetto tone. Aslan raised his head. He knew *watch me* meant to look at her face. Once she had his attention, she started over the line. She strode out as Shelly had taught them, hoping beyond hope that he would follow. And he did! He trotted a few inches behind her instead of right by her side, but he didn't stop to sniff—not even once! The fifteen steps went by faster than she'd expected, and in a flash, they crossed the finish line. Again, the class erupted in cheers.

* * *

Near the end of class, four of the five skills had been tested, and all of the puppies were passing, including Aslan. He'd been a rock star so far, but before each test, Shelly had to remind Krissy to keep her voice light and happy.

Krissy hated to fail, especially in front of others, and while they'd done well so far, the public aspect of the test had been torture. She twined her hands and pushed them into her lap to hide their trembling. Why was she putting herself through this agony? Just for a S.T.A.R. Puppy certificate? Just for proof they could move on in their agility quest? If she hated this, what would agility competitions be like?

All the pups had already passed walking on a leash past other people without lunging or excessively pulling on the lead. This had been hard for Honey and the terrier mix, both of whom loved to greet people. Their owners used food lures to bring their pups under control, and they squeaked by with passing scores. Next had been sitting on command, which was pretty straightforward, and as Aslan's best behavior was a sit, he aced it. In fact, all of the teams nailed their sits. Calling the leashed pups to come to their owners from five feet away had also been easy for everyone, as food, voice, and hand clapping could be used to get the puppies to obey.

The last step in the test was still to come—the drop. While the drop was a basic behavior, it had been taught later in the six-week course, so it was a newer skill for the pups. As such, many of the puppies in class, including Aslan, had floundered during lessons. To perform a proper drop for the puppy test, a dog had to lie on the floor with both front elbows touching the ground, if only for a second. In training, most pups had lain in a sphinx position with their hind legs bent and front legs forward, so their entire stomachs rested on the floor. Others had taken the sphinx position and then flopped onto one hip. Jeeves liked to roll completely onto his side when asked to drop. He even went to sleep like that in one class. As long as they hit the sphinx position at some point, they were all good.

While Jeeves was a drop pro, others found it difficult. The Chihuahua sucked at it. She would try to drop, but the moment her hairless tummy hit the cold linoleum floor, she'd bounce up with a scowl on her big-eyed face. Aslan found the cold floor uncomfortable, too, and he didn't like to drop in class. He did much better on the carpet at home than on tile or concrete. He was also slow and sometimes wouldn't put his elbows on the ground even when practicing on carpet.

When Shelly began explaining the criteria for passing the drop, the anxiety in the room ratcheted up. For this task, the dogs didn't have to be in the center of the room, and the drop could be performed at their seats. The handlers could stand, sit in their chairs, or sit on the floor, and even use treat lures to get their pups to drop.

As before, Mike and Honey were the first to go. Mike chose to get on the floor for the drop, which turned out to be a huge mistake. As soon as he slid to the ground, Honey's expressive hairy face lit up, and she leaped at him, licking his nose. Then she sprang to the end of her leash, turned on a dime, and flew at him again, this time giving his ear a quick wash before hopping away to attempt the ambush anew. Mike giggled and repeated "drop, drop, drop," which caused Honey's bouncing to increase in both velocity and amplitude.

Shelly tried to intervene. "Mike, get your treats out and have her play Watch Me or The Name Game. No, don't laugh. No. Stop pushing her away. That's making her think you're there to play. Mike, stand up. Use your treat to get her focused on you. Put the treat directly in front of her nose, not over her head so she has to jump for it. No, no, Mike. Hopping on your toes and laughing at her isn't going to help her focus."

By then, Honey was in full zoomie mode. The only thing keeping her from running full-bore around the room was the leash, which Mike—now standing and laughing almost hysterically—worked to unwrap from around his legs. Honey's rollicking play affected the other pups, and they pulled at the ends of their leashes, too, trying to join in this boisterous game.

After several minutes, Shelly regained control of the class. Honey was barely restrained, standing in front of Mike, looking at him with dancing eyes. "Okay," Shelly said, striving to keep exasperation from her voice. "Let's catch our breath here. I'm sorry, Mike, but I have to be a fair examiner. Unfortunately, that was a failed attempt at the drop."

Mike let loose a loud guffaw and bent over in near hysterics again, one hand on his ample stomach. Other class members laughed as well. "But she had so much fun flunking," Mike said when he'd gained control of himself. "She really knows how to bomb."

"That she does," said Shelly, "but today is about the puppy test. If I were testing zest for life, she would be a star. But I'm not. I'm testing for puppy-level obedience behaviors."

Mike's wide smile never faltered. Neither did Honey's.

Shelly continued, "Fortunately, the evaluator's guide says if a puppy fails only one step of the test, she can be retested on that step. So, let's give Honey a break to calm down, and we'll see if you two can't give that drop another go at the end."

Mike sat, pulled Honey close, and told her how much he loved her.

Krissy found herself smiling along with everyone else. How could they not?

Abby and Jeeves went next. Abby chose to sit in her chair for the test. Lowering her hand palm-down to the floor, she said,

"Drop." Jeeves fell as if shot, hit the sphinx position before flopping on his side, and then let out a low, contented sigh. He even closed his eyes.

"There ya go!" Shelly exclaimed. "That's a great job. You can wake him if you want, Abby."

"He looks a bit tuckered out. I think I'll let him sleep," Abby said.

Shelly laughed and said, "That's going to be a handy behavior for you. If you need him to sleep, ask him to drop and *poof.* Lights out." She turned away from Abby and Jeeves to face Krissy. "Okay. Krissy and Aslan are next."

Aslan's eyes were still on Honey, although Mike massaged her ears, trying to calm her and keep her from distracting the other puppies. Krissy gave a few light taps on the leash to grab Aslan's attention—to no avail.

"Remember, a nice, happy voice," Shelly said.

Krissy froze her facial muscles so as not to betray her annoyance. Yes, she remembered. She commanded Aslan to watch her, keeping that internal frustration from her tone. He turned his head and stared into her eyes, hoping for a treat.

In that moment, she replayed Mike's response to Honey's meltdown. He hadn't been embarrassed or mad. He hadn't raised his voice. Instead he laughed at his dog, loving her for who she was. And Abby had been pleased with Jeeves's instant snore drop because it exemplified who he was, too.

So, why couldn't Krissy be happy if Aslan decided the linoleum was too cold on his belly? Would it ruin her life if her dog wasn't perfect? Would his perfection bring world peace? She frowned at herself and the queasiness in her stomach.

She closed her eyes for a long second, opened them, and, in the most relaxed tone she could muster, said, "Drop." As she said it, her hand lowered, palm down. And her eyes widened as she realized her mistake. She'd meant to use a treat to lure him into position for this behavior. Aslan wouldn't drop onto the cold floor without it.

He studied her hand signal. Then, inch by slow inch, he lowered himself to the floor. Krissy leaned sideways in her chair to see if his elbows hit the ground. They hovered about half an inch above it.

"All the way." Her voice stayed surprisingly calm considering the nervy fear and the undefinable thrill that simultaneously flowed through her.

Aslan looked into her eyes and lowered his elbows to the ground.

"Okay!" Krissy said, releasing him from the behavior. The class once again erupted in claps and cheers. Grinning, she glanced over at Dad, who sat on the edge of his chair clapping, newspaper on the ground next to him, forgotten.

* * *

After class, the students lingered in small groups, both basking in their test successes and unwilling to say goodbye to their newfound friends. Honey had passed her second attempt at the drop. It'd been a close one, but after consideration, she'd decided to lie down for a split second. Shelly had pronounced Honey's attempt good enough, so all of the puppies were now part of the American Kennel Club's AKC S.T.A.R. Puppy Program. Krissy couldn't wait to find a place on her bedroom wall to hang Aslan's certificate.

"Will you be starting Shelly's Tuesday basic obedience class next week?" Abby asked, turning to Krissy.

"Yeah. Shelly thinks Aslan needs more work before starting puppy agility classes."

Abby tucked a loose strand of her straight brown hair behind one ear. "I've decided to take a puppy agility class with Jeeves, too, but we're doing the basic class first. I don't know if he'll like agility, but I'm having so much fun training. Mike said he and Honey will be in the basic class. It'll be like a puppy class reunion."

Krissy smiled. "I'm glad. I get nervous working around strangers. It'll be good to have people I know there."

"You're doing awesome. Aslan's a phenom. We'll show those older dogs in basic how it's done. See you Tuesday!"

Krissy collected her training gear and went over to Dad, who'd been speaking with Mike. "I just found out Mike and Honey will be in your basic obedience class," he said. "He's vaguely considering doing agility, too."

"Honey would be great at agility," Krissy said. She headed toward the door, Aslan by her side. "She's a monster."

"Aslan will give all the agility dogs a run for their money," Dad said, following. "Your hard work paid off tonight."

The puppy obedience work had paid off, but agility would be another matter. She hadn't faced any physical challenges tonight. What about when her body's athletic ability was tested?

In spite of the worry, she left Positive Pups smiling. It had been agony, yes. But it had been kinda fun, too.

CHAPTER 9

Poop and a Poop Bag

October: Twenty-Eight Weeks Old

Mom stared at her, eyes narrowed. She took a step forward and tugged at the large gray lawn-and-leaf bag engulfing Krissy's frame.

"I'm having a hard time reading it," Mom said. "Stand tall and square your shoulders."

Krissy pulled her spine straight and threw her rounded shoulders back in an attempt to add a few inches to her height.

"That's better. I can see *poo bag* although the last *p* in *poop* is getting lost in a fold." Mom reached out to pull some more at the plastic bag. "At least poo is an acceptable form of poop."

Violet, sitting on a maroon chaise lounge in Krissy's parents' bedroom, snickered. It was incongruous to see Krissy's normally reserved and decorous mom, dressed as always in heels, speaking freely about poop.

"Be sure to stand tall," Mom said. "Otherwise people won't have a clue what you're supposed to be."

Krissy turned to the full-length mirror. She slouched, and sure enough, almost the entire word *poop* disappeared within the folds of the bag. She'd cut holes in the light-gray bag for her arms and head and had written poop bag on the front. The back read *please discard in an approved receptacle.* It was an innovative, cheap costume. The problem was, lawn-and-leaf bags didn't come in small, medium, or large, so she was a small swimming in an extra-large.

Aslan's ears drooped as he waited by her side. He wore a toddler's T-shirt. Attached to the back of the brown tee were brown tubes of faux suede material each sewn, stuffed, and precisely arranged by Mom to resemble a pile of dog poo. He had a brown, mini-tube tied to his head, and behind the pile of poo sewn on his back was a small stuffed ball that hung down by his tail and represented the "dingleberry"—the piece of poo known for getting stuck on long-haired dogs' fur as it fell from its origin.

The total effect was unmistakable. They were Poop and a Poop Bag. Only the odor was missing.

Aslan glanced at the mirror and turned away as if his reflection revolted him. The poor guy had drawn the short end of this costume stick, and his head hung as if he knew it.

"Do you think we can win?" Krissy asked. "There'll be dog people there, so they shouldn't get too grossed out by the poop theme."

"I think you've got it in the bag," Violet said and fell back on the chaise in a fit of giggles at her decent pun.

The costume had been Krissy's brainchild after learning of the "Howl-o-ing for Rescues" doggie Halloween costume party. They had a prize for the funniest dog/human duo's costume, and she'd begun planning for it several weeks ago. Tonight, the costume would debut, hopefully to prize-winning acclaim.

Violet, also dressed for the event, was a clown, her honey-colored hair in pigtails, her face painted white with a wide red smile and a red nose. She wore baggy overalls and a red bandana tied around her neck. Heidi was costumed as a white-collar worker. She wore a short-sleeved white dress shirt and tie, her front legs sticking out of the arms of the dress shirt. Boxer shorts substituted as pants and were put on backward, so Heidi's tail wagged from the fly.

"Boxer shorts?" Krissy asked.

"Dad's shorts wouldn't fit," Violet said. "So, we got the best of my brother's old boxers out. I was hoping their dark gray color would look like slacks."

"Hmm." Krissy evaluated the look. "You know, it kinda does. You're going to make boxer slacks all the rage, and Heidi seems comfortable in her business suit, especially compared to poor Aslan."

It was true. Heidi sat erect like nobility in her costume. She cut a much different figure than Aslan slouching in his poop shirt.

"Sun's pretty much set," Violet said. "Let's go." She stood and called Heidi to her as she left the room.

"It's a good thing it's a temperate night," Mom said, following Violet. "You girls shouldn't need coats. It would be a shame to have to hide that cute clown outfit under a jacket."

Krissy glanced one more time at their reflections in the mirror, hoping Poop and a Poop Bag would win whatever prize came with the funniest costume.

* * *

A small light-brown dog covered in flouncy white material paraded past Aslan. He took a step toward the dog, trying to sniff the white thing covering her body, but she didn't slow. He glanced back at the tube-pillows stuck on the shirt that the girl had forced him into. The brown stuffed pillows slipped to one side at the turn of his head, and the girl reached down to straighten them.

This was another human puzzler. His girl and her friend had dressed him and the big German shepherd in clothes. Then, they'd gotten in the car and driven to this place with trees and grass—and lots of other dogs wearing clothes. As far as the place went, he liked it okay. His girl had picked up treats at different tables and given some to him, and he'd gotten to sniff a few friendly dogs. Even so, the pillows on his back made him pant, and his fur snagged and itched under the shirt.

While the place was okay, the people weren't. They pointed and howled at him, and him alone. The German shepherd got lots of smiles and nods, and she strutted and wagged her tail in response. But it was different for Aslan. People cackled when they saw him. Actually cackled. He was mortified. All the dogs at this place wore clothes of some kind. So, what made people hate him? Aslan trudged through the crowd, dodging feet and keeping his eyes lowered to avoid the jeering faces.

A man in front of a table yelled, and people assembled around him. Krissy joined the crowd, pulling Aslan behind her. They passed a man and woman with a big dog covered in a white bed sheet, and the woman glanced at Aslan and snorted. He lowered his head, causing the pillow fastened there to flop over his eyes. The girl bent down to adjust it as the yelling man continued to speak. Aslan ignored him. He wanted to leave. He wished he could go sniff in the trees behind the tables, away from the staring and smirking.

The crowd cheered as a lady and her dog approached the yelling man, who gave them a bag. The small dog, mantled in bright feathers like a bird, had a weird orange muzzle, but most surprising were the golden wires encircling her. People clapped and grinned at her. She wagged her feather-covered tail, which poked through the wires.

The man yelled again, and with a sneer, pointed at Krissy and Aslan. The leash grew taut, and his girl pulled him to the front of the crowd. He slogged behind her, his ears flattened and tail curled between his legs. This was a terrible human game. When they reached the man, Aslan couldn't raise his head to meet the crowd's critical, snickering faces. The yelling man handed the girl a bag, and she spoke in excited, happy tones. She reached inside it, pulled out a treat, gave it to Aslan, and—joy of joys—removed the annoying head pillow as he chewed.

The treat and absence of the head gear renewed his spirits, and it gave him the courage to peer up again. He stepped back in shock. No one was sneering at him. Instead, they clapped and smiled. His girl's face glowed radiant. He'd missed something. Everyone seemed happy now, not mocking at all. His girl moved back into the crowd, nodding to people who talked to her as she passed.

When they'd returned to the German shepherd's side, his girl retrieved two more treats from the bag. She fed one each to him and the German shepherd, then scratched him behind the ears, telling him he was "good and brave." He wagged his tail and crunched the treat while she dipped back into the bag. After swallowing, he licked her hand and sniffed the glittering thing she'd pulled out for him to see. The top of it was silver, and the bottom was a smooth white rock. The girl inspected it with a wide grin. Her friend motioned for the thing, and, after taking it from his girl, examined it closely, too. The girls giggled. He barked his playful puppy bark and danced on his toes.

This clothes event was looking up. The fact was, nothing made him happier than when the girl. . . No. She was more than just *the girl.* She was *"his Mistress,"* a well-deserved title. . .Nothing made him happier than when she smiled really, really wide the way she was right now. For that smile, he'd follow his Mistress to the front of all sorts of crowds—whether they cheered or jeered.

* * *

With one sneakered foot, Krissy pinned the edge of the paper plate to the asphalt, so Aslan could lick the remains of the tacos from its surface. He seemed more relaxed now that he was out of his costume, which was stuffed in her new tote.

"We've got about ten minutes till your mom shows up." Violet stared at the time on Krissy's old-fashioned flip phone before setting it on the plastic picnic table. Heidi sat on the ground by her side, looking not the least bit tired after spending the evening prowling the festival's various booths and activities.

"Do you want anything else from the food trucks?" Krissy asked. She had eaten three gourmet tacos from Big Truck Tacos, but Violet had gotten only one.

"I'm good." Violet stared into the park without interest.

Krissy turned to scan the crowded booths scattered throughout the park behind them. Orange pumpkin lights draped across many of the booths, and black netting and orange and black crepe paper fluttered everywhere. Laughter echoed from inside the "Haunted Forest" where several cheesy, child-friendly Halloween tableaux had been located along the path through the trees.

Barking erupted behind them, and the girls spun in their seats to see a Saint Bernard dressed as a monk stroll past the adoption booth, causing a ruckus from the crated homeless dogs. "How about visiting the dogs up for adoption again?" Krissy asked after the adoptable dogs had calmed.

"Nah. It would just make me want that spotted puppy." Violet turned forward as two non-costumed, denim-clad teens approached the picnic table.

"Hey, ladies." Evan wiped off the bench across from Violet with his hand before sitting. "How's tricks?"

"These dogs are adorable!" Jessica squealed and pointed to a passing small tan dog in a purple-and-pink dragon suit.

A wide grin brightened Violet's face. "What are you guys doing here?"

Evan leaned back, a mischievous grin on his face. "We came to find you."

"And Krissy," Jessica added. "We tried to text, but we couldn't get you."

"My battery's dead," Violet said.

"You should've called me. My phone's okay." Krissy picked up her flip phone from the table and waved it like Exhibit One.

"You can't get texts with that stingy plan your parents got you," Jessica said. "So, we texted Violet's mom. She said you were here, so here we are."

Krissy's brows knit together. "You could have called me. My phone does do calls."

Jessica waved a hand dismissively. "You have to talk your parents into getting you a real phone. That thing is scary. Maybe someone should put it on their dog's back and spook the kids with it. 'Here's technology from hundreds of years ago. Ooooooh.'"

"So, why did you come to find me?" Violet asked before Krissy had time to decipher Jessica's bewildering phone comment.

Jessica laughed. "Oh, yeah. Dahlia is having an impromptu Halloween party. Nothing big, but some of us are bringing over our folks' leftover Halloween candy and watching *Night of the Living Dead*. We came to get you."

"I can't go," Krissy said. "My mom is coming by any second to take us home."

Violet frowned. "Yeah. It sounds fun, but Krissy's mom expects to take me home. Plus, I've got Heidi, and I'm dressed like a clown."

Evan grinned. "You'll be the cutest clown at the party. We can drop Heidi off at your house on the way, and you can tell your parents."

Violet pursed her lips. "I don't know."

"It's Dahlia. Dah-li-a." Jessica leaned forward and pronounced every syllable. "Like, who turns down the opportunity to hang with her tribe?"

Krissy reached down and scratched Aslan behind his ears. Dahlia's parties were legendary, but not in a good way. Rumor had it her parents didn't care what she did, so she did whatever she wanted. At school, the phrase "Dahlia's House Rules" had become synonymous with no rules. But eating candy and watching an old horror flick sounded pretty tame. Krissy's parents would never let her go, though, and this time, she didn't mind.

She turned to Violet and shrugged. "My folks won't go for it, but if your mom's good with it, you can go."

Evan rolled his eyes. "Of course your folks won't go for it. They're so clean, when they speak, bubbles float out. Look what they allow you for technology." He nodded at Krissy's phone on the table.

"Hey, are those dogs over there for sale?" Jessica pointed to the cages of rescue animals.

"It's a fundraiser for a local rescue. They're up for adoption," Violet said.

A silver Avalon pulled into the parking lot. "My mom's here." Krissy put her scary old phone in her bag. "I gotta go."

"Evan, come with me. I've got to see how much they're selling those dogs for." Jessica grabbed Evan's arm and pulled him to the adoption booth.

"They're up for adoption, not sale," Krissy called to them as they left.

Jessica threw a glare back, her red hair flying. "Duh. It's the same thing."

Shaking her head, Krissy slung the bag with her trophy and prizes over her shoulder and looked at Violet. "You can go with them to Dahlia's if you want."

"Can't you come with us?" Violet asked, trailing her to the car. "Like Jessica said, it's Dahlia. She's so cool."

"She's kind of wild," Krissy said. Should she push Violet to come home with her? It was only a horror movie, and Jessica would be there.

"She's just a free spirit," Violet said. "I've always wanted to be more like her."

They'd reached the Avalon, and Krissy put her hand on the door but didn't open it. "I think I'll pass. You go have fun—but not too much fun. Don't go all wild on me."

"The worst thing that can happen is a stomach ache from a chocolate binge. I'll call you tomorrow," Violet said as Krissy opened the car door and, holding Aslan, slid inside.

Krissy watched the orange-and-black festival grow small as the Avalon pulled away from the park. Her round frowny face reflected ghost-like in the car's window.

Violet had caught up with Jessica and Evan, and Evan's arm slithered around Violet's shoulders before the darkness engulfed them.

CHAPTER 10

The Second Step

November: Seven Months Old

In the Johnson house, dinner was served at six-thirty on the dot every single weeknight. Dad would come home at six-fifteen, and dinner hit the table fifteen minutes later. It was a standing rule. No one dared be late.

There were other rules, too.

1. One never missed dinner without permission.
2. The whole family ate together.
3. No electronic devices or books were allowed at the table. Only eating, talking, and family time.
4. Manners mattered. No elbows on the table. "Pleases," "May I's," and "Thank you's" were required. No talking with one's mouth full. Forks, spoons, knives, and napkins were to be used formally and arranged in their proper places.
5. Every meal included a meat, vegetable, starch, and salad.
6. One ate what was served. No matter the meal, each family member had to swallow at least a few bites.

Historically, Rule Six had caused Krissy the most trouble, and tonight was no exception. Because tonight, Curried Egg Bake sat stinking on the table. Of all the meals in Mom's repertoire, Curried Egg Bake was Krissy's least favorite, and being forced to eat it on a nervous stomach right before her first agility lesson with Aslan was a whole new brand of epicurean torture. She hated curry, and combining the powerful spice with hard-boiled eggs was flat-out sinful.

Her parents shoveled in bite after bite of the atrocious entrée as the smell of rotten eggs leaked from the covered casserole dish. Her roll, corn, and side salad eaten, all that remained on her plate was the nasty, watery egg bake. Even Peter had managed to eat half of his. Her tummy roiled at the smell of the scoopful plopped on her plate. Mom monitored the requisite two bites from the corner of her eyes. She knew curry was not Krissy's thing, but Rule Six would be honored.

Holding her breath, but not being so rude as to pinch her nose between two fingers (which would violate Rule Four), Krissy took a small fork-load of a sliced hard-boiled egg in the puke-yellow curry sauce and swallowed the bite whole. Before taking a breath, she grabbed her milk and drank several gulps. Her stomach knotted in preparation to retch, but a deep breath controlled the urge. One more bite to go.

"We need to leave soon," Dad said, unaware of the gastronomical drama occurring to his left. "It'll take about thirty-five minutes to get to Okie Dokie Rover, and we'll need extra time to find the place and get situated."

She straightened. Mom would never let her leave the table, even for her first puppy agility class, until she forced down that last bite of egg bake. She didn't want to be late. As far as she knew, none of the dogs from basic obedience had enrolled at Okie Dokie Rover, so it would be a whole new group of students. Bracing herself, she took another deep breath, swallowed a second small forkful of the vomit-resembling stuff without chewing, and chased it with milk.

"May I please be excused?" she asked, gasping a bit.

"Have you taken your pills?" Mom asked.

"They're down." Krissy always took her immunosuppressant pills for her kidney transplant before dinner, and Mom always double-checked. Her transplant would fail if she missed doses.

"Then yes," Mom said. "Take your dishes to the sink please. And don't forget to take the new dog treats with you. I went to three pet stores before I finally found them at that specialty store on Britton and May. I hope the new trainer approves."

Dad pushed his chair back from the table. "Get Aslan and meet me in the car."

Peter glowered at Krissy as she jumped up from the table and took her plate and glass to the sink. Was he mad she'd gotten the last bite down without whining or jealous because she was going to classes? Why would he care? He didn't want to do agility.

She lowered her eyes rather than glaring back at him like she wanted. Her illness seemed to have upset the family's emotional apple cart, and since the problem stemmed from her, the solution should, too. So, Krissy forced a smile onto her face and turned back to the table. "Are you through, Peter? I can take your dishes to the sink since I'm up."

He stared at her with a confused, slack-jawed expression. "No thanks. I'll be walking right by the sink in a second. I'll drop them off then."

Krissy's smile faded, as she went to find Aslan. How could she make everyone happier if they pushed her away?

Well, she wouldn't let his sour attitude spoil her mood. She was beyond excited. Tonight, they'd take the first real step in Aslan's agility training. Her level of anticipation surprised her—she'd tried to talk herself out of agility, figuring neither she nor Aslan were a good fit for it. Yet here she was, her stomach twisted in anticipation.

Either that, or the egg bake was fighting back.

* * *

Forty minutes later, Krissy's gloved hand gripped Aslan's leash as she followed Dad past a darkened fenced-in lot and toward a rectangular metal building. Shadows grew from the ground in the silent field, forming into the ghostly shapes of agility equipment as they neared. Dad opened the door to Okie Dokie Rover's training building, and they entered a well-lit but unheated horse arena. Well, dog arena, really. Pieces of colorful agility apparatus scattered across the expansive dirt floor. The blue and yellow A-frame, teeter, tunnels, and dogwalk sent a shiver through her. She longed to put Aslan on the stuff, eager to see how he'd do. He trotted by her side, nose to the dirt, giving the novel place a good examination.

As at Positive Pups, Dad found a plastic patio chair along the edge of the arena, dusted it off with his hand, sat, and opened his anachronistic newspaper.

Cooing to Aslan to get his attention, Krissy approached several other owners and puppies huddled in the middle of the arena, who were listening to a teenager about Krissy's own age speak. A tall willowy girl with chocolate-brown hair pulled back with barrettes, she held herself with authority—back straight, head up—and the adults seemed more than willing to submit to her.

"That's why y'all need to set your crates up over there." As the teen pointed to the south side of the arena, Krissy realized each owner lugged not only a pup and a training bag, but also a crate of some sort. Some of the wire crates were collapsed and leaned heavily against the handlers' legs, while others were soft-sided crates folded into neat, easy-to-carry bundles.

Krissy's brow scrunched. "I don't have a crate," she told the girl, not meeting her eyes. "I didn't know I was supposed to bring one."

"It was told you in your welcome email." The girl put a hand on her hip and cocked her head, causing her hair to flop to the side.

"My dad got that." Krissy waved a limp hand in his general direction. "I guess he forgot to tell me."

The girl let out an exasperated sigh and pointed to several empty wire crates lined against the wall. "For tonight only, you can use one of those, but bring a crate next week. Them crates are for our dogs, not students' dogs."

Small dust clouds puffed around Krissy's boots as she scuffed toward the wire crates in the far southwest corner. Careful not to clang the metal door, she put Aslan inside one of the large sandy crates, hoping to avoid any more negative attention.

As the students set up their crates and portable chairs, the teenager stood in front of the class and spoke. "I'm Mia. I'm the training assistant for this class, and my mom is the instructor. She's finishing dinner and will be down from the house in a few. First though, I want to make sure who's here."

As Mia called names off a list, Krissy took stock of the other students. There were two border collie pups, a westie, a Labrador, a medium-sized mixed breed with pointy ears, a German shepherd mix, and what appeared to be an Australian shepherd. Dogs had to be between five and ten months old to enroll in the class, so all the pups were clumsy with their too-long, adolescent legs and gawky bodies. Several of the class members giggled when the German shepherd mix chased his own tail, tripping over his rangy legs as he spun in circles.

Mia stopped reading names and glared at Krissy. "I said, is Krissy and the sheltie Asiain here?"

Krissy hadn't heard her name called over the laughter. She raised her hand, ignoring the fact that Aslan's name had been mispronounced. Mia rolled her eyes and continued. "Get your treats out. First, we're going to work on sits, drops, and stays to see how good your dog's obedience skills are."

The class spread out around the south end of the building and proceeded to train sits, drops, and stays on-lead. Krissy found an isolated space between the crating area and a bright purple tunnel, pulled out some treats, and asked Aslan to sit. He did, plunking his furry butt on the ground and gazing at her with eager, hungry eyes. "Good boy! That was fantastic! Okay." She remembered to keep her voice light and happy as Shelly had taught her.

Out of the corner of her eye, she saw a lady who looked to be a carbon-copy of Mia enter the barn through a side door. Krissy guessed this was Charlotte, the head instructor. The lady's gaze immediately fell on Aslan, and Krissy tensed.

Standing straight, Krissy turned back to Aslan, and, palm moving to the floor, said, "Drop!" Her command came out too sharp. He stared at her with a blank expression, as if he'd never heard the word before.

"Drop," Krissy repeated, trying to put the smile back in her voice. The lady moved toward her. Krissy bent over, and, using the treat as a lure, brought Aslan into the sphinx position on the dirty arena floor. "Good boy! Okay!" she said, releasing him from the command.

"Hi. I'm Charlotte, your instructor. You never use a lure," the lady said by way of introduction. "You can't take treats into the ring with you to lure your dog around the agility course, so you don't use them here. If he won't drop, pull on his collar to force him into position." Charlotte grabbed Aslan's collar and pulled his thin neck toward the floor until his legs folded. His eyes widened as she tugged him to the ground. "Give him a treat," Charlotte said after letting go of the collar. "Remember, always reward your dog for good work."

Krissy held the treat out to him with shaky fingers. Rather than his normal behavior of snatching and gulping it whole, he hesitated and took a small nibble. His eyes darted between her and Charlotte, ears limp and head low. Krissy had never seen him like this.

Was he scared? If he was, she couldn't blame him. Shelly had taught her to lure. Was Shelly wrong, or was agility training different because of the rules? Krissy didn't like the idea of jerking Aslan to the ground. If agility training required much harsher corrections than this, she wasn't sure she'd have the stomach for it.

* * *

Krissy and Aslan waited in line for their turn at the PVC agility jump. Her foot tapped, burning anxious energy. Earlier, Charlotte had explained how dogs competed in different jump height classes based on the measurement of each dog at the withers. That way a Chihuahua didn't compete against a super-fast border collie but only against other small dogs. She then went around the class, eyeing the pups, and telling the owners what jump height group their dog would be competing in. When she got to Aslan, she said, "He's gonna jump in the twelve-inch height class. He's scrawny, so he looks smaller than he is. But he's gonna be a twelve-incher. Don't let anyone tell you otherwise. For now, you'll jump him at four inches because he's a puppy."

After assigning jump heights, she'd said jumps were, by far, the most used piece of agility equipment. Following a brief explanation of their first jumping exercise, Charlotte's border collie had demoed the jump. She'd made it look easy.

Krissy quieted her tapping foot and in lieu fingered Aslan's lead as she awaited their turn. When the pointy-eared mixed-breed in front of them finished his attempt at the jump, Charlotte motioned for Krissy to take her place in front of the class.

Krissy set Aslan ten feet in front of the jump as she'd been told, and Charlotte repeated the exercise's instructions, sounding like a bored flight attendant repeating flight safety instructions. "Keep him on lead and run by the jump. Make sure to hold the leash high enough so you don't hit the jump stanchions. Just run him to the jump, and he'll take it."

Krissy let out slack on the leash. Game face on, she thrust her feet into the deep sand and told her body to run toward the jump. Instead, her body merely trotted. Aslan followed, bird legs pumping in an even rhythm. Then, without warning, instead of gathering to leap over the jump, he skidded to a halt inches in front of the bar, a cloud of dust billowing around him. Krissy, focused on keeping the leash from becoming entangled with the stanchion, continued forward. Her momentum ate the leash's slack, and she jerked Aslan straight into the jump bar, which fell to the dirt. Krissy's right wrist—the wrist with the fistula—had dropped due to his weight pulling on the lead, and she took out the jump's entire left stanchion. Frightened, Aslan yanked back from the clattering jump pieces, almost pulling free from his collar.

"No!" Charlotte's volume increased to just shy of a yell. "I said *run* to the jump. You weren't going fast enough, so he didn't have the speed to jump. Plus, your arm was too low. I said keep it up, so the stanchion doesn't fall." She waved her hand in a gesture of dismissal. "You'll get to try again later. Next dog."

As they trudged to the end of the line, Krissy avoided glancing at Dad. If he was disappointed in her bungling, she didn't want to see it. Once back in line, she raised her wrist to her ear. The familiar *whoosh, whoosh* greeted her. Relieved, she examined her arm, seeing no signs of injury. The memory of the hoof pick incident with Whickery played, and the old fear tugged in her chest.

Their next chance at the jump, Aslan sat in the dirt like a stubborn donkey, unwilling to move. When Krissy took out a treat to lure him over the jump, Charlotte reminded her, "Lures can't be used in the ring and aren't allowed here, either." After a few more failed attempts to get him to move, they were sent to the back of the line and didn't get another opportunity at the jump.

* * *

After class, Dad and Krissy collected her training gear. It had been an utter disaster, and she was ready to go. The rest of class had gone about as well as the obedience and jump training had, which was to say horrid. True, Aslan had done okay with the tunnel, but agility obstacles weren't all tunnels. Later Charlotte had yelled at her again for not running fast enough during the A-frame training.

The egg bake was in downright revolt now, and she fought to keep the nausea at bay.

Dad glanced up, alerting Krissy to Charlotte's approach from behind. "So, what's keeping you from running?" Charlotte was abrupt and all business.

The blunt statement took Krissy aback, but Dad interceded. "She was on dialysis and later had a kidney transplant. Complications caused some issues with her joints."

Charlotte barely glanced at Dad before focusing on Krissy. "Well, agility is an *athletic* sport." Her voice was dispassionate, matter-of-fact. "It requires the handler to run fast. You can't trot around the course. Plus, your sheltie doesn't seem very interested in the game. I think you'd do better with obedience or nosework where you don't have to run."

Although Charlotte wasn't looking at him, Dad spoke. "I've seen videos of people in wheelchairs doing agility. It seems it can be done whether a person can run or not."

"That's just novice level—beginning level—agility," Charlotte said. "At the advanced level, you have to run. There's no sense spending all that time, effort, and money for Aslan to be forever stuck in novice because your daughter can't run."

"Will we get a refund?" Dad asked calmly. Krissy stared at him, mouth open. He was giving up on her? Just like that?

"I usually don't give refunds, but in this case, I'll refund everything but tonight's class fee. You took obedience classes from Shelly, right? I suggest you talk to her. She can help you with competition obedience classes. I have your address from the on-line entry form. I'll mail you the refund."

Krissy picked up Aslan and petted his velvety head. She followed Dad out the barn door, her head lowered so her hair would hide her face and the tears that blurred her vision as she walked away from yet another failed dream.

CHAPTER 11

Trees, Toys, and Trust

December: Eight Months Old

Sedate music played low in the background as Aslan snuggled next to his young Mistress's warm denim-covered thigh. His comfy spot on the pillowy sofa contrasted to the cold rain pattering against the patio door, and he let out a moan of deep contentment.

It'd been another good day. Today his Mistress had stayed home instead of leaving the house from morning to mid-afternoon. Together, they'd played several games, like Sit, Drop, Come, Walk With Me, and the new game, Stand. When not playing games, he'd followed her around the house.

And he'd avoided Ruffis. The large collie had made it perfectly clear he didn't care for the sheltie pup. Whenever Aslan got near him, Ruffis would quiver his upper lip just enough so Aslan would notice, but the humans wouldn't. The subtle warning screamed, "Stay away from me." On the few occasions when Aslan had gotten bold enough to try enticing the old collie to play, Ruffis had snarled and snapped at him.

Aslan still remembered the place with his mother, his littermates, and all the other shelties, although the memory now came to him as if through a mist. Thinking about it caused an odd ache in his throat.

He loved his Mistress, though. She laughed, talked to him, and petted him. The best fun came when she got out the treats and asked him to play. The challenge of figuring out what he needed to do to get a treat hurt his brain sometimes but in a good way. If she spoke Dog better, they'd progress faster, but they were improving. The treats came with more regularity and less confusion.

Dog tags rattled, and Aslan raised his head to track Ruffis, who slogged on stiff legs from his sleeping spot in the middle of the den floor to the fluffy dog bed. Maintaining constant vigilance around the elderly dog exhausted Aslan, but he couldn't risk accidentally getting too close. The collie flopped onto the thick foam bed between the dark fireplace and the new fake tree.

This fake tree often captured Aslan's attention, and he studied it once again. The tree had appeared a few weeks ago. Dad and Peter had hefted the big chair from the corner of the den by the fireplace to the garden room. Then the humans carted cardboard boxes from the garage until the den floor was covered with them. With grunts, they lugged a fake tree from the garage, too, and everyone worked to raise it in the corner of the den vacated by the chair. Why they brought a tree that wasn't a tree into the house was a mystery. At first, he wondered if it was for his personal toilet use, yet it didn't smell like a tree, the outdoors, or urine. And it would feel strange to pee on it indoors—like peeing on furniture.

The family then pulled things out of the boxes and placed them on the tree. A tremor fluttered through him. The things resembled toys! A fake tree covered in dog toys was a stellar idea. Anticipation built as multi-colored balls and long tug toys made of shiny silvery material were plucked from the boxes, exclaimed over, and hung all over the tree. There were also stuffed toys that looked like mice, birds, and curious white-bearded people. The family chatted and pointed, coordinating the placement of the toys. In addition, colored lights sparkled on the tree, but their function remained incomprehensible.

A toy tree made perfect sense, and Aslan wished the humans had thought to bring him one sooner. While they artfully placed the toys on the tree, they ate cookies and drank hot liquid.

His Mistress gave him pieces of cookie for a few spontaneous games of Sit and Drop. Her cheeks were rosy, and she giggled when he flopped to the floor on command. She'd seemed sad since they'd gone to the place with the sandy floor, so he was eager to flop-drop just to see her smile. He wagged his tail as they played games. He even forgot to keep an eye on Ruffis in his excitement over the tree party.

The atmosphere later changed from festive to dull after the tree had been covered from top to bottom with toys and the empty boxes had been removed. Aslan had lain by the tree, waiting for one of the family members to show him how to play with the toys. Instead, his Mistress grabbed a book and curled on the sofa, staring at it, Mom sat at the kitchen table and shuffled papers, and Peter and Dad went upstairs. Ignoring all of it, Ruffis wandered into the entryway to lay in the hall where he liked to sleep.

Time passed. Aslan whined, yet no one showed him how to play with the tree of toys. Was he supposed to help himself? Unsure, he studied the dust-scented branches covered in toys. Soft toys. Crunchy-looking toys. Toys that smelled old and moldy. Some that looked like food. He crouched, and, slow step by slow step, approached the tree. He sniffed a brightly colored stuffed bird hanging from one of the branches at the very bottom. When his nose touched it, the feathered creature swayed temptingly to and fro. He stared at it for several moments. He glanced at his Mistress, her nose in the book. What should he do? It *looked* like a toy. It didn't look like a shoe or a sock, which were not to be chewed or touched for any reason.

Yes. It had to be a toy. Decision made, he didn't hesitate. He lunged, snatched the bird in his jaws, and yanked it off the tree. The tree rustled at the indiscretion. It wasn't the rustle a real tree would make if a squirrel or the wind disturbed its branches. It sounded more like his Mistress's hairbrush when she cleaned it.

With the toy clenched in his jaws, guilt flooded him, although he couldn't imagine why. Toys were all over the tree after all, and he'd always been allowed to play and chew any toy within his reach. But his Mistress's eyes snapped up from her book. With a turn of his head, he tried to hide the stuffed bird from her view.

"Aslan. No!" She dropped her book on the sofa and rushed toward him, hand extended to grab his treasure. In shock, he bolted to the garden room. Surrounded by plants, two dog crates sat with their doors open, and he dove into the little wire one, toy clutched between his teeth. His Mistress got on her knees, reached in, and pulled him out. Without hurting him, she pried his jaws open and freed the bird.

"No." She shook the toy in front of his face. "No. This is a no. You cannot touch the Christmas ornaments. Bad dog."

He didn't understand much of the human language, but he knew well what *no* and the accompanying tone meant. He lowered his head, ears drooping. Drawn by the commotion, Mom rushed into the room, and after the two humans spoke in their language, they'd returned to the tree and rearranged the toys.

Now, as Aslan sat on the sofa with his Mistress, he examined the tree. All of the toys that rang when touched—which had originally been placed in a haphazard manner all over the tree—were repositioned to the bottom branches in a devious trap. A few days ago, he'd tried to sneak the bird away again, but as he'd been tugging it from its branch, the tree had rung an alarm, sending Mom running into the room in a sour mood.

So, from afar, Aslan admired the tree of toys in complete mystification. The family was as mystified by it as he was, as they also spent lots of time staring at it in wonder.

He lay his head on the soft sofa cushion and pressed against his Mistress's leg. Humans were a constant source of fascination.

* * *

Krissy crossed her eyes slightly, making the passing Christmas lights blur in the fogged side window of Dad's SUV. On the rear seat next to her, Peter leaned his head back and rubbed his forehead, while up front, Mom critiqued the choir's performance at that evening's Christmas Eve candlelight service.

"*Christmas Medley* was beautiful, until Marjorie came in too early on the last stanza." Mom sounded disgusted. "I went over and over that with them."

"It was fine," Dad said. "Nobody noticed."

"How do you know? You were in the choir loft, not sitting with the congregation. How could someone not hear Marjorie's lone A in discord with the piano's B-flat?"

"It's a small choir," Dad said. "Nobody expects perfection. We did quite well."

Although only fourteen, Krissy also sang in the church choir her mother directed, and Dad was right. The choir lacked members, but Mom demanded perfection from the twelve singers anyway. Usually she got a pretty good facsimile of it, but tonight Krissy had heard Marjorie's early, off-key entry and had known it would plague Mom.

Dad pulled into their driveway, and Krissy exited the car. A light cold mist fell, casting their house, outlined on both stories in cobalt LED lights, in an ethereal blue haze. White twinklers sparkled in the yard's river birch as well, creating a mini winter wonderland.

"And the basses came in fortissimo on the chorus of 'O Come, O Come Emmanuel.' Fortissimo! They gave a perfect pianissimo in practice."

Dad didn't respond as he unlocked the front door.

The dry warmth of the house and the smell of Grandma's chili lingering from dinner wrapped Krissy in comfort. It smelled like Christmas Eve should. Mom was big on holiday traditions, and as such, every Christmas Eve, the family sat down to a meal of Grandma's chili, which wasn't really chili at all, but egg noodles and hamburger in a tomato-based soup. Then, they'd rush to get ready for Christmas Eve service. Mom, nervous about choir, would charge about, issuing orders. Following tradition to a tee, Dad always ran a few minutes late, making Mom wring her hands and repeatedly yell for him to hurry. Krissy and Peter knew better than to tempt Mom's wrath when choir was on the line and would both be dressed, standing at the door, and waiting for Dad. At the last minute with Mom in a total frazzle, he would fly down the stairs, coattails flapping, and the family would flee out the door to church. It was the same year after year.

Krissy put a brown paper sack filled with old-fashioned ribbon candies, unshelled peanuts, and fruit the church had handed out after the service on the counter by the sink. If given the choice between going to church on Christmas Eve or getting Christmas presents, she'd choose church. The warm candle glow and familiar hymns followed by Christmas greetings from friends always filled her with good cheer—like a Norman Rockwell painting. Reaching into the bag, she grabbed one of the hard candies. She popped it into her mouth before trotting into the den past Peter, who was pulling Christmas gifts out from under the tree, to the darkened garden room to release Aslan from his crate. Long ago, Ruffis had ceased needing to be confined to his crate when the family left the house, but Aslan was a puppy. Even though he was potty-trained, the ornament heist of a few weeks ago had proved he was not yet trustworthy enough to have full access to the house.

Calling his name, she led him to the patio door and let him out for his business. The small sheltie trotted to the patio's edge and tiptoed onto the dormant brown Bermuda grass, where he squatted like a girl dog to pee. He hated wet grass and would be back at the sliding glass door in a minute, seeking shelter under the eaves from the mist.

While he did his thing, she took a step back from the patio door to get a good view of Violet's house through one of the floor-to-ceiling garden room windows. She and Violet would have shared a backyard fence except for the headwaters of Deepfork River, which flowed in a small stream between the two yards. Violet's bedroom window glowed golden in the dark. Krissy smiled. Her best friend was probably getting ready for bed, excited about gifts in the morning. Violet's family was a Christmas morning family, so around noon tomorrow, Krissy would call, and they'd chat about their present haul.

Done with his business and looking forlorn, Aslan stared in through the glass door, none too happy with the cold, wet weather. It was too bad temps wouldn't drop low enough for a white Christmas, but those were rare in Oklahoma.

She opened the door, and he pranced inside. As she slid it closed, he lifted his grateful face to hers. Although in the awkward adolescent stage, he'd grown cuter. His mottled-buff coat would never be thick like conformation shelties, but she couldn't see through to his skin anymore. His body had become streamlined, all of the puppy fat turned to stringy muscles, yet he still had those birdlike legs. His plumed tail wagged at her, and his big round eyes reflected the shine of the outside porch light.

Charlotte had been right. He was scrawny. But Charlotte had also been shortsighted. Aslan was so much more than his looks. She'd missed his heart.

And, Dad must've missed not only Aslan's heart but Krissy's, too. He hadn't stood up for her at the lesson. He'd said nothing, and his silence had said it all. He didn't believe she could do it.

She swallowed against the lump growing in her throat. If her own father thought she couldn't, then, it was time to move on. She needed to stop thinking about agility—to stop wanting to do things she couldn't. She was who she was. Aslan was who he was. And together, they would find something else to do.

A second choice.

"You're a good pup, Aslan," Krissy said, her voice thick with emotion. His tail continued to wag in recognition of the praise, and he trotted, head high, into the den.

* * *

Peter ran his fingers over the blade on a blue windshield scraper—the pile of unopened gifts by him diminishing. On Christmas Eve, they each took turns opening gifts, and he'd just unwrapped the scraper.

Dad nodded at it. "That's a metal blade. It's great on ice, but be careful not to scratch the glass with it."

Krissy sat on the floor next to the tree with Aslan lying by her side. When she'd first begun unwrapping gifts, he'd been interested in what the boxes contained, but after he'd tried to eat some of the discarded Christmas paper, she'd gone to the freezer to snatch him a Kong toy filled with leftover chicken meat as a distraction. All of his attention was now focused on getting the frozen meat out of the rubber toy's innards.

Her turn up, she chose the smallest of her remaining gifts—a package wrapped in her favorite foil paper. Little frosted-blue reindeer gamboled on a silver background before she ripped through them. With the silvery foil removed, she opened the cardboard box. Inside lay a crisply folded piece of paper. She unfolded it and read: *One year of agility classes at City Dogs Agility School with instructors Daniel and Judy Furuta. Also included are six jumps, one tunnel, and one set of weave poles.* Bordering the paper were cartoon clip-art dogs weaving and climbing A-frames.

She glanced at her parents, her lips stuck in a half-smile to mask her lurching innards. "What's this?"

"That," Dad said with a grin, "is your new agility school. I went out there last week and met with the instructors. I told them what happened at Okie Dokie Rover, and they were disappointed to hear about it. We talked for a long time. They assured me you can do agility at any level you want with the right training."

Krissy's throat tightened, and she couldn't swallow. "But, I've given that idea up." Or at least, she'd tried. "I've never even heard of City Dogs, and I did a lot of research on local trainers. Who are they?"

She wasn't prepared for this. Agility was behind them. The moment she'd returned home from Okie Dokie Rover after Dad had given up on her, she'd gone to the dog corner of her room, torn the pics of shelties doing agility off the wall, and thrown them in the trash. Only regal collies and a new photo of Aslan remained. She'd been pondering getting into rally obedience or something more fitted to her abilities. Nosework maybe?

"You don't have to go," Dad said, "but these are wonderful folks. I called Shelly and told her what happened at Okie Dokie. She was horrified and apologized profusely for recommending them. She'd suggested Okie Dokie thinking you and the young girl assisting class there might become friends. Instead, she told me to contact City Dogs. Daniel Furuta said you absolutely *can* do agility and even compete. He also said it sounds as if Aslan has the earmarks of a great agility prospect. So, if you want to do agility, you can. Nothing's stopping you. The Furutas are willing to help train you and Aslan, knowing your abilities. They're eager to have you join their team."

Krissy stared at the paper, her heart pounding. Things had changed. In just two weeks, they'd changed a lot. She knew she should thank her parents for the gift, but she didn't want this. If she tried agility again, she'd wind up failing—again.

Searching for something to say that wouldn't be a lie, she asked, "Why six jumps, a tunnel, and weaves?"

"Daniel recommended those pieces of equipment for a beginning distance trainer."

"A what?" Krissy asked.

"Daniel explained that you'll probably need to work Aslan at distance. Turns out you don't have to run adjacent to him. You can teach him to go out and do the obstacles on his own. Dan showed me with his own dog. His dog was about thirty feet away from him, doing the A-frame and weave poles. It was eye-opening." Dad spoke with uncharacteristic animation using hand gestures to mimic the shape of the A-frame and a waving motion for the weave poles. "Dan said lots of people in agility don't run as fast as their dogs. Some do, but many use training to overcome that deficit."

He paused, staring at his now silent hands. "You can do this if you want. But, there's no pressure."

She'd never heard of distance training and couldn't envision the agility she'd seen on the internet being done with a dog thirty feet away from his handler. How would the dog know where to go from that far away? Dad made it sound possible—but how? People like her couldn't do agility. Charlotte had said as much.

She continued to study the paper. It was tangible proof that Dad had never stopped believing in her—that she'd been wrong about him. Her eyes burned, and she blinked back the tears. If she did this, she'd risk more humiliation. If she failed agility this time, she might not have enough confidence left to pick up the pieces and summon the courage and desire to attempt a second-choice dog activity. He'd said she could say no, but he'd gone to so much effort to find this place. And he was so fervent about it.

So hopeful.

She stifled her emotions for Dad. He'd tried so hard. "Thank you. I will give it some thought."

Dad nodded. "That's good enough."

"I believe I'm next." Mom broke the tension and lifted a gift onto her lap. With care, she pulled the tape from the paper.

Krissy watched without seeing. Her hand stroked Aslan's soft fur as he licked frozen chicken bits from his toy. Was Dad right? Could they do agility? Were there any videos out there of distance agility? Krissy had watched video after video of teams competing at Worlds, and the handlers ran with their dogs. The moves they did required the handler to run, slam on the brakes while turning or spinning, and then tear out at top speed in another direction to beat their dog to a far obstacle. Dogs were cued to leap from both the front and back sides of jumps. Handlers had to be at the jump to cue that. Right?

Dad believed in her. Could she ride the wake of that belief and try again? She had to. She couldn't disappoint him. Her illness had caused enough emotional trauma in this family. She'd pick herself up and put herself back out there for Dad, and maybe for herself, too.

Carefully, she folded the piece of paper and placed it back in the lidless box. When she looked up, Peter was staring at the paper, brows furrowed, eyes flashing. What was wrong with him lately? Mom held a pair of earrings to her ears, and smiling, thanked Peter for them, causing him to shift his attention. As he turned his head toward Mom, his features changed, and he grinned at her, all signs of anger, jealousy, or whatever, gone. Behind his back, he dropped the windshield scraper he'd been holding onto the carpet.

Aslan made greedy piggy noises with his toy as Krissy set the box and its disorienting contents aside.

CHAPTER 12

Reprise - Second Step

January: Eight Months Old

Déjà vu made Krissy's head swim. Once again, she and Aslan walked past a darkened agility field into a metal building filled with agility equipment. There were differences between last time and this time, though. This time, she wasn't excited-nervous. She was scared-nervous. This time, the building wasn't an indoor horse arena but a small metal building about the size of a tricked-out four-car garage. Also, Dad seemed more aware, more engaged. Picking up on her anxiety, Aslan walked on his toes.

After the darkness of the parking lot, Krissy squinted into the bright lights of the training building, and agility equipment fuzzed into view. Most of it was folded and neatly stored along the metal walls, but several jumps created an arc around the edges of the training area. Green indoor soccer turf covered the floor, springy and soft under her sneakers as she walked across it. It was warm in the building compared to the freezing January evening outside, and the space felt cramped but cozy in contrast to Okie Dokie Rover's large cold arena.

This time, she came prepared for class. Dad had made sure she had all the necessities. He hefted a new soft-sided crate for Aslan, two bagged camp chairs, her training bag toting treats and toys, his newspaper, and a cup of coffee. She carried her purse, a bottle of water, and Aslan's leash with Aslan attached. She hoped they had everything she'd need.

Like at the Okie Dokie Rover class, students congregated around someone who appeared to be in charge. As Krissy neared, a middle-aged woman with long blond hair pulled back in a ponytail turned toward them and excused herself from the huddled group. The woman, dressed in a track warm-up, was thin, strong, and athletic—like Charlotte.

"You must be Krissy and Aslan. My name is Judy. Welcome." Her voice was warm and comforting. She nodded to Dad in greeting. "Feel free to set up your crate and chairs against that wall. We will be getting started in a—"

"Krissy!" The familiar voice caused Krissy to grin before she even turned. Mike shuffled over, a big smile on his face, too. "I was hoping I'd see someone I knew from Positive Pup here, and look who shows up." He clapped Dad on the shoulder. "Hello, Doc. This is like old home week."

Judy smiled at the reunion and left to greet another student. "How's Honey?" Krissy asked, searching the other students' crates lined against the wall for the blond beardie as she and Mike followed Dad to the crating space.

"As smart as ever. Shelly talked me into trying agility. She thought it'd be a good outlet for Honey's energy. I'm not exactly fit, so I'm hoping Honey will put up with this laggard." He patted his ample stomach. "Need help with that, Doc? These soft-sided crates can be a puzzle to assemble."

Mike and Dad fought with the new crate while Krissy surveyed the room. Finding Mike and Honey there eased some of her anxiety, and her muscles relaxed.

The door opened, and Abby and Jeeves walked in.

"Mike! Did you know Abby was in this class, too?" Krissy pointed at the team walking toward them.

"Abby and Jeeves!" Mike exclaimed, closing the gap to give Abby a welcoming hug. "Another Positive Pup alumnus."

"Can I set up here?" Abby lifted her hand holding a bag of dog treats toward an empty spot next to Aslan's crate. Her shoulder-length brown hair was pulled back with two barrettes, and her cheeks were pink from the outdoor chill. Jeeves heeled by her side, his short coat shining with health under the fluorescent lights.

"Please do," Dad said. "It's great to see you two."

"I'm so excited to be starting agility." Abby looked at Krissy. "I knew you were going to do agility, but Shelly thought you were enrolled at Okie Dokie Rover."

"We were, but we changed schools," Dad answered cryptically.

"I'm so glad," Abby said with a smile. "So, the S.T.A.R. Puppies continue. Sort of like the Three Musketeers."

"Make that Two Musketeers and their hilarious sidekick, Honey." Mike glanced at his beardie, who had a seam of her pink soft-sided crate between her front teeth. "Honey, no! That's new!" Mike rushed over to stop the destructive escape attempt.

The roiling in Krissy's stomach eased. It was so good to see Abby and Mike. Like the cavalry, they'd arrived at just the right time. She wasn't alone in this venture. She had friends.

Minutes later, Judy walked to the center of the room and called for everyone's attention. Just as at Okie Dokie Rover, she asked everyone to get their pups out and work their sits, drops, and stays on leash. Dread sneaked its way back into Krissy's gut as she freed Aslan from his crate and put treats in her pocket. She found an isolated corner and practiced sits and sit/stays. She didn't work the drop. Ever since Okie Dokie Rover, Aslan's drops had deteriorated.

Aslan's bright, round eyes focused with eagerness on the treats in her hand, and when commanded to sit, his butt hit the turf with rocket speed. She marked the sit with a "yes," gave him a treat, and released him. He pranced, expectant eyes waiting for her next command. A man—Daniel, perhaps—ran his fingers through his thick, black hair as he stood to the side, watching Aslan perform sit after flawless sit.

After a few repetitions, the man approached. "Can you ask him to drop?"

Krissy's mouth drew into a straight line. Pressing her palm to the ground, she said, "Drop." Aslan wouldn't look at her, pretending to be distracted by the nearby dogs working with their owners. She repeated the command. Again, he avoided eye contact.

Shelly had suggested using a treat to lure him into a drop, and then fading the treat and lure over time. But since Charlotte had said to never use a lure in agility, this man would surely expect her to yank on the collar. She cringed. She hated doing it, but grabbing his collar, she pulled it down until he lowered to the floor, bewilderment written on his face. She rewarded him and released him. He bounded to his feet and backed away.

"Yeah. Pulling the dog into the drop position seems like it would be a good thing to do when he doesn't respond, doesn't it?" the man who was probably Daniel asked as he came and knelt by the pair. "But, agility needs to be fun for both the dog and you, so let's use your treat to lure him." He reached for the treat in her hand to show her how to do it, but she closed her fingers over it.

She'd heard the "agility is a game and must be fun" speech before. Wanting to show she wasn't that far behind and knew how to lure, she snapped the treat in front of Aslan's nose and brought it to the ground at the precise angle Shelly had shown her.

"That's it!" the man exclaimed as Aslan lowered himself to the ground, following the treat with his nose. "Now we'll need to work on fading the treat lure."

"Normally, he'll drop without the lure," Krissy said. "He might be nervous tonight."

The man smiled, his dark eyes sparkling in his handsome face. "Yeah. The first class at a new place can be stressful."

His disarming smile eased her shyness and gave her courage. "Shelly, my obedience instructor, taught us to lure, but at the other agility school, they said never to lure because you can't have a treat with you in the ring."

"It's important to make this fun, so luring, removing the lure, and then working the behavior in a variety of different environments until the dog is solid with his job is best. Soon, you'll have Aslan doing drops regardless of whether or not you have a treat or what's going on around him. Working the behavior in increasing distractions is called *proofing,* and we'll help you learn that." His voice was strong but patient. "For tonight, lure him down with big praise and treats each time he's successful. Make it a game. Make it fun!"

The man petted Aslan's head. "You'll find we train many things differently than Okie Dokie Rover. From basic obedience behaviors like this to taking our time teaching the dogs proper jumping style, we focus on going slowly, letting the pups grow, and making it fun. Strong, fun foundations are key. So, training here will be different."

He rose. "It's good to meet you and Aslan. We'll enjoy instructing you two."

He crossed to help a white poodle mix. The cute mix greeted the instructor's arrival by wagging her tail so hard she couldn't hold her butt on the floor to sit. The owner, a thin young man in his twenties, tried to get control, but the dog's excitement increased to a near-Honey impersonation.

The dark-haired trainer introduced himself to the poodle mix's owner. "I'm Daniel, Judy's husband and co-trainer here."

Mystery solved.

The advice Daniel had shared sounded a lot like Shelly's, making Krissy more comfortable and confident. Other teams scattered across the room practiced their sits and drops. Honey bathed Mike's face rather than laying down, reminiscent of the puppy test. Judy knelt next to them, giving Mike advice. Jeeves performed perfect sits and drops with long stays. Abby didn't even have to bend and point to the floor for him to obey.

Other class members included a red-and-white border collie, a Pembroke corgi, and a Doberman pinscher, who sat tall and watched his middle-aged handler intently, waiting for her to release him from his stay. The handlers smiled as they worked with their dogs. The atmosphere was light, and even though some of the dogs struggled to focus, everyone was having fun. It was a stark contrast to Okie Dokie Rover. Smiling too, Krissy turned back to Aslan, who waited at her feet for the next command.

* * *

The hour flew by. In that short time, the class had learned exercises to improve rear leg awareness, an important skill for agility dogs, as well as hand targeting. Then each dog walked across a long plank raised a couple of inches off the ground. Being small with a low center of gravity, Aslan had excelled at this, and after a few repetitions, he'd galloped, tail high, across the board.

There had been no embarrassing incidents, thank heaven. As in puppy obedience class, Aslan wasn't the best dog, but he wasn't the worst either. Maggie (the Doberman) and Jeeves had been the stars. And, as Mike predicted, Honey was the humorous sidekick.

None of the dogs had gotten on the agility obstacles. They hadn't climbed the A-frame, jumped a jump, or run through the tunnel. Judy had explained why. "Puppy agility class concentrates on foundations. These skills lay the groundwork for your dog's future in agility. Skimp on the foundation skills, and your team will struggle later. There's much to learn before these pups will be ready to tackle the agility obstacles. Plus, their bodies need to grow strong before they can absorb the pounding forces involved in full-height agility. We don't want injuries."

At the end of class, Krissy was stowing Aslan's treats and toys in the training bag while Dad broke down the soft-sided crate.

Daniel approached. Her breath caught. It was just like the end of class at Okie Dokie Rover.

Daniel spoke. "If you have a few minutes, I'd like you to stay to meet my border collie."

Her shoulders fell in relief, but she still glanced at Dad, unsure why they'd been singled out. "We've got extra time," Dad said, setting Aslan's folded crate on the turf.

Daniel nodded. "There's about ten minutes before the next class arrives. Come on over, and I'll introduce you to Q."

They followed Daniel to a plastic crate that housed a small black-and-white border collie. "Q is five years old. She competes at the Master's level and has earned her agility championship."

He opened the door, and the small border collie burst out and jumped on him. He smiled, and, like a magician pulling out a hidden string of multi-colored handkerchiefs, he yanked a tug toy from the pocket of his warm-up pants. "A good dog trainer is always prepared." He grinned at his eager dog, who leaped in the air to grab the toy.

"I understand you've been told that a person who can't run well can't do agility. Q and I would like to put that myth to rest. I'm not physically limited. I can run, and I do. But, I also know the power of having distance skills in agility, so I trained them. I want to show you how a handler can do agility without needing to run. Then, if you'd like, you can handle Q."

Krissy blanched. "I'd like to see you handle her, but I don't think I can."

Daniel smiled his kind smile. "Okay. How about you watch us first, then."

As Daniel walked over to a jump, Judy joined them. "Daniel's going to set Q in front of that jump," she said. Krissy followed Judy's outstretched finger to an orange cone marked with a big number 1. "Then he's going to lead out past the first jump. He'll call Q over the first jump and then turn and push her out over that arc of three jumps without running to them. Q will be about, oh.

. .fifteen feet away from him at the furthest point and will cover all of that distance on her own with Daniel telling her where to go, not running right with her to show her. Then he will call her back to him and over the last jump there."

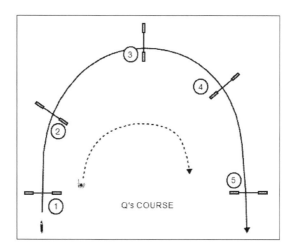

Krissy stood transfixed as Daniel told the border collie to stay. He led out past the first jump and called the dog over. Q took off like a firecracker had blown her from her stay. She sailed over the first jump and ran to the second, gaining speed with each stride. Daniel called "Out!" as she gathered to elevate for the second jump. She whipped away from him toward Jump Three. With continued yells of "Out!" from Daniel, Q never slackened her pace as she worked the promised fifteen feet away from him, clearing the third and fourth jumps and then turning in line with him for the final jump.

The whole thing had taken no more than a few seconds. Q ran so fast that if Krissy had blinked, she'd have missed a jump. Daniel threw the toy for Q, who ran and snatched it off the turf, shaking it to and fro in a mock kill.

"Now, it's your turn," Daniel said, turning toward Krissy.

Her eyes widened. "I could never do that. She's too fast. I couldn't even think that fast."

He laughed. "I think you can do it—even tonight. Come here, I'll give you a few pointers."

She followed him with reluctance. She didn't want to appear rude, but this wasn't going to work. In the end, Daniel and Judy would share a look of unspoken agreement and tell Krissy that perhaps she should try a less active dog sport. It was the prelude to more humiliation.

A couple of minutes later, Daniel finished with, "Remember, she's well trained. If you say 'out' and keep your shoulders squared to each jump, she'll do the rest." He handed Krissy Q's slobbery tug toy. "I'll cue her for her stay. You release her with an 'Okay.'"

Daniel sat Q several feet in front of the first jump, and Krissy led out past the first jump. Sucking her lower lip, she looked back at Q, whose golden eyes locked on her with a frightening intensity. Krissy said, "Okay." Q flew over the first jump before Krissy finished turning to the second jump. Shocked by the dog's speed, she gave the out command well after Q landed the second jump. Q left her behind, taking the third and fourth jumps in a few heartbeats. Krissy turned and signaled the final jump, and Q responded, soaring over it less than a breath later.

"Reward her. Throw the toy." Daniel's voice sounded as if it had come from a distant tunnel. She threw the toy a yard beyond where Q waited, paws dancing in expectation of her prize.

Krissy's heart raced. She'd taken only a few steps as Q ran the arc of jumps, and yet she was out of breath. Those brief seconds were like nothing she'd ever experienced in her life. She'd handled lightning! A small border collie made of lightning!

Laughing, she turned to Daniel, her shyness temporarily banished. "That was fun!" Dad stood a few feet behind Daniel, grinning.

"You can do this," Daniel said. "It'll take a lot of work to train Aslan to read you at distance, but you can do agility with him."

She looked at Aslan sitting by Dad's feet and blinked against tears. What if Daniel were wrong? What if she could never run that lightning again? She wasn't even sure how to describe it, but that feeling. . .She wanted to relive it over and over. Could her sheltie runt be taught to do that? Could she handle him?

As if reading her mind, Judy said in her soft voice, "You've got this if you want it. With hard work and dedication. . .it's all yours."

CHAPTER 13

A Half-Cent Sparrow

February: Ten Months Old

Aslan leaned against his Mistress's too hot body as she finally slept. For most of the day, she'd either been in a tossy-turny doze or watching a small flat thing with moving images that made noise. Her face seemed peaceful now, although it remained flushed, and wisps of sweaty hair stuck to her temples.

Instinct told him she didn't feel well, and although his body ached to be up and doing something, duty demanded he lie quietly by her side in the bed. He would be deeply concerned, but the other humans didn't seem to be worried. Mom came in the room every now and again, touched his Mistress's forehead, and brought in new things for her to drink or eat, but Mom didn't seem upset. When Mom left, his Mistress would give him bits of her food. He liked that.

Otherwise, it had been the most boring, trying day he could remember. There had been no play, no games, no giggles. The entire day had been spent lying by her side. He hated it, yet he knew he couldn't leave her. She was sick, and she might need him.

Unable to sleep after the inactive day, he listened to music coming from the flat thing. He wished Mistress would get up and play that new game called Easy. They could play it indoors or outside, and he'd learned it fast. When his Mistress held her hand down and called "Easy!" he would run and touch his nose to her palm. Brainless. She often sneaked the command in during daily activities. For instance, if she was in the kitchen clinking glasses, she sometimes stopped and yelled, "Easy!" No matter where he was in the big house, he ran to her hand, hit it with his nose, and got a treat.

So fun to get a treat for something so simple. It was a great game, and the faster he ran to her hand, the happier she became. He loved to hear her call him, "Good dog. Good boy." The memory made the tip of his tail raise and lower in a small wag.

But his favorite trick of all was the Out game. It required more running than any game he'd ever played. Well, other than Go Get It. His Mistress would set a bucket in the middle of the backyard and walk several steps away from it. Then she'd gather him by her side, stroll in the direction of the bucket, push her arm out toward it, and yell, "Out!" As with all of the games, he'd been confused at first, but she'd taken her time to show him what she wanted. He soon learned to run around the bucket and then run back to meet up with her. The faster and farther he ran around the bucket, the happier she was. When he ran especially far without turning back, she gave him extra treats and praise. He'd run to the bucket from all sorts of angles and distances. It was so much fun to go fast, but sometimes he got confused about a hard angle or distance and turned back to her to make sure he was doing it right. She didn't seem to like that much.

He longed to go play the Out game again. He stretched one hind leg straight to ease the soreness of inactivity.

The door to the room opened, and Mom crept in. On silent feet, she tiptoed to the music device and pressed it, stopping the sound. Without disturbing his Mistress, she picked him up off the bed, turned out the light, and closed the door as she left. Carrying him downstairs, Mom whispered to him. He recognized the words "potty" and "outside." Now that she mentioned it, he did need to go potty and was glad she'd thought of it.

Mom opened the patio door, and he and Ruffis headed into the dark backyard. Leaving Ruffis to his guard duties, Aslan wandered under the trees in the far back of the yard, sniffing for the perfect spot to relieve himself. As he squatted, he glanced back at the big house. The bright light that lit up the yard at night wasn't shining. Odd. He finished his business in the dark and then trotted back to the big house, giving the collie a wide berth as the bigger dog sniffed with interest at a pile of bricks stacked against the stockade fence. Aslan went to the door and waited for one of the humans to come and let him in. He paced as the late-winter wind nipped his nose and ears, anxious to return to his Mistress.

Without yipping, he lingered at the door for several minutes. Ruffis finished his guard duties and wandered onto the patio, but he didn't join Aslan in his backdoor vigil. Ruffis never came inside at night. He preferred to stay outside, which suited Aslan fine. When Ruffis hung out in the house during the day, Aslan had to pay attention to where the big dog was at all times, so he could avoid his snapping jaws. This meant Aslan loved his nights in the warm house, relaxing and sleeping unafraid by his Mistress's side.

From the edge of the patio, Ruffis glared at him, waiting for him to leave. Ruffis viewed the backyard as his domain, and Aslan was an intruder. Ruffis had made that clear from the beginning.

Aslan peered through the sliding door and gave a small, treble yip when the lights on the first floor of the big house went dark. A strange loneliness enveloped him. He turned and looked questioningly at the big collie, who eyed him with suspicion. Where were the humans?

Ruffis walked off the patio for another sentry turn around the yard. Aslan stared through the glass of the patio door into the vast darkness of the house. He whined.

No one came.

After staring into the empty house for a long time, he started shivering. The cold always bothered him. With his thick coat, the big collie seemed oblivious to the chill, but Aslan detested the biting winter wind. It parted his thin fur and froze his tender skin. He circled in frustration. Although he'd lazed about all day, he was tired, cold, and wanted to be asleep in the comfy bed where he could keep tabs on his sick Mistress.

He cast around the patio. In the corner created by the house and the square box that roared and blew hot air in the summer, a pile of windblown leaves had congregated. From that vantage point, he could keep an eye on the patio door in case one of the humans came to let him inside, and the box would block the winter wind. He walked over and sniffed the nestled leaves. They smelled of moist decay and a dead insect, but they'd offer some warmth and cushioning. He circled over the leaves several times, pressing them down with his paws before lying on them. The box provided a nice wind block, although he still shivered. If only the box would blow the hot air like it had in the summer.

An insulated doghouse sat vacant on the opposite corner of the patio. Once before, he'd pushed his head inside the leather flap covering the entrance. It was lined roof-to-floor with clean carpet. It would be much warmer than the small bed of leaves on the frigid concrete, but the doghouse reeked of Ruffis. After his first investigation, Aslan had never crawled back inside it. With a heavy sigh, he lowered his head onto his small white paws, and against his will, his drooping eyes closed.

With a start, he jerked his head up. What was that noise? Throwing off a moment's disorientation at waking up on the patio, he stilled himself. It had sounded weird. Something he'd never heard before.

Accch. A sound like a throaty human sneeze came from the backyard by the stockade fence. He rose and peered around the box into the dim recesses of the big yard. The ambient glow of the nearby street light cast enough illumination for him to make out the ghostly figure of Ruffis rearing on his hind legs, front paws up on the stockade fence.

Accch. The sneezing sound—no, not sneezing really, but a gagging sound—came from near the collie.

Aslan stood, ears pricked, as Ruffis's body torqued sideways, his front paws remaining on the fence. Then without warning, the big dog thrashed his head back and forth, making the noise again, which this time ended with a strangled whine.

Aslan's skin tingled. The collie had never made a noise like that before. The big dog stopped struggling and returned to his original position, hind legs on the ground and forepaws on the fence. His breathing was labored as if he'd been playing a hearty game of fetch.

Aslan took a few wary steps away from the big house and toward the darkness of the yard. If he got too close, Ruffis would growl and snap at him, maybe even pinch his skin. He faltered, and halted, not knowing what to do. His curiosity warred against his better judgment.

Again, the collie writhed by the fence, breathing heavily.

Arrrrrch! It was a distinct cry of anguish.

Aslan no longer hesitated. He ran to investigate, slowing only when he neared. Ruffis's head was pushed sideways against the fence. The old dog reared on his hind legs, and his forelegs gripped the fence's middle horizontal support board, claws extended, scraping in desperation at the wood. His leg muscles quivered with the effort of holding the unnatural position, and his breath came in panting gasps.

Why was Ruffis standing like that? Was he looking through a hole in the fence to the road outside? With great caution, Aslan tiptoed to the collie's side.

And went rigid with horror.

The grand collie's collar had hooked onto a nail sticking up from the middle support board of the fence. The collar had slid way down over the nail, and it was clear neither the nail nor the collar was going to budge. His eyes swiveled to Aslan, and he tried to turn toward him. But Aslan darted away at the big dog's movement. Ruffis's collar twisted and tightened further, making him gasp for air. He groaned.

Aslan trembled, but this time, it wasn't from the cold but from fright. Once, he'd pulled on his leash, and his collar had tightened just as he had tried to inhale. The loss of that one breath had taught him that collars could constrict breathing and needed to be respected. Now, his enemy was noosed, unable to get air. And with each passing moment, that enemy weakened.

Ruffis needed human help, and he needed it now. Aslan ran to the house and barked at the patio door. Terror and pleading coursed through his high-pitched voice. For long minutes, he barked and barked and barked.

The house remained silent and dark.

He stopped his pleas for help and listened. More gasps and cries came from the collie, and, if possible, they seemed more frantic than before. Aslan wheeled and ran to the fence. One of Ruffis's forelegs was twisted under him—that leg's grip on the middle support board gone. Only his shaking hind legs and a weakened front leg clawing into the middle board kept his full weight from hanging by the strangling collar.

Ignoring his fear of Ruffis, Aslan scurried to the fence and pushed in as close to the big dog as possible. The collie remained motionless as Aslan raised himself on his hind legs and shoved his nose toward the collar. But even stretching as tall as he could, his muzzle remained far from the taut leather. He fell onto all fours and paced back and forth as Ruffis whimpered between gulps of air.

Aslan glanced helplessly around for an answer. There was a column of bricks stacked next to the collie, but the gap between the bricks and the hooked collar was long. Plus, the bricks were piled to a level a bit higher than the fence's horizontal board. He would have to jump three times his height to reach the top. The thought of slamming into the sharp-cornered bricks in a failed jump attempt scared him, but the collie's deteriorating condition demanded he try something.

Anything.

Backing several steps away from the pile of bricks, Aslan turned and focused hard on the top of the stack. He'd never jumped that high before, but he was strong for his size. With a burst of speed, he ran at the bricks, coiled, and sprung his body airborne. The top edge of the column slammed hard into his ribs, making him cry out in pain. While his back legs dangled, his front claws scraped at the top layer of bricks, futilely seeking purchase. He began to slip.

Refusing defeat, he brought up a back leg and scratched along the side of the brick stack. As his front paws slid, his rear leg found a small clawhold. Straining, he hoisted himself further up onto the bricks until most of his upper body lay across the top surface. With a final effort, Aslan heaved himself onto the column. He lay unmoving, breathing against the pain in his chest from hitting the edge of the stack.

Ruffis rasped, and Aslan, ignoring his own pain, scrambled to his feet to investigate the situation from his new elevation. He found himself a bit higher than the collar and nail, but since the collie's twisted forepaw caused him to list toward the bricks, his neck lay between Aslan and the nail. Aslan would have to crawl out, hind legs on the bricks and front legs somehow balanced on the fence's horizontal support board, and reach over the collie's neck to release the collar.

It couldn't be done. The reach from the bricks was too far.

Aslan's paws danced up and down on his tower. There had to be an answer—but what?

Then, he remembered recently walking into his Mistress's closet and finding a toy made of straps of thick skin attached to flat rubber. It just lay on the floor emitting a faint smell of animal doused in chemicals. The animal scent had been so attractive, he couldn't stop himself. He had seized the toy and chewed it, enjoying the toothsome feel of the animal hide in his mouth. The toy was a slobbery blob when his Mistress discovered him in the closet. She'd scolded him, and that day he'd learned not to chew anything in the closet, even if it looked like a toy.

The memory gave him an idea, but it would mean breaking a standing house rule. Steeling himself, he stared at the choking golden dog and crept to the edge of the bricks. Reaching out with his right paw, he stepped with care onto the middle support board, then slid his paw bit by bit across the board while shifting his weight as much as he could to his right side. When in position, he pushed out with his left paw toward the support board, keeping his rear paws on the bricks. His left paw landed just in front of his right paw, and, using his core and leg muscles, he fought to maintain balance.

Perfect! The back of the collie's neck was at his feet. Slowly, ever so slowly, Aslan lowered his head forward, body rebalancing as his neck stretched. He opened his mouth and bit the collar circling Ruffis's neck.

The collar dug into the old dog's skin, making it hard to chew the strap and not chew the collie. At first, only his front teeth found any hold on the soft leather, but after much frantic nibbling, Aslan had enough of the leather pulled away from Ruffis's neck to get his front molars involved in the job. Several times, he accidentally chewed live flesh instead of dead hide and tasted blood. Ruffis never protested. He held still as Aslan continued his feverish work to free the exhausted old dog.

The smells of leather, slobber, blood, wet fur, and fear assaulted Aslan's nose, and his front leg muscles weakened. If he fell, he wouldn't have the strength left to mount another assault on the bricks. Redoubling his efforts and caring less about drawing blood, he maneuvered the collar onto his best back molars and ground at the leather. His neck began to spasm from the angle of his chewing, but he didn't stop. Hope rushed through him as part of the collar gave and separated. He readjusted his head for a better bite.

At his movement, the collie's left foreleg slipped. The big dog dropped almost all of his weight on the collar. Aslan's balance tipped as well, and in a blur, the fence, the beautiful dog, and the bricks passed by.

Aslan landed hard on his side—his breath escaping in a single *whoosh*. He lay stunned for an instant before jumping to his feet to avoid the thrashing collie.

Ruffis was fully choking now. His body twisted, his back against the fence, all four of his legs flailing in the open air in a failed attempt to find support and relieve the tightened noose on his neck. Horrified and helpless, Aslan watched as the collie threw his body back and forth in silence, all gasping gone—he couldn't breathe to make noise. Desperate to help, Aslan sized up the jump to the top of the bricks again, but he sensed that even if his tired legs could make the leap, he wouldn't be able to free the collie in time. Only moments remained.

Dying, the old collie threw himself into a final, violent twist, and a snap echoed in the night. Ruffis plunged to the ground with a dull thud and lay in a heap. Stuck to the nail, the collar swayed, ripped in two where the leather had been weakened by tiny jaws.

Aslan slunk to the old dog and sniffed. Ruffis drew in big lungfuls of air but didn't move. Other than his pants, the backyard loomed silent. Trembling from both his balancing efforts and fear, Aslan lay next to Ruffis and put his head on the old collie's back. Eventually Ruffis fell asleep, but Aslan stayed awake, guarding his enemy through the long, cold night.

* * *

Krissy examined the collar dangling from her fingers, holding it up to the early morning light filtering into the den. She sat on the sofa wrapped in a blue afghan, her fever gone. The collar had been chewed through except for a quarter inch or so that was shorn. Little teeth marks pitted both sides of the tear.

"Seriously?" She looked at her mother, whose expression was a mix of wonder and shock. "You found this on the fence?"

"Yes," Mom said. "I couldn't believe it. When I saw Ruffis's bloody neck, I noticed his collar was missing. I went out to search for it, and there it was. Hooked on a nail."

Dad, sitting next to Krissy, reached for the collar to inspect it, though he'd done so many times already. "If we hadn't left Aslan out by accident. . ." He let the rest of the statement lie.

Ruffis sat at Krissy's feet, or, rather, at Aslan's feet, as she held Aslan in her lap. Since coming inside, the big collie hadn't let the little sheltie wander more than a few feet away. Aslan's facial fur was dark and slobbery from the kisses the big collie had bestowed on his hero. It was strange to see how Ruffis's attitude toward the little pup had done a one-eighty literally overnight.

"Is the vet's office open yet?" Dad asked Mom, setting the collar aside to look at the bloody wounds and missing clumps of fur on the back of Ruffis's neck.

"I think I can get someone now. I'll call and get him in this morning." She walked to the kitchen for her phone.

Dad picked up the ruined collar again, tags jingling. "We almost woke to a dead dog today. 'Are not two sparrows sold for a penny? Yet not one of them will fall to the ground outside your Father's care.'"

The familiar scripture hung like mist in the air as he reached down to scratch Ruffis' ears.

CHAPTER 14

Zombies and Bleacher Battles

March: Eleven Months Old

E yes wide, mouth agape, Krissy halted at the top of the broad open staircase overlooking two green indoor soccer fields. On the soccer pitch to her right, a border collie wove through an agility course of blue-and-yellow equipment. White jumps and weave poles had been arranged into a course on the left pitch, but no dogs competed. Instead, a herd of humans walked the course without their dogs, arms extended toward jumps, bodies swiveling and bending—for all the world looking like a *When Zombies Attack* movie.

In between the two pitches, an expansive space held a colorful sea of dog crates, travel chairs, and bags of training gear. It looked like her agility training class times one hundred. A constant hum matched the visual overload. Dogs barked, and people gathered in small groups, laughing and sharing stories about their most recent runs.

"This is way bigger than I thought it would be," Violet said, taking in the mass of people, dogs, equipment, and crates.

"Yeah," Krissy said. "This is super cool."

Holding Aslan under one arm, she grasped the hand rail and, with slow deliberation, descended the stairs into the hotbed of activity on the level below. Like always, she hesitated at each step, making sure her footing held before continuing down.

When Judy had told her about the AKC agility trial being held minutes from her house at Soccer City, Krissy had begged her parents to let her go watch. Both of them had plans, but they acquiesced when Daniel and Judy said they'd look out for her. Her parents' overprotective natures probably stemmed more from the incident at Okie Dokie Rover than worry over her safety. So, trusting her to Daniel and Judy, Mom dropped her and Violet off, and in about two hours, Dad would pick them up.

The real problem was that two hours wouldn't be nearly enough time to soak all of this in.

They stood at the bottom of the stairs, apparently looking like Puritans at Woodstock, because a middle-aged woman dressed in a shirt that said *Red Dirt Rocks—Red Dirt Agility Club* asked if she could help them.

"I need to find Daniel or Judy Furuta," Krissy said. "I'm one of their students."

The lady's face brightened. "Oh, sure! Let's see. They're crated over against the jumpers with weaves ring." She pointed to a line of crates lined up against the plexiglass surrounding the soccer pitch with the white jumps and weave poles. "You'll see their crates and chairs. It's all City Dogs' royal blue."

Violet nodded in that general direction. "I see it."

"Thank you." Krissy followed Violet into the sea of crates. Sure enough, one large and one medium dog crate covered in heavy royal blue material with *City Dogs* embroidered in large white letters snugged up against the jumpers' ring. Royal blue captain's chairs with *City Dogs Agility School* emblazoned on their backs faced the ring. Bags of gear surrounded the crates, but Judy and Daniel were nowhere in sight.

Violet sat in one of the chairs. "If this is their stuff, they'll show up at some point."

Posture stiff, Krissy also took a seat nestling Aslan in her lap. The facility smelled like old sweat, soccer balls, concrete, and tension. Excitement filled the air. Nearby, a dog howled.

"Kraymer, hush!" yelled a woman walking around the course with the jumps and weave poles. The dog quieted, and Violet giggled.

"Like the lady said, this must be the jumpers with weaves class." Krissy motioned to the ring they faced. "It's got only weave poles, jumps, and sometimes a tunnel. In agility school, they told us each course is different for every class, and before they compete, the handlers get to walk the course for eight minutes without the dogs to decide how they're gonna handle it. It's called a walkthrough. It's supposed to be really important because if a handler chooses the wrong handling strategy, it can all fall apart. I think they look like zombies out there, though—all those people pretending to run in slo-mo without their dogs."

Violet stared at the handlers who walked in circles, arms out, seemingly lost. A grin formed on her face. "Yeah. They do. That's spooky."

"I'm waiting for someone's arm to drop off, or someone's skin to start dragging on the turf behind them." They both giggled at the mental image.

A loud buzzer went off, and the crowd of zombies left the course.

"Hey, Krissy!"

She turned. Judy skirted crates and chairs with her beautiful, grinning golden retriever, Autumn, whose tongue lolled out of her mouth. Krissy had met Autumn at class. A Master Agility Champion—aptly called a MACH—Autumn had qualified for the American Kennel Club Agility National Championship four times. Her name was a perfect fit as her golden coat possessed many of the colors of fall. Krissy was in awe of the talented dog.

"How do you like it so far?" Judy asked, gesturing in a wide arc at the show.

"This is the coolest place ever," said Krissy, and she meant it.

"I'm thrilled your first impression is positive," Judy said between quick breaths.

"Did you just run?" Krissy asked. Both Autumn and Judy were winded.

"We did."

"How'd you do? What was it like?" It had to be killer to run a course at a trial like this.

"We didn't qualify, but we had so much fun. I gave a late command, which caused her to go off course, but she was spectacular. One thing you learn quickly in agility—almost all of the mistakes are the handler's fault, not the dog's. The dogs are a lot better at this than we are." Judy scratched behind Autumn's ears.

"I can't wait until Aslan and I get our turn."

After a moment's silence, Judy glanced at Violet, and Krissy reprimanded herself for her lack of manners. "Oh, sorry! Judy, have you met my best friend, Violet?"

"I haven't. It's nice to meet you, Violet. Do you have a dog?"

Violet shook her head. "Only my brother's German shepherd, Heidi. I'd love to do this with her, but my brother already thinks I spend too much time with her."

Judy tilted her head toward the concession stand. "How about I get you two something to drink, and you can sit in the bleachers to watch the action? Agility people are nice. You can ask them any questions you'd like. They love to talk about their dogs and the sport."

Soon Krissy, Violet, and Aslan were perched on a short stack of metal bleachers facing the colorful Standard ring with its large pieces of painted equipment. An A-frame, dogwalk, teeter, table, weave poles, tunnels, and a variety of jumps appeared to have been arranged like a puzzle across the artificial turf of the soccer pitch. Aslan squirmed in Krissy's lap eager to get down and sniff, but she held him tight.

Her brows knit in concentration as a large black mixed-breed ambled over a jump and trotted onto the up-ramp of the dogwalk located right in front of the bleachers. His owner, a pretty twenty-something woman dressed in a sleek running suit, ran ahead of him, pleading with him for more speed. When the dog hit the down-ramp of the dogwalk, the handler pointed to a sizeable yellow-painted rectangle at the very end of the ramp.

"Hit it!" she yelled. The dog trotted toward the painted yellow area and, nearing it, leaped off the dogwalk.

"Oh, he bailed that." A middle-aged lady in a red T-shirt sitting a few rows down from Krissy motioned at the dogwalk. "That was totally blown."

The judge raised both hands, indicating a fault.

"Oh! No, no, no!" A lady with silver hair teased into an updo sitting next to the woman in the red T-shirt nodded toward the dogwalk. "He had a full paw in the yellow. The judge has been getting contact calls wrong all day. She's out there raising her hands as if she's exercising with Richard Simmons."

"Maybe she's missed a few calls, but not that one," Red T-Shirt said. "He completely missed the yellow. Good call."

Silver Updo threw her hands in the air and looked at her seat partner with exasperation. "Come on, it's right in front of you! He had his whole paw in the yellow. Another bad call."

Violet leaned toward Krissy and whispered, "What are they arguing about?"

Krissy whispered back: "On the contact obstacles—the big ones with yellow paint at the bottom like the A-frame, dogwalk, and teeter—the dog has to put a part of one paw into the yellow safety zone at the bottom of the down-ramp. It's a rule. You have to train the dog to run into the yellow. Otherwise the dogs might jump off the obstacles from high up, making it dangerous. The judge raised her hands and called the dog for a missed contact."

A thin elderly man wearing striped shorts and a *Dogtag Agility School* T-shirt sitting behind the women interrupted the ladies' ongoing debate. "Ropa's paw was clearly in, but either way, the call has been made. It's a shame because Liz and Ropa are close to their MACH. But, Liz finished with energy. Good handling in a bad situation."

Krissy whispered in Violet's ear, "If you blow a contact, it means the dog has failed the course. The team continues running, but they can't earn any ribbons."

Red T-Shirt shook her head at the elderly man. "Roger, your vision's so bad, you can't even drive anymore. How would you know if Ropa's paw was in the yellow?"

"Do you need glasses?" Silver Updo said to Red T-Shirt. "Maybe you and the judge could share some binoculars?"

"I can see just fine, thank you." Red T-Shirt stood. As she turned, she was wearing a smile. "But you, my dear, might need Lasik."

Silver Updo laughed as the other woman walked off.

"What do dogs get for passing the course? Money? Can you make money at this?" Violet's eyes glittered, her whisper gone.

"No. No money. When a dog passes a course, he earns a Q—a qualifying score. The Qs add up over time, and the dog earns titles for so many Qs. I don't know how many Qs it takes for a title, but I know the titles get more prestigious and harder to earn as the dogs advance. The top title is called a Master Agility Champion—MACH for short. Autumn has a MACH."

"So how long will it take for Aslan to earn a MACH?"

"He'll never get one. Judy said few dogs earn them. I think most people do this for fun, ya know? Some want the big titles, but others just want to play with their dogs. It takes a really good team to get a MACH. We aren't like that."

Roger, the elderly man, stood and turned to them. "Sorry to be eavesdropping," he said with a pleasant smile, "but I'd be happy to tell you why it's so hard to get a MACH."

Krissy waved a hand, motioning him to continue. "Please do."

"Well at the top level, like what we're watching, a team can't make any mistakes to get a Q," Roger explained. "There are several types of mistakes, too. A blown contact like you saw is just one. A dog can't run by an obstacle she is supposed to take or run up to an obstacle and stop or spin. That's called a refusal.

She can't go off course. That's called a wrong course. And then there's dropping bars, leaving the teeter before it hits the ground, leaving the pause table early, the handler touching the dog during the run, and oodles of other things that are also faults. It's darned demanding, and a team has to be perfect."

Silver Updo, who had turned to face Roger, nodded. "It's true. My dog didn't make time today. He ran clean but was over time. Boom. NQ for us."

Roger said, "My Brittany and I have been in agility for eight years, and we're nowhere near a MACH. It's a great achievement, but there are other titles and successes to chase in this sport. That's one of its best parts. Even an old geezer like me can compete and be successful."

Violet flashed him a toothy grin. "You're not old."

"Then you're the blind one." The man smiled back before walking away. Laughing, Silver Updo stood and followed.

Violet's face scrunched, either confused by the rules or the "blind" comment. Krissy was about to explain what little more she knew when a familiar and unwelcome voice spoke from behind.

"Well, hello!" Charlotte said. She hiked a leg and boosted herself to the third level bleacher next to Krissy. "How are you doing?"

Krissy hesitated, unsure what to do. Violet knew what had happened at Okie Dokie Rover, but she didn't know what Charlotte looked like. Mom's advice would probably work best in this situation—manners first.

"Hello, Charlotte," Krissy said using her most polite, all-manners-in-play tone. "I'd like you to meet my best friend, Violet. Violet, this is Charlotte. She owns Okie Dokie Rover."

All sugary-sweet, Charlotte said, "Nice to meet you, Violet. It's wonderful you both could come and watch the competition. What do you think of it?"

"I can't wait to get out there." Krissy figured it might needle Charlotte that she hadn't taken her advice to seek a different dog sport, but her eagerness to compete was the truth.

"Oh? What dog sport have you chosen to compete in?" Charlotte asked.

"Agility."

Charlotte pasted on a pitying smile. "But we had decided you should go with another sport more suited to your abilities, like rally or nose work."

Movement behind Charlotte's shoulder caught Krissy's eye. Daniel was darting through the crowd toward them.

"No. I'm training in agility. We're having a great time." She patted Aslan's soft head.

Charlotte frowned and opened her mouth to speak, but Daniel's arrival interrupted her. "Charlotte! I see you've met my new student." He looked past her and met Krissy's eyes. "Hey! It's great to see you and Aslan here."

Charlotte turned away from Krissy to glance at Daniel, which was unfortunate. Krissy was dying to see the look on her face. It must have been a mix of emotions because her next statement rankled.

"Krissy told me she's thinking of competing in agility," Charlotte said, her voice full of mock concern. "You know, she took a class with me, and I felt she and Aslan were better suited to another, less physical sport. We'd agreed she would pursue one of those."

Krissy frowned, and Daniel saw it.

"Yeah," he said. "We've talked about it. There's no reason Krissy and Aslan can't compete successfully in agility. She's training for distance, and they're doing fantastic."

Charlotte glanced at Krissy, and then, turning back to Daniel, she leaned forward and lowered her voice to a stage whisper, which of course Krissy could still hear. "Daniel, I think she's had enough disappointment in her young life without working hard in agility only to find she can't cut it."

His face reddened, and his mouth stretched into a thin line. "There are a lot of talented agility handlers who happen to be handicapped. Valarie from Topeka is one who comes to mind."

"Yes, and she runs a border collie. With their natural distance abilities, they're much easier to handle from afar than, say, oh, I don't know, a *sheltie*."

"Well, Frank from St. Louis handles a cocker-mix from his wheelchair," Daniel retorted.

"I guess it's not my problem." Charlotte stood, her volume rising with her. "It'll be yours when she comes to you in tears after realizing this sport is too much for her." She stepped off the bleachers and left in a huff.

Only then did Krissy realize Violet was standing on the bleachers, too, her face red. It reminded her of when Violet had kicked in their band director's desk. What part of Charlotte had she been planning to boot?

"Seriously?" Violet demanded, enraged. "I cannot believe she just did that. Who does she think she is?"

Daniel ran his fingers through his hair, anger still flashing in his eyes. He lifted himself up on the edge of the bleachers to sit in Charlotte's vacated seat.

"I am sorry," he said. "I wish I could tell you all agility competitors were kind. Most are wonderful, encouraging people who root wholeheartedly for each other, but there are always a few rotten apples. Charlotte isn't all bad, though. She's a hard-working volunteer and a strong advocate for agility. Unfortunately, she's also a stage mom. Her daughter is the only teenager doing agility in the area right now, and I suspect Charlotte doesn't want another teen sharing Mia's spotlight."

"So, she's jealous?" Sarcasm laced Violet's voice. "Of Krissy? Who isn't even competing yet? What kind of nutter is she?"

Violet's comment stung, but Krissy didn't have time to digest it before Daniel spoke. "She's like any overzealous little league parent. She wants her kid to excel. It's common in all youth sports, and agility isn't immune."

Violet sniffed and sat, arms crossed, eyes forward.

Daniel turned to Krissy. "You do believe me when I say you can do this?" Deep concern radiated from his dark eyes.

"I ran Q," she said. "I felt it, you know, how it could be. How I could handle a dog at distance. So, yeah, I believe you."

He smiled. "Good. Please don't let someone like Charlotte get to you. This sport is well within your grasp, and Aslan will be a fantastic teammate."

Her little puppy sat in her lap staring at her, concern showing in his eyes, too. He must have caught the tension. She smiled at him and kissed the top of his silken head. "It's okay, Little Man." She used her new nickname for him. "We'll do great at this." Gently, he licked her hand and lay back down on her lap with a sigh.

"You said when you ran Q you 'felt it.' Do you know what we call that?" Daniel didn't wait for a reply. "Hitting the zone. It means that as a team, as two distinct species, we think like one, dance as one. Sometimes, we hit the zone for a few obstacles. On rare occasions, we hit the zone from start to finish. At City Dogs, we call that the 'Zone of Totality,' like the zone in a solar eclipse, where, for a few minutes, the world goes dark. When you hit the zone, everything slides to slow motion, yet your mind is totally present. You feel it all—your dog's power, her personality, her eagerness, her movement. And you feel yourself in a new way, too—your breath, your heartbeat, your muscles moving. Everything is experienced at once and yet individually. You are totally absorbed in the moment. In the run." His voice broke. "One with your dog."

Daniel turned away, fingers combing his hair again, and continued after a moment. "I think you did something rare with Q that first night. I think, for a few obstacles, you hit the zone. And in those few jumps, you lived this sport's power."

A chill ran up her spine. After a few seconds, she whispered, "Maybe I did feel something like that."

Gathering himself, he smiled and pointed to the Standard ring where a Belgian Tervuren single-stepped through the weave poles. "Do you have any questions about what you've seen so far?"

"A million," Krissy said. "How much time do you have?"

"I've got a walk-through in jumpers in about thirty minutes. Yeah. Until then, I'm yours. Ask away."

* * *

Krissy's head felt like it was stuffed with wet sand, and if she added one more grain of information, it would explode and splat on the tile floor. Daniel, and later Judy and a few of the other adult City Dogs competitors, had given her way more information about agility competitions than she could absorb. It'd been awesome. Much, much better than she'd expected. She couldn't wait until she and Aslan could compete.

Violet typed on her phone as they topped the stairs and headed to the soccer facility's front door. "Hey, Evan says he's nearby and wants to pick me up. Is that okay? I don't want to leave you alone with that. . .that. . .*lady* around. How far away is your dad?"

Krissy looked out the front glass doors. Evan's green car threaded its way through the parking lot. Was Violet going on a date with Evan? Why hadn't she said something before this?

"Dad said he'd be here at one. He should show up any second. Why didn't you tell me you were going on a date with Evan? That's kinda big news."

"Oh, it's not a date." Violet waved a dismissive hand. "A group of us are meeting at Dolese Park to play Frisbee golf. But, if that lady bothers you again, call me. We'll come back." She glanced over her shoulder, looking for Charlotte.

Krissy worked hard to add a nonchalance she didn't feel to her voice. "It's no problem. If she shows up, I'll go find Daniel, Judy, or other folks from City Dogs. I'll be fine." This was a lie because it was a problem. Krissy had figured they'd go home and hang out this afternoon. She folded her arms across her middle to ward off her building insecurity and disappointment.

Evan's car pulled up to the front doors. The car's tinted windows kept her from seeing his long blond hair. "It's a beautiful spring day for Frisbee golf. Throw a hole in one for me." Krissy forced a tight smile.

"I will. Call me tonight." Violet waved as she left.

The back door of the car opened. Jessica's red hair gleamed as she leaned out and said something to Violet, who opened the passenger door and hopped in. They both laughed and closed their doors. The car tore out into the lot, earning nasty glares from two competitors walking their dogs nearby.

A shroud of loneliness fell on Krissy. Why hadn't she been invited to play Frisbee golf? Maybe because Evan was Peter's best friend, and he viewed her like a little sister? But Violet hadn't even mentioned the afternoon's plans until now, and why hadn't her best friend invited her along?

For a brief moment, Charlotte's words echoed. *A sport more suited for your abilities.* In other words: *Your disability is so obvious. You're plainly unable to do this.*

And, Violet had said, *She's jealous? Of Krissy?* Like, who'd be jealous of poor disabled Krissy? Was her transplant an embarrassment to Violet? With the exception of her fistula, most of Krissy's scars—like the long scar on her abdomen where the kidney transplant was—were hidden. The emotional scars were, too. People couldn't see she wasn't normal. Could they? Did her face look wrong? Her body?

Had she not been invited to Frisbee golf because she looked stupid doing anything athletic? She'd played Frisbee golf before. While not great, she hadn't completely sucked at it. It didn't require running, thus emphasizing her odd trot. Was it another sport that didn't "suit her abilities?" Or, was she simply not suitably cool? The odd transplant kid who was just different enough not to fit in?

No. No. None of that could be true. Violet wouldn't have stood up for her like she did today if she didn't want to hang around her.

But Violet was the ultimate people pleaser. She wanted everyone around her to be happy. Maybe Violet stood up for her just to make Krissy feel better, not because she really wanted to?

"There you are! Mom said you was here." Krissy pulled herself away from her introspection as Mia skipped toward her, a little Jack Russell puppy bouncing off lead at her feet. Mia wore a plastic smile, and her ponytail waved with each step.

"Hi," Krissy said, trying unsuccessfully to push the thoughts of being different from her mind. As the puppy neared, she tapped on Aslan's leash, and he moved closer to her side.

"Did you see my new puppy? He's going to run like a spitfire. I just love him. His name is Cool." Mia's voice sounded syrupy fake-nice, but, unlike her mother, at least she seemed to be making an attempt at being cordial.

"He's adorable." Krissy knelt, calling the puppy to her with excited cheeps. He pranced up, sniffed her hand, gave a play bow to Aslan, and after spinning in a circle, darted toward the door as a young woman entered with her papillon. Reacting with a burst of speed, Mia reached Cool just in time to scoop him in her arms before he escaped the building.

"That were close." She kissed Cool on the head. "We almost had us a game of parking lot chase there."

"He is a spitfire." Krissy fidgeted with Aslan's leather leash and glanced out the front doors, but Dad's SUV wasn't in sight.

"If you ever do compete, I think Cool and your sheltie—what's his name again—will be in the same jump height. That'll be so much fun!"

Her too-sweet-for-iced-tea accent was well rehearsed, but this could be the real Mia. Some girls seemed to ooze sugar. Yet, that didn't align with how she'd acted during Krissy's one class at Okie Dokie Rover.

Then, Dad rolled up in his SUV, like a white knight. "My dad's here," Krissy said. "I've got to go. It was good to see you."

"You too! Hopefully we'll see each other again, and Cool and your pup can play." Mia waved as Krissy turned and made her escape.

CHAPTER 15

The Third Vault Veto

June: Thirteen Months Old

E yeing the agility map in her hand and calculating the distances between jumps in her head, Krissy dragged one of the white plastic jumps across the backyard's short green grass and angled it into position in the yard. She found course building an exercise in frustration, but they had to train this specific drill. As Aslan got faster, sequences such as this one had become mandatory.

The yard looked more like a real agility ring every month. The light-blue tunnel, six jumps, and twelve weave poles she'd gotten for Christmas littered the lawn along with the brand-new, blue-and-yellow teeter her parents had given her for her fifteenth birthday in early May. Judy had insisted Krissy get approval from their vet before they purchased the teeter, but an x-ray and exam showed Aslan was ready for full-height agility.

"Dogs mature physically and emotionally at different rates," Judy had said. "We have to be sure his bones and body are ready for the rigors of weave pole, teeter, and jump training. You have all of the basics down, so once Aslan is physically ready, we'll focus on raising the equipment to full height and finishing his beginning foundations."

To celebrate Aslan's leap—she grinned at her pun—into full agility training, her parents had presented Krissy with the regulation teeter. A short month later, Aslan could boldly run to the end of the teeter, and, crouching in the yellow contact zone, ride it down to bang on the ground before hopping off. He'd even learned to weave all twelve poles since the beginning of May. Judy had said that while that was no small accomplishment for a new trainer with a new dog, she wasn't surprised. Krissy trained every day and followed her coaches' instructions to a tee, and the dividends had paid off. Aslan weaved, jumped, hit his contacts, and followed directions with accuracy and speed.

The speed thing was both an electric charge and a concern. As Krissy and Aslan understood the sport better, his speed increased. This meant she found herself farther and farther behind, especially as the obstacle sequences became longer and more difficult. Daniel helped her, teaching her to train Aslan to respond at distance, but it was hard work. Aslan did great when she ran with him at a lateral distance where he could keep her in his peripheral vision, but when he ran ahead of her in a straight line of three or more jumps, he almost always spun back before the third jump to visually check in with her and make sure she still wanted him to take the jump. This spin was bad. If a dog stopped or turned right before an obstacle he was supposed to take, it was marked as a refusal. This was a fault, and in the top levels of the sport, it would mean they wouldn't qualify.

Commanding your dog to run ahead of you is called a *send*. She could hear Daniel's voice in her head: "The send seems like it would be the easiest of cues, but actually, it's the hardest distance skill to train. Invariably, dogs will do what Aslan is doing. They'll be okay going one or two jumps ahead, but that third jump takes the dog about thirty feet away from you and out of their vision. They're working only on voice at that point, and since voice is your weakest cue in agility, they want to turn back to make sure your forward motion, shoulders, and hand signals are still indicating a send. It's rough. It gets in their head, and it gets in yours.

Training a dog to respond only to verbal cues when running this fast and this far is a very advanced skill."

Krissy stared at the line of jumps she'd set up. The sequence seemed easy. Aslan was supposed to run as fast as possible down a line of three jumps and then roar straight into a tunnel. He loved tunnels, and his small size and speed allowed him to bank the side of the macaroni-shaped tunnels as he ran through, like Indy cars bank their oval race tracks.

The straight run into his favorite obstacle might entice him to continue forward on verbal cues alone. Hopefully, this sequence would build his confidence and help him overcome the third jump spin.

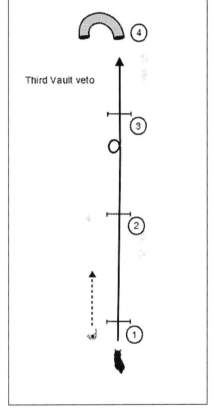

Third Vault veto

As she surveyed the jumps, Aslan danced at her feet and barked in excitement, tail wagging in that slow sheltie style of his. Agility had transformed him. His favorite thing to do was train, and even when outside on his own, he would run through the tunnel and sail over jumps with a wide doggie grin.

"Prince lives for that sport," Peter had said a few days ago, calling Aslan by his royal nickname. It was true. Prince did live for agility.

Smiling at the impish, loud dog, Krissy clapped her hand against her thigh and cued Aslan to follow her to the first jump. When they were about eight feet in front of it, ensuring he had a straight visual shot down the seventy-foot line of jumps to the tunnel, she commanded, "Sit. Stay." His butt hit the grass, and he quieted. She led out a few steps toward Jump One.

* * *

Of all the commands his Mistress gave him, *stay* was the hardest. And to be expected not to move a paw with a line of agility jumps straight ahead was torture. Aslan's body trembled as he leaned forward onto his front toes, yearning to run and fly over the jumps. When would she say *okay* so he could go? Why did she always make him stay first? She knew how much he wanted to go and jump the jumps. He couldn't leave without the *okay* though. If he did, she'd stop him, and all of the fun would go away. She'd put him back in front of the first jump, and they'd have to do it all again. Best to obey, even if it didn't make any sense.

"Okay!" Finally! He sprung from his sit and, in two long strides, gathered himself for the first jump. When it came to jumps, this was his favorite part. Pushing hard with his legs, he exploded into the air—and flew. The wind generated from his speed whipped his ears back, and his fur flattened against his body. During his flight, his Mistress yelled, "Straight!" The cue came late, so it was a good thing he'd guessed right and took off extending toward the jump ahead of him. He landed and blew past his Mistress, who trotted as fast as she could, which wasn't very fast at all, beside the line of jumps. His muscles strained as he gained speed with each stride. He could never run fast enough. Ever.

A small bark escaped as he coiled for the next jump. "Straight!" This command was better-timed but still a bit late. Fortunately, he was on the straight path. She trotted behind him now, and he couldn't see her anymore. He tried to turn his head as he flew again, but he couldn't catch her in his peripheral vision. His speed took him toward the next jump, but as he neared, he worried. She'd said *straight*, yet sometimes she said one thing while her motion and hand signals indicated another. If he could see her, he would know for sure. She would trot toward the jump, her shoulders would point to it, and he would know. He could hear her footsteps pounding the ground behind him. Was she slowing? Was she turning? Although only a stride away from the jump, he needed assurance. He turned to look.

Yes, she was trotting down the line of jumps, her face contorted in a grimace of effort. She repeated the cue. "Straight! Tunnel!" He spun with confidence back to the jump and once again became a bird, if only for a second. After returning to the earth, he hauled for the tunnel. He loved tunnels. He could run into them so fast his body would turn sideways and his paws would run along the tunnel's side. As he entered it, the ambient noise of the breeze, birds, and his Mistress's thumping feet disappeared, replaced with the rumble of his paws on the bottom sides of the tunnel. Another small bark of frustration escaped. He'd wanted to really bank the tunnel this time, but his spin before the last jump had cost him speed. He exited and spotted his Mistress standing by the second jump. Dashing back to her, he barked his enthusiasm and desire to do it all again.

* * *

Krissy ran a hand over her face. She wanted to tell him no, but Judy had been adamant she not bring verbal punishment into the game. "Aslan's a bit of a softie emotionally," Judy had warned. "He will shut down if you add in punishment."

Instead, they retried the sequence. Again, a spin before Jump Three. So, they ran the sequence again and again and again. Only one time out of eight attempts did Aslan make it through all four obstacles without a refusal at the third jump. The time he did, Krissy rewarded him with lots of treats and praise, but her annoyance with their inconsistency intensified. Exasperated, she left the sequence behind and instead worked Aslan on the teeter.

After training, she rested on the patio settee, a water bottle on the table and Aslan in her lap. He panted, finding little relief in June's warm evening breeze. His narrow tongue stuck out and curled up at the tip like a miniature pink spoon. With each exhale, he made a cute little huffing noise. She ran her hand along his long soft fur feeling his petite yet muscular body under her fingers. He turned his head to her, round eyes bright and smiling, and said, "This agility stuff is my favorite thing in the whole world!" Well, that's what he wanted to say, anyway—she was sure of it.

Even with the aggravation of trying to tell a non-English-speaking dog that spinning at the third jump was a no-no, she understood. "I get that," she told him. "I really do."

* * *

Early the next morning, flute in hand, Krissy slid to the ground and leaned against the chain-link fence enclosing the football field. Small streaks of mauve lingered in the sky from the sunrise, and the cool but humid dawn air refreshed her as she inhaled, filling her lungs. Early morning band camp was bracing.

Violet plopped next to her on the ground. Raising her knees, she crossed her arms on them and put her head on her arms. Her alto clarinet, exchanged from the bass version for marching practice, dangled from one limp hand. She groaned.

"Are you okay?" Krissy asked.

"My stomach is not happy," Violet muttered.

"Go home, then. Marching practice is no place to be if you're going to upchuck breakfast."

"Oooh," Violet moaned to the ground. "Please, don't mention food."

Jessica approached and sat cross-legged on the grass in front of Violet. She giggled. "Feeling green?"

Violet raised her head to glare at the red-head.

"You were so wasted last night," Jessica said. "It was hilarious."

Krissy's jaw dropped. Sensing she was gaping, she shut her mouth and stared at Violet with wide eyes. Wasted? On alcohol or drugs? Or both? What on earth was happening? A numbness crawled up Krissy's limbs.

Violet glanced at her but didn't hold eye contact. Instead, her glare returned to Jessica. "Shut up, Jessica. I wasn't that bad."

"Oh? You cried for an hour about losing a button on your overalls. It was so funny. Evan couldn't stop laughing." Jessica grinned. "Don't you remember?"

Violet's eyebrows furrowed. "Sort of. Man, that's the last time I do something like that before early morning practice."

The band director blew his whistle to signal everyone to take their pre-field formation. Violet grimaced at the shrill sound. They stood, and Krissy followed Violet and Jessica, who continued reliving last night's escapades as they trekked onto the field. Her head swam.

She slowed, letting the other two girls move ahead of her, but they didn't notice she'd lagged behind. Staring at her feet as she trudged, she struggled to take it in. Her best friend had gotten drunk last night. To make matters worse, Violet had told Krissy she was staying home to watch a movie with her folks, not going out partying with Evan and friends. Apparently, she didn't remember that little fib this morning. Evan and Anthony, a trombonist in the band, rushed to Violet and Jessica, laughing and teasing. Anthony began to mock-cry, moaning about losing a button. Violet pushed him and laughed.

Krissy had been distracted with Aslan's training, but when had her best friend started drinking, or whatever? As Krissy shuffled to join the line of flute players, Violet and Jessica whispered together in the clarinet section. Krissy stood on the outside looking in, and she had no idea when it had happened. And what she found herself looking into was something she wanted no part of. There was no way she would risk her kidney by putting chemicals into her body. That wasn't a choice. Not even to be popular. Not even to be Violet's friend.

Yet in spite of the surety she was better off left out of it, there was a hollowness inside. She had one best friend. If Violet and Jessica kept hanging around the partying clique, where would that leave her?

There was only one answer.

Alone.

CHAPTER 16

Camping

August: Sixteen Months Old

Aslan's fly-away fur tickled her cheeks as Krissy buried her face into his neck for a goodbye hug. The hug served two purposes. It hid her tears from her family and allowed her to surreptitiously wipe them off on his fur. The love exchanged from the hug was a bonus.

It was dumb as dirt to cry. In a short forty-eight hours, she'd see him again, but the tears had come out of nowhere. She fought to knock back the unexpected emotions.

She let Aslan escape her moist embrace and set him on the kitchen floor. "You'd better watch him like a hawk," she told Peter and Dad for the umpteenth time. "And watch for hawks, too. Seriously. Anything could happen out there."

Dad glared at her from his seat at the table. "He's going to be fine. We'll watch him. He'll spend most of the weekend in his crate by the fire."

"Not too close to the fire," she said.

"It's a metal crate," Peter said, exasperated. "It can't catch fire."

"He can, though. And he can get too hot." Every family member glared at her, their expressions oozing frustration. She was supposed to help ease family tensions, not create them, but she couldn't help herself. Aslan would be out of her care for the first time. All the bases had to be covered.

"For heaven's sake, let's go," Mom said. "They'll take good care of him. We'll call them and check on him regularly."

"If cell service even reaches out in those boonies." Krissy bent to scratch Aslan behind the ears one last time, then stood and picked up her purse from the kitchen counter. "And keep that tick collar on him. I just know he's gonna get covered in ticks and get some tick-borne disease." Eww. Ticks. She shivered. "Do I really have to leave him?"

Mom met her eyes and said in a stern, slow tone, "We're going, and that's final."

Krissy turned to snatch one last look at her adorable dog and stomped to the garage. What if that was the last glance she'd ever have of her sweet bitty puppy? It was a stupid thought, yet a sickening knot formed in her stomach.

She hadn't wanted to go to the mother/daughter retreat at church in the first place. A weekend of speakers, relationship-building activities, and structured "fun" didn't sound like, well, fun. Not only would she miss a practice session at City Dogs, but Aslan would have to go camping with Peter and Dad. Desperate pleas for Aslan to be boarded at the vet for the weekend had fallen on deaf ears. Dad hadn't wanted to spend the money, so both Ruffis and Aslan were going camping with him, Peter, and Peter's friends Evan and Dillon. Anything could happen—especially with Evan there.

Slumping onto the car's passenger seat, she willed the tears to stay at bay. She shouldn't be throwing this tantrum. She should be sowing peace in the family, healing what her illness had wrought. That had been her plan. But how could she leave her nine-pound sheltie to the mercy of the Oklahoma wilds?

In the car, Mom pushed the button on the garage door opener. As the motor rumbled, she turned to Krissy. "He's going to be fine. I talked to your dad, and he promised he would be in charge of Aslan. I suggest you forget about it and control your attitude, or this is going to be a very long weekend."

Powerless to stop herself from sulking, Krissy stared out the passenger window as the car reversed out of the garage.

* * *

Aslan blinked and turned his sensitive nose away from the smoke drifting into his cage. Ruffis's big body lay on his side in an adjacent cage, his rib cage rising and falling in a slow rhythm as he slept in the tree-dappled morning sun. Aslan had seen fire before, but never outside of the fireplace in the big house. This fire sat bold-faced on the ground, and though he wasn't close enough to feel its heat, the smoke drifted everywhere, the smell burning his nostrils.

Today had been perplexing. First, his Mistress hadn't been home all night, and he'd been forced to sleep in his crate in the garden room. He missed the soft bed and his Mistress's warm side. Then, before the sky turned light, Peter had woken him, fed him breakfast, and put him back in his crate, which had been relocated to the car. After riding in the car for a long time, they'd arrived at this most amazing place. Leaves and sticks covered the ground between tall trees, and the smells from the earth and the air intoxicated him: squirrels, rotting food, burnt wood, dog urine, animals whose scent he didn't recognize, and more. He ached to sniff and search, letting the scents carry him where they would. Instead, after being allowed to relieve himself, he was forced back into his crate with no toys, just a bowl of water.

Stuck, he'd watched as Dad, Peter, and two other boys—one with long yellow hair who came often to the big house and the other a brown-haired boy he'd never seen—worked in a small clearing under the trees. They made the fire on the ground, put up three canvas crates big enough for humans, unfolded the chairs his Mistress used at dog class, and carried food and jugs of water from the car. Another puzzler. Aslan's ears lay back against his head. The uncertainty of it all made him long for his Mistress.

The boys and Dad had chatted happily as they worked, and soon they huddled around the fire holding hot dogs speared by metal sticks over the flames. Aslan loved hot dogs. His Mistress sometimes used them as treats when they played their games. She would break off little pieces for him when she was happy with what he'd done. His mouth watered at the smell of the cooking meat, and his annoyance with the stinging smoke lessened.

He made a soft, whiny sound in an attempt to attract attention—and maybe a hot dog—but the boys and Dad were too busy creatively placing their hot dogs in the middle of bread. Aslan loved bread, too, and the thought of the combination almost drove him wild. With despair, he circled in his crate as the meat and bread disappeared into the mouths of the humans.

After eating, the boys grabbed towels and jogged off in the direction of the water. Aslan smelled the water, although he couldn't see it. It smelled like lake, which brought back vague memories of lots of dogs playing in a large yard, but he couldn't recapture the details. The memory had left him feeling comforted, though, and he'd been lost in that warm-blanket emotion when he fell into a deep sleep.

* * *

When he woke sometime later, a refreshing breeze had dissipated the fire's smoke, at least for now. Aslan wanted to go potty, but Dad stared at a book he held in his hands, oblivious. The boys' noise and smell announced their approach, and soon, wet with lake water, they came into view. Dressed only in shorts, they walked barefoot, tiptoeing over sticks and sharp rocks. One of the boys—the one with the long light-colored hair—shoved Peter, who fell to his knees. Laughing, the boy continued on while Peter picked himself up and brushed moist dirt off his damp legs, a scowl on his face.

Sitting in his chair, Dad watched the boys enter the clearing. He spoke to them in a tone that sounded like discipline, and he gave Peter a command. Peter went to a box containing food and opened the lid. He pulled out a couple of cans and brought them to Dad, who said a few more gruff things and pointed at Aslan.

The boys put on shoes and dry shirts, and Peter came over with the leash to let Aslan out. Energy pulsed through him at the opportunity to escape his confines, although Peter seemed to be in a bad mood. Peter leashed him, and all three boys headed toward one of the trails leading off the clearing, Aslan trotting in anticipation by Peter's side.

At last, Aslan could explore some of the interesting scents that had assaulted his nose whenever the breeze drove the smoke from his crate.

Lowering his head, he inhaled something that smelled sort of like squirrel but not quite. Eager to discover what creature carried that scent, he took a few steps off the trail to follow the spoor, but when the slack in the leash ended, Peter tugged him back onto the trail.

Undaunted, Aslan continued on the path, picking up strange odors along the way. He caught the familiar smell of dog urine right by the trail, and he sprinkled his scent on top of it. As he sniffed his way farther into the woods, Peter and the other boys talked. Their talk held a light tension, but Aslan was too busy deciphering odors to pay it much heed. This was one of the best walks he'd ever been on, and he was happy to trot along, nose on the path.

They were far from the clearing when all three boys halted. The light-haired boy reached in the pocket of his shirt. Aslan lifted his nose off the ground for the first time since starting down the path. Treats lived in pockets. His Mistress and everyone at the agility school carried treats in their pockets. Aslan listened for the rustle of a treat bag, but, instead, the boy pulled out two white oblong treats. Aslan sniffed but could detect no odor. Cheese, maybe? Cheese was sometimes white.

All scents on the trail forgotten, he waited, mouth watering, as the boy held the small treats out for the other boys, a smirk on his face. Peter responded with an outburst of anger, his voice gruff like Dad's had been. Aslan stepped back, stunned. How could someone be upset over the unexpected appearance of food? Food was always good.

Then, with the speed of a squirrel, Peter slapped the light-haired boy's hand, and the treats fell to the dirt right in front of Aslan. What a boon! He stepped forward to sniff the dropped bounty and caught the barest whiff of chemicals coming from the treats when Peter lunged for them. Aslan acted. Any time food was dropped on the ground, it was fair game. Right? He refused to lose this opportunity. He opened his mouth and snatched up the two treats and some dirt.

At this, Peter screamed. Aslan froze at the sound, watching in shock as two hands flew toward his mouth and the food held there. He tried to swallow, but Peter was too quick. He closed one hand around Aslan's upper jaw and the other around his lower jaw and forced his mouth open. Aslan squirmed against the cruel treatment, but Peter held his jaws in a vise grip, forcing Aslan's nose toward the ground. Peter's fingers filled his mouth, making him gag. Unable to move his tongue to swallow or keep the white cheese inside, the treats fell to the dirt. Peter grabbed Aslan's collar and yanked him away while simultaneously picking up the two cheese pieces.

For a brief second, there was only a stunned silence. Aslan shook his head and tested his sore jaw. Licking his lips, he attempted to remove the ghost-feel of Peter's hands manhandling his mouth. A bitter, chemical taste coated his tongue, and he salivated against it. At first, the three boys stared at Aslan, but then in slow synchronicity raised their faces to stare at each other.

Then, face red, Peter yelled at the light-haired boy and stepped off the path and into the underbrush. Putting his hands together, he split the treats in half, and, as he turned his palms down, a fine, white powder drifted to the forest floor.

The light-haired boy said something in a low, menacing growl. Peter took a few quick steps closer to the boy, yelled again, and pointed a finger at the boy's chest. In a louder, more frightening growl, the boy spoke, but at the same time showed submission by taking a step back. Aslan took a step backward, too. Sensing his opponent's weakness, Peter rushed the boy, and this time jabbed his finger straight into the boy's chest. Angered by the finger attack, the boy shoved Peter, who fell with a thump onto his backside. The light-haired boy stepped toward Peter and snarled something in a tone that threatened imminent violence.

For several long moments, no one moved. The air thickened with combustible emotion. Then, the light-haired boy turned and charged away on the footpath toward the clearing.

Peter bounced up, eyes flashing, and ran after him. Both took off running down the trail. The third boy, who had taken the role of dazed observer during this exchange, trotted behind.

Aslan stood alone on the trail, his leash ground into the loose soil of the forest floor. He didn't know what to do. Stupefied by the show of aggression between the two humans, he sniffed his leash. Once at training class, his Mistress had accidentally dropped his leash while she carried his crate and a chair. When the leash fell, he'd stopped walking, unsure of what to do. His Mistress figured out her mistake within moments and returned to praise him for his stay. Stay was a game, but with the exception of the day when his Mistress had dropped his leash, it always started with a human pointing at him and saying *stay*. Peter hadn't.

Did the dropped leash mean *stay* like that time with his Mistress? Was this a game? If he played it well, would he get some white cheese?

He inhaled the moist woodsy air. The strange odors called to him. Without Peter to pull him back on the path, he could see if any of that destroyed cheese remained on the ground and then go explore those unknown scents and discover what made them.

But if this was a stay game, he wasn't supposed to go following spoors.

Puzzled, he sat on the ground. It would be best to wait a bit and see if Peter returned. Aslan did want one of those white treats.

Time passed. A rustling sounded in the underbrush not far off. He stood and lifted his nose to the breeze, trying to smell what could be making that noise. A bird? Something more exotic? The desire to give chase intensified, almost overwhelming him. His muscles tightened in preparation to dart into the woods and investigate the noise when a frantic call echoed through the trees.

"Aslan!" The rustling silenced, and Aslan swiveled his head toward his name. It came again, shrill and loud, accompanied by the pounding of several feet. "Aslan!"

Thinking fast, he plunked his haunches back on the ground in a sit. His best bet to snag those white treats was to be sitting pretty when the humans came into sight.

Peter and the two boys rounded a bend in the trail. Peter rushed to him, pulled him into his arms, and hugged him so tightly that Aslan's eyes widened.

"Good boy. Good boy," Peter repeated over and over. Relief flooded his voice.

Ah. So, it was a stay game after all. Apparently there would be no food rewards for his stay, which didn't seem quite fair after having the white treats forcibly removed from his jaws, but praise rewards were good, too. Although he could do without the tight squeezes.

* * *

"So, there we were." Dad leaned forward on the sofa in the den, his hands mimicking holding a pot over an imaginary fire. "Pork and beans warmed in the pan, but no utensils to eat them. It was catastrophic. Four hungry men staring at hot food with no possible way to feed themselves. I poured the beans on each man's plate, anyway." Dad mimed slopping beans from the pretend pan onto a circle of plates. "The last rations. 'We're gonna starve!' Evan cried. 'We're done for,' I agreed. But Peter wasn't scared. His mouth was too full. He'd used his potato chips like a spoon to scoop up those beans. He was scarfing them so fast, I think I heard him grunt. The fact that we're here to tell the tale is proof of his heroism." Dad finished the story with a flourish of his hand.

"Sounds like you were the chevalier of the camping trip, Peter," Mom said.

Peter bowed his head in mock humility. "I always eat my beans on potato chips. It wasn't a big deal. I'm just an average guy."

"Did Aslan get any beans?" Krissy asked.

Peter hugged the sheltie sitting by his side on the blue sofa. "No, but he got loads of potato chips. He slept with me in the tent, too. He's like a warm teddy dog at night."

Krissy ignored the *teddy dog* mixed metaphor, figuring it was intentional. "Was he any trouble?"

"No," Dad said. "He and Ruffis spent most of the time sleeping under the trees in their crates. Other than a few long walks in the woods, they rested. I told you they'd be safer camping with us than boarded at the vet's."

Peter's grin faded to a frown, and his eyes narrowed. He pulled Aslan closer to his side in a protective hug. Krissy's inner warning bells clanged. Had Aslan been in danger? As her mouth opened to interrogate Peter, she remembered her tantrum at the beginning of the weekend, and it stopped her. She was supposed to be spreading peace, not conflict. And what would she accuse him of? Plus, Shelly had said to avoid arguing in front of Aslan.

She shut her mouth and gritted her teeth against the accusations that warred for release. Whatever may have happened, Aslan was fine, and Peter seemed to like him better.

She needed to just let it go. This making-everyone-happy thing was hard.

CHAPTER 17

Agility to the Rescue

September: Sixteen Months Old

T he warm wind from the car's open window whipped Krissy's shoulder-length hair forward and then back in an angry tornado-like spiral as Dad drove along the highway. Aslan exhaled a loud, contented sigh and snuggled in his crate in the backseat. A year ago, she'd let him ride free in the car. A year later, she'd learned how dangerous that was, and now he rode in a lashed-down, crash-tested crate.

Funny how much could change in one year.

One year ago, he'd passed his S.T.A.R. Puppy test. Now, he was headed to a mock agility trial. One year ago, she'd been best friends with Violet. Now, especially after this afternoon, their friendship was very much up in the air.

She and Violet had fought today. It was Friday, and all over the school, kids had been making weekend plans. For once, Krissy had plans, too. She'd been looking forward to the mock trial for weeks, but as it neared, she'd begun to wonder whom she'd hang around with between runs. All of her agility classmates were adults. They were great people, and Abby, in particular, was fun to talk with. But Krissy had never hung around with them outside of class. It'd be odd sitting around chatting with adults while she waited for her run.

So, last minute, she'd decided to ask Violet and Jessica to join her. It had been a long time since the three had done anything together. Evan consumed a lot of Violet's time, and they usually hung with Jessica and her latest hot dish. Jessica liked to try new and always hot dishes—often.

All those people wanting Violet's attention probably made her feel pretty loved, but she also probably felt stretched thin, too, especially with her overriding need to please. A girls' night out seemed like a solid answer for everyone. Krissy hadn't heard any more about Violet drinking, but with Evan in the picture, Violet was surely partying. Another good reason to spend the evening catching up, away from guys.

But even before Krissy asked Violet if she wanted to go to the mock trial, Krissy's day had been bad. First, she'd gotten a C on her Algebra II test. She hadn't studied, but still. Then she'd found out the football player she'd been crushing on had a girlfriend. Not that he even knew who Krissy was, but still. Then she'd read the list of chair positions posted on the band room's door. Seventh chair flute, *again*. Not that she was good, but still. In a bad mood, she'd tromped to Violet's locker, where she found her friend bent over, loading her backpack.

"Hey." Krissy rubbed at an ache in her forehead. "Aslan and I are going to a pretend agility trial tonight. Do you and Jessica wanna come? We can watch a movie or something after."

"I can't." Violet straightened. "We're going to the Gamble Red concert at Riversand Casino."

"Is that the band Gamble Red, or are you just going to the casino to gamble? That sounds fun. Sitting around with the gray hairs pulling levers on slot machines and smoking cancer sticks one after the other." She'd mostly meant that to be funny, but it rang snarky.

Violet wheeled on her, one hand on her hip, head tilted. "What?"

"You can't get into the concert. You have to have an adult to get into casino concerts."

"Evan's brother is taking us." Violet scowled and turned back to her locker.

Disappointment topping a lousy day loosened Krissy's tongue. "Well, have fun then. Don't get too drunk."

"I'll do what I please," Violet shot over her shoulder, voice cold.

"I'm sure you'll do what Evan wants you to." Realizing that could be taken two ways, Krissy stammered. "Uh. I mean, Evan seems to run your life." The amendment was possibly worse than the original comment. Krissy's cheeks burned. She'd gone too far.

Violet slammed her locker and spun around. "No one runs my life." Her eyes narrowed. "But I'm thinking a dog runs yours."

Stunned, Krissy hadn't replied and instead stalked off, waves of guilt, anger, concern, and, lastly, loneliness crashing through her. How could someone feel so many emotions all at once?

As the car sped toward the mock trial, Krissy pushed the memory away and rolled up the window, not wanting the wind to so tangle her hair that she couldn't comb it out with her fingers. She'd forgotten to put a hairbrush in her purse. Aslan's slicker brush was packed in the training bag, but *yuck*. Even she, who apparently let a dog run her life, couldn't bring herself to use her dog's brush.

Minutes later, the SUV's tires chewed the gravel as it rolled across a long driveway to a small indoor horse arena owned by a rancher on the outskirts of the city. Outside the arena's open barn door, Daniel and Mike were hefting one of the dogwalk planks off a flatbed trailer. Mike saw the SUV, nodded, and smiled, unable to wave with his hands gripping the heavy ramp. The pair and ramp disappeared into the arena.

Aslan had never run on a dirt agility surface before. He trained at home and at City Dogs on grass or, during bad weather on class days, indoors on turf. According to Daniel, most of the regional agility trials were either on indoor soccer turf or dirt, and he'd wanted the students who were headed to competition to get a feel for agility on dirt, too.

After gathering her gear and Aslan, Krissy hurried to the arena. Her bad mood lingered, but the opportunity to run a course in a horse arena, like a real show, made her smile for the first time that day. Aslan pranced at her side, tail wagging, unfazed by the new environment with its myriad smells and sounds.

"Hey, kiddo!" Mike yelled as he walked out the barn doors toward her. He gave her, training gear and all, one of his trademark bear hugs. "I set up Honey's crate along the concrete apron by the bleachers inside. All the beginners are there. It's a squeeze, but it'll fit our needs tonight." He turned to Dad. "Hello, Doc. How's the laboratory?"

Krissy skipped into the building and spotted several crates and chairs in a line where Mike had described. The crates were within feet of the arena floor, so the dogs could watch the action from the comfort of their cushy beds. The square arena was small with dirty white walls and the strong smell of horse manure. Judy, Daniel, and several of the Furutas' students worked in the ring arranging agility equipment.

"You need to go help." Dad came up from behind and reached for Aslan's leash. "Part of agility is volunteering."

Krissy swallowed hard against a sharp *well, duh* reply. Instead, she plastered on what was supposed to be a sweet smile but might've been a little lopsided. "Great idea, Dad. Thank you!" Dad's eyebrows furrowed, and one eye squinted in a bemused expression. The feeding-her-family-happy-healing-emotions thing hadn't worked quite yet. They seemed more confused than relaxed by her change in attitude, but she was determined to continue. Handing him the leash, she trotted onto the arena floor to ask what she could do.

"Krissy!" Judy set down the jump she carried and trotted to Krissy, putting an arm around her shoulders in a welcoming hug. "I'm so glad you could make it. Are you ready to run?"

"I'm stoked." Krissy smiled for the second time that day. "How can I help?"

"First, let me introduce you to Basma. She's one of our advanced students, and I'd like her to be your mentor this evening and for your first few trials. She will help you with everything from entering a trial, to checking in, to getting to the ring on time. And she knows all the secret rules of dog show etiquette no one bothers to tell new people. I want you to feel comfortable asking her anything. It's hard to be new in this sport, and it will be good for you to have someone ready to help you."

Judy, her arm still around Krissy's shoulders, guided her through the crowd of people carrying various pieces of agility equipment and marking distances with a yellow measuring wheel. A short stout woman with olive skin and dark hair that framed her round face in loose curls dropped a load of PVC jump bars along the arena's border with a clatter. Her face lit with recognition as the pair approached. She looked to be around sixty, but honestly, it was sometimes hard to tell the ages of older people.

"Here she is, Basma," Judy said.

"Well, my word." Basma's southern-influenced drawl indicated she'd been raised in eastern Oklahoma. "Would you look at her. She's as cute as a bug!" She stuck out her dust-covered hand, and Krissy shook it. "Judy said this is your first agility event? Is that true?"

"Uh. Yes." Krissy was a bit cowed by the woman's vibrant personality.

"You are gonna love this. We have the best time doing agility. You run a little Shetland sheepdog, correct?" Basma's delivery was all rapid fire, southern charm.

"Uh-huh."

"I have shelties, too!" Basma exclaimed with genuine enthusiasm. "My word, but I can hardly handle them. Shelties are hooligans, aren't they?"

"Basma is being modest," Judy said. "She's earned eight agility championships on two of those hooligans of hers."

Krissy gawked. Was that eight total or eight on each dog? Either way, it was astounding.

Basma squeezed Judy's shoulder. "You can tell what Judy does for a living, can't you? It's just like a counselor to boost her client's morale. I got lucky to find good hooligans, that's all." She wrinkled her nose and made a sort of snorty sound Krissy guessed was a laugh. Krissy smiled back.

"Well, we need to get to work, or this course will never be built. Have you ever built a course before?" Basma asked Krissy.

"Only in my backyard."

Basma slid into her mentoring role. "When building a course for a trial, the judge can get plenty picky. There are tricks course builders use. Let me show you the measuring wheel."

* * *

Krissy sat swinging her legs on the wooden bleachers between the other two musketeers, Mike and Abby. Alonzo, the thin young man who ran the white poodle-mix named Star and the fourth member of the original puppy class, sat behind Abby. About twenty-five other handlers attending the fun run watched from the bleachers or milled around the arena, chatting. The Three Musketeers and Alonzo were dressed the same as everyone else, in shorts, tees, and sneakers, like mismatched school uniforms.

The Three Musketeers were doing well in agility. Of course, Abby and Jeeves were the best. Jeeves wasn't blazing fast, but he was super accurate, and Abby was so athletic. Daniel had predicted lots of titles in their future. As shocking as it was, Krissy and Aslan might be the next best team in class. That was because of hard work, though, not any particular talent on her part. Aslan loved agility—lived for it, even. The serious puppy had disappeared, replaced by a buff bullet. He couldn't wait to work and gave her his all every practice session. The "Third Vault Veto," as she called the spin before the third jump, still plagued them, and they lacked some essential distance skills. But overall, they'd made consistent progress.

Even Mike and Honey had skills. Honey enjoyed having a job and excelled at weave poles. She had some issues keeping jump bars up, but her incredible speed and wide grin made her so much fun to watch.

However, poor Alonzo and Star struggled. At the beginning of summer, Star had been practicing the teeter in class. She'd run to the end of it and ridden it to the ground like Daniel had taught the small dogs to do. As it hit the ground, Star went to hop off as usual, but the teeter bucked on the hard ground, smacking her rear feet on the rebound. She'd flipped in the air and landed hard on her side. She was uninjured, but the accident left her with a strong and understandable fear of the teeter. Daniel told Alonzo if he remained determined and kept his teeter training sessions happy, Star would work her way through it, given time, but it could take months. Everyone knew Alonzo would stick it out, though. He had ulterior motives to stay in class. He liked Abby—a lot.

"Let's take bets." Mike put his bottled water on the ground between his sneakered feet. "How many times will Daniel make his grimace face on the course tonight?"

Abby laughed. "Oh. I know that face. He does it every front cross."

"All we have to do is figure out where he'll throw front crosses, then," Krissy said.

The four discussed the course, examining handling options and deciding where Daniel might throw front crosses. Crosses were maneuvers performed by handlers to turn their dogs on course. There were several different kinds of crosses, including fronts, rears, and blinds.

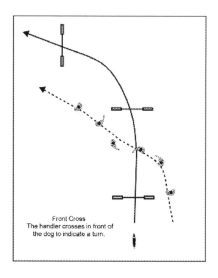

Front Cross
The handler crosses in front of
the dog to indicate a turn.

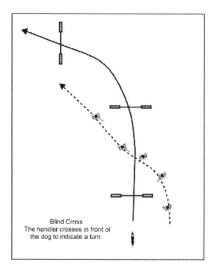

Blind Cross
The handler crosses in front of
the dog to indicate a turn.

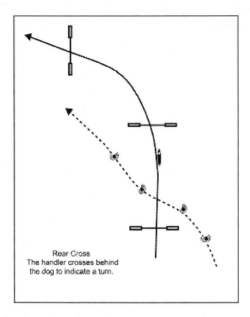

Rear Cross
The handler crosses behind
the dog to indicate a turn.

Handlers had to decide when to use which cross, and choices differed from team to team and sequence to sequence. So, figuring out how many front crosses Daniel might throw proved challenging.

The Musketeers weighed options as the first of the advanced dogs ran. The experienced dogs competed first on a more difficult version of the course, and when they finished, an easier version would be built for the beginner dogs. While the advanced teams ran with speed and skill, the Three Musketeers plus Alonzo studied and joked on the sidelines.

When Daniel and Q walked into the ring, Mike said, "Let's firm those bets. Alonzo, you say two grimace faces. Krissy and I vote for three, and Abby is going all out with four. Correct?"

Heads nodded. "I'm going to go to the other side in case he flashes a grimace face y'all can't see from here," Alonzo said, scrambling off the bleachers.

"Run!" Abby said. "He's about to lead out."

Sure enough, Daniel set Q on the start line. After commanding her to stay, he led out past the second obstacle, a jump.

"Okay," he said, releasing his dog. The black-and-white border collie blurred, arcing over the first two jumps before whirling toward the dogwalk. As she blasted across the dogwalk down-ramp, three paws hitting the yellow safety zone, Daniel pivoted in a front cross, turning his face toward the bleachers. His nose scrunched and eyebrows contorted in concentration—a grimace.

"One!" Mike yelled, and the Musketeers, standing now, cheered.

A few obstacles later, Daniel threw a blind cross after the A-frame. Running straight at the bleachers, he grimaced.

"A grimace on a blind." Abby waggled a slender finger. "I knew he'd grimace there."

Q turned for a jump, and Daniel cued her to wrap tight around the jump's stanchion and come back toward him, front-crossing as he did. However, he faced the other side of the ring away from the bleachers.

"Three!" Alonzo yelled from across the ring. The Musketeers whooped.

"We're on point!" Mike yelled, holding a high-five hand to Krissy. She slapped it.

"No more! No más!" Krissy yelled at Daniel, who now stood motionless by the pause table. On the table's top, Q leaned forward on her tiptoes, anxious to be released. Daniel glanced at the cheering bleachers quizzically during the five-second pause at the table, but when the countdown finished, he had to refocus for the last section—three jumps that would require some kind of cross to turn Q to the right. Krissy and Mike rooted for a rear cross. Daniel's chances of grimacing during a rear were less. Abby yelled for a front. Above the din, Alonzo, on the opposite side, called for a front and a win for Abby.

Releasing Q from the table, Daniel ran toward the last three jumps. Instead of a front or a rear, he blinded, his face in profile.

His lips pulled back, his nose scrunched, and his eyebrows knitted. The fourth grimace.

Mike and Krissy groaned. Abby cheered and circled in a victory dance. Alonzo whooped from the far side of the arena.

"To the victor go the spoils!" Mike yelled, leaning past Krissy to clap the winner on the back.

"What's going on?" Daniel walked toward the bleachers breathing hard and pulling Q by a colorful tug toy held in a death grip between her teeth.

"We all bet on how many times you'd make the grimace face," Mike said. "Abby won. You grimaced four times."

"We didn't realize you grimaced during blinds as well as fronts," Krissy pointed out.

"I knew that," Abby said, "but I kept that handicapper's tip to myself."

"Grimace face?" Daniel asked as Alonzo trotted up to the group.

Abby scrunched her face, opened her mouth, and pulled her lips back. She stuck her tongue out for effect.

"That's perfect!" Mike nodded at Abby.

"Yeah. No way. There is no way I do that," Daniel said. "That looks like a confused troll or something."

"And yet Q is willing to run with you, anyway," Krissy said. "She's quite the dog."

Daniel imitated Abby's version of his grimace. His face crinkled, his eyes scrunched almost closed, and his tongue lolled out of a twisted mouth. Q looked at him, dropped her tug toy, and whined.

Once again, the bleachers roared with laughter.

* * *

An hour later, Krissy shifted her weight from one foot to the other as she waited in line at the ring gate. Energy surged through her, and her stomach fluttered. Even though this wasn't a real trial, it felt real. For the first time, she would run Aslan in front of strangers—not just her agility class members and the Furutas. She rolled her shoulders and bent to touch her toes in a failed attempt to stretch her nerves away.

Aslan, on the other hand, looked relaxed. His eyes danced, and he pranced at her feet in anticipation of treats, but his energy wasn't the nervous kind. Just his usual happy kind.

Happy. His *usual* happy. When had that happened?

She didn't have time to reflect on it, though. When Abby had won the bet, Daniel gave her the right to choose the running order for the beginning dogs. She'd chosen small to tall, meaning the shortest dogs ran first. Aslan measured in at twelve inches, one of the smallest dogs. In a moment, he would step to the start line at his first agility event.

The Master's students had stayed to help build the novice course, and many loitered around the arena, talking in small groups or leaning on the metal panel fence to watch and cheer the new students. As the border terrier in front of her turned toward the finish jump, Krissy's butterflies transformed to wasps. For a brief moment, she couldn't move.

"Okay. Next is Aslan," said the ring's gate steward, a motherly-looking advanced student. "You can go in now. Have fun!"

Krissy huffed in and out several times, calming her wasps, and she and Aslan stepped into the ring. Several feet in front of the first jump, she removed his leash with shaky fingers. His eyes shined. His ears pricked. His body tensed. He saw the agility equipment and knew they were about to play the game—his favorite game. He smiled at her, and with that confident doggie grin, her wasps reverted to butterflies.

Krissy dropped the leash on the dirt, pointed at him, and said, "Stay!" She led out past the first jump and looked back, reached her left arm toward him, and said, "Okay!" Released, he tore over the first jump. She took several steps in place before forcing her body to move forward, indicating the dogwalk. In her confusion, she forgot to call the obstacle's name, but he read her motion and leaped onto the long sleek obstacle. Tail down, ears flattened against his head, he galloped at top speed along the twelve-inch-wide plank and reached the down-ramp several feet ahead of her. Wits collected, she commanded, "Contact. Stay!"

He hit the bottom of the dogwalk's down-ramp with his two back feet on the contact zone and two front feet resting in the dirt. It was a perfect two-paws-on/two-off contact performance, exactly what they'd spent hours training for. Knowing he was to hold the position until released, he didn't move a paw, although his body quivered in anticipation of her next command. She turned, then yelled "Okay!" and trotted toward the next obstacle, a panel jump.

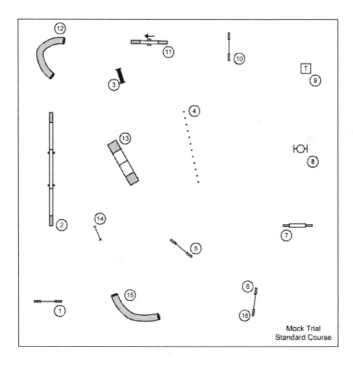

Mock Trial
Standard Course

And then it happened.

The world slowed. The ambient noise of the arena dimmed, and Krissy heard her breathing, her heartbeat, and the distant sound of her voice calling commands. Aslan ran with silky speed, knowing what to take next as if he could read the orange number cones placed beside the obstacles. His compact body compressed and sprang open with each stride, muscles rippling under the long coat. Joy emanated from his athlete's heart.

"Here weave! Here! Back! Here! Straight through! Straight pause!" The commands sounded from her mouth but weren't a part of her. He responded like a high-end sports car, weaving, jumping, and finally coming to rest on top of the pause table.

Judy, who was acting as the judge, counted down from five. Krissy took the five-second pause required on the table to lead out toward the next obstacles—a jump to a teeter. When the countdown finished, she yelled, "Okay. Over! Straight teeter!" His nails ripped at the pause table, clawing to gain purchase. Footing found, his hind legs powered his body off the table, over the jump, and to the teeter. "Hit it! Straight tunnel! Straight A-frame!"

The commands and body signals flowed once again, flowed as if she'd always known this language.

"Contact! Stay!" she yelled as he soared over the A-frame's pointy apex. He hit his two-on/two-off position at the bottom of the obstacle and held, and she moved to get ahead of him to push him over Obstacle Fourteen, a jump.

Then, something went wrong. The sounds in the arena came back into focus—cheers and Daniel yelling something. She stubbed her big toe on an uneven place in the dirt as she released Aslan from the A-frame and stumbled, catching herself before she fell. The moment vanished. Whatever it had been, it was over.

The sync lost, Aslan crossed in front of her to dart into the Obstacle Fifteen tunnel—not Fourteen. Judy raised her hand, palm open, marking the off-course. Krissy gathered him back as he barked his irritation with her poor handling, and she re-sent him to jump Fourteen. After that, he ran to the tunnel again.

"Straight, over!" Krissy indicated the last jump with voice, hand signal, forward motion, and shoulders, but instead of heading to the jump after exiting the tunnel, he pulled toward her and barked, causing a refusal at the last jump. He hadn't read her send. She gathered him again and sent him over the final jump, which stopped the clock.

Those remaining in the arena cheered. The two mistakes at the end of the course didn't diminish her thrill. Jumping up and down, she hopped to her dog—her teammate—and whooped. He barked his cheers back, his eyes sparkling and shiny, his mouth open in a large doggie grin.

"You rocked that, Little Man!" She pumped her fists at him. He trotted to her side and bounced like a Super Ball next to her in celebration. Mid-air on his third bounce, she snatched him into her arms, and, from the safety of her hug, he barked again.

Daniel, with a toothy smile spread across his face, met them as they exited the ring. "That was spectacular! You hit the zone, yeah?"

She leashed Aslan and put him on the ground. He barked and pranced in anticipation of treats and more praise. Holding out her trembling hands, she said, "Look at me shake. Yeah. We did. Wow! It was. . .beyond words. I want to run that again."

Daniel laughed. "That was beautiful to watch. The zone! And before you've even competed! Be careful, or you'll become a zone addict."

"It's adrenaline." Basma rushed up and pointed to Krissy's shaking hands. "It's addictive. That was incredible! My word, his contacts were flawless. Watch out, twelve-inch jump height class, Aslan's coming at 'cha!"

Krissy laughed, smile wide, breath coming in gasps.

"And that distance!" Basma continued. "For a novice dog, he can move out."

"We have to reward your dog!" Daniel scanned the area for her treat bag. "He needs his treats and his praise. Good boy! Great run!"

* * *

Krissy kicked the bed sheets, unable to sleep. The infectious laughter of her agility friends rang in her ears. She smiled, remembering Daniel's grimacing face and Abby's hilarious imitation of it. These new friends helped ease the sting of her social life, or lack thereof, at school. She was welcomed and accepted, even loved, at agility. A part of—not apart from.

And to think she'd worried it would be awkward to hang out with adults. Had Violet had as much fun at the concert? No possible way.

Krissy relived Aslan's run—the zone—the beauty of it all. It wasn't that she and Aslan had become one. Instead, they'd each kept their individuality yet mixed together somehow. For a while there, she knew his mind. Knew his spirit. Understood his thoughts and shared his emotions.

But best of all, for a few moments there, she'd left her broken body behind, joined Aslan, and knew what it was to fly. Really fly.

True, it'd been a simple course. Agility courses got harder and harder as teams advanced, and while Judy had said today was a success for Team Aslan, they hadn't run clean. It proved she could handle the easy beginner courses at distance, but what about the hard Master's courses where if you made one simple mistake, you wouldn't qualify?

She rolled over and pulled Aslan's warm teddy-bear body to her stomach. She kissed his silken head, and he sighed.

He was a talented gift from God, but could she do this gift justice? Could they someday run the tough courses clean?

CHAPTER 18

The Third Step

October: Seventeen Months Old

K rissy stood on the concrete parking lot, Aslan on lead at her feet, and stared at the huge metal building. Inside, Aslan would soon compete in his first real agility trial. Barking escaped the open barn door. Shouldn't whinnies be the animal accompaniment for a horse arena?

The faintest odor of manure hung in the moist morning air. The familiar earthy scent evoked the memory of Whickery's tail as the trailer door closed. Of her fear of the horse.

Of her failure.

Her insides lurched. What was she doing here? It would all happen again. Failure with yet another animal.

She glanced at Aslan. He seemed to sense her hesitation as he stared into her eyes. His own eyes exuded excitement and confidence. He wanted this new adventure. He suffered no anxiety, no concern for defeat. He felt only the thrill of the game.

She closed her eyes to recapture the feeling of the zone they'd experienced weeks earlier at the mock trial. In her mind, she relived the run. Felt the thrill. Felt the mistakes at the end. Her eyes squeezed tight as she dug deep into the memory and seized upon the emotional high that had allowed her to accept that the mistakes hadn't mattered. They weren't important. It was their relationship. The zone. The rush.

"You're gonna fail," Daniel had told their class one night. "You won't qualify more often than you will. You'll have periods of time—perhaps long ones—where you never catch a Q. If we moved through the ranks with ease, Qing every run, agility would be dull. So embrace the fact that *you will fail.* Learn from your mistakes. Train the problems away, and then you'll qualify more often. But even then, you will never reach perfection. You will always fall short. Hug that concept."

Embrace failure. Krissy had tasted success—the partial zone run. Then they'd slammed into failure at the end, and she'd hugged it. If they failed today, she would not—*would not*—let it stop her from trying again and again and again. Aslan would not become Whickery. She wouldn't let her fears win and destroy his joy.

A loud *thunk* broke her reverie, and Aslan danced in place at the familiar sound. The expected, more muffled, second *thunk* resounded as a teeter in the building ahead of them returned to its original position, the competing dog having left the obstacle.

"Let's go dance, Little Man," she said to him. He barked his treble, happy bark, and they walked through the arena's open doors.

Dad came up next to her as she stopped to scan the scene. His arms clutched trial gear—crate, mat, chairs, training bag. Behind him, Mom, dressed in black slacks, a red plaid jacket, and black loafers, pulled a rolling ice chest.

"Where do you want to crate?" Dad asked, also surveying the trial site.

Reddish-brown dirt covered the floor of the large square building. Near the middle, two agility rings were sectioned off by rusty galvanized-metal tube fencing. The ring by the door was the Standard ring, with its colorful contact obstacles arranged in a Master's-level course. A black Standard poodle, his face lit with laughter, capered around his handler as she asked him to weave for the third time. The far ring held jumps, a tunnel, and weave poles. In it, zombie people walked the Jumpers with Weaves course, strategizing and memorizing their cues.

Krissy remained rooted for several moments, taking it all in. It was show time.

"Hey, you guys!" Basma, dressed in a bright purple jogging suit, waved before carefully extracting herself from a tall stand of bleachers in front of the Standard ring. Once free, she trotted over, her dark curls bobbing. "How exciting is this! Your first show! Follow me. All of the City Doggers are crated over here."

Basma's machine-gun chatter continued as she led them through crates, camp chairs, handlers, and dogs. Aslan didn't walk by Krissy's side. He pranced. The intensity in the air fed him, and he loved it. "I set this mat down to save your space." Basma pointed to a red woven beach mat similar to Krissy's own. "Just pick it up, put yours down, and set up your gear. After that, I'll take you to get your course maps and get you checked in."

Glancing at the nearby crates, Krissy found the Furutas' gear and recognized some of the dogs lying in surrounding cages as belonging to other students at City Dogs. After her mat and gear were set up, Basma returned and, leaving Krissy's parents with the gear, led her to the maps. Soon, Krissy had the novice course maps in her hand and had checked Aslan in for both of his runs.

"Now, you get to sit and wait." Basma's words tumbled out in her thick Okie accent as she walked Krissy back to the crates. "After you study those course maps, if you have any questions, grab me, Daniel, or Judy. And feel free to wander into the stands and visit with the other competitors. Agility is a social sport, you know. My word, we sit and jabber for hours between our runs. At some point, you should also walk Aslan along the outside of the rings and around the building to let him get a feel for the place, its sounds and its smells. Daniel and Judy have an ice chest filled with goodies and drinks. Help yourself and relax. Your class won't start for at least an hour."

Setup and check-in done, she breezed away and left Krissy with her parents, who already had drinks resting in their chairs' cup holders while Aslan slept in his crate. Mom read a book, and Dad watched the last of the Master's dogs compete in the Standard ring.

"It'll be about an hour before I get to walk novice jumpers with weaves." Krissy shuffled her course maps as she spoke.

"Sounds like we got here at the right time," Dad said. "One hour early. Sit and relax."

Krissy sat on the edge of her canvas chair, but there would be no relaxing. She bent her head to read the maps, but they blurred in her shaky hands. She closed her eyes and repeated her mantra. *Aslan isn't Whickery. If I fail today, I will try again.*

Moments later, the trembling subsided, and she tried again to study the maps. The Jumpers with Weaves course started with a tunnel. That was good. Aslan loved tunnels. After the tunnel, a sequence of jumps veered to the right and, at the back of the course, turned left. A turn required a cross. Her forehead scrunched in concentration. She should probably rear-cross Aslan between Jumps Four and Five.

Then she gasped. Four jumps in a row snaked from one side of the ring to the other across the back of the course. A Third Vault Veto! And to make matters worse, the third jump in the line, Obstacle Number Eight, was offset! It would require Aslan to execute a difficult and subtle change of direction to find it. Normal handlers ran right next to their dogs for such maneuvers, pushing their dogs toward the slightly out-of-position jump. But she wasn't normal. She would be way behind Aslan by then.

This was disastrous. It was the Third Vault Veto on steroids. How would she ever do this? Her confidence plummeted. The Furutas had said she was ready for this. Obviously not. In truth, she was nowhere near ready.

Cold crept through her, and the map shook again. She rubbed a hand over her face in an attempt to control her fear. Maybe she could find a creative way to do this at distance? After her rear cross between Jumps Four and Five, she would be trailing Aslan as he darted over Jumps Six and Seven. She could yell, "Straight," but giving the straight cue for Eight would send him on a direct line to the wing of Jump Nine. She could do a rear cross, but that would cause him to turn too sharply off of Seven.

Her cheeks burned. She'd failed before she'd taken one step in the ring. Her eyes filled with tears, and she blinked hard.

No. If I fail, I will dust myself off and try again.

She flipped her maps and examined the Standard course. There was a tricky box of obstacles in the upper-right corner of the ring where a dog could easily go off course, but the Furutas had drilled her on how to handle those. It would be hard, but at least it was doable. The vise grip on her chest eased.

Daniel trotted up with a big grin on his face. "Hey, Johnsons! Welcome to your first trial!"

Her parents smiled and greeted him. Krissy ground her teeth and pretended to study the map in her hand as Daniel grabbed a nearby chair and pulled it next to her. "I see you've gotten the course maps already. What's the news today?"

She yanked the Jumper's map to the top. "There's a Third Vault Veto here." She slapped the map with the back of her free hand. "Look. It's four jumps—*four* jumps—all across the back of the course."

Daniel took the map and examined it with pursed lips. "Yeah." He nodded. "This will be a challenge for you."

"It can't be done, not by someone like me." Her voice sounded shaky.

He shifted and looked straight into her eyes. She hoped he didn't see any remnants of tears. "This can be done at distance. It's true. You may not have this particular skill yet, but it can be done. It takes longer to train for distance. There are so many skills like this that need more work than the average bear, but it isn't impossible. I told you this at the beginning, remember?"

Krissy nodded, unable to trust her voice.

"We'll teach you how to train this, but for now, let's look at your handling options with the tool box you currently have. Remember, you can make mistakes in Novice. You don't have to run clean to qualify."

That was true. In Novice, she could make a few mistakes and still qualify. If they ran clean everywhere but the Third Vault Veto, they might be okay. She studied the map in Daniel's hand with new eyes, and together, they worked on a plan.

* * *

Basma and Krissy leaned on the rusty metal fence surrounding the novice Jumpers with Weaves ring, pointing and talking strategy as the judge tweaked the course for accuracy. A middle-aged man, the judge laughed and teased with the course-building crew as jumps were aligned and distances measured.

"Hello, ladies!" Smiling, Charlotte approached from behind and leaned on the fence next to Basma. "I see City Dogs' youngest protégé is debuting today."

"How are you, Charlotte?" Coolness dampened Basma's voice. She must've been told about Krissy's previous run-ins with Charlotte because Basma's attitude flipped from helpful mentor to protective mother bear in a millisecond.

"We had another great day," Charlotte said, ignoring Basma's frostiness. "Lil' Boss and Oreo both earned Standard Qs, and Cool Q'ed in Jumpers and Standard. One more in each, and Mia will be in Master's with him. They are kicking butts and taking names."

"Congrats." Basma didn't sound as if she meant it. She turned back to Krissy and pointed. "Do you see where you start at the tunnel? When you take his leash off—"

"It looks like a runner's course out there today," Charlotte interrupted. "Good luck with that, Krissy." She smiled and without waiting for further comment, walked off.

"My word." Basma's brow creased, and her voice dripped with disgust. "Don't pay her any mind. She's kind of a loon and goes bonkers sometimes. We all ignore her when she gets like that."

But Charlotte's comment bounced around in Krissy's head in spite of Basma's admonition. *It looks like a runner's course.*

It did. It was.

Krissy frowned at the four jumps lined up along the back of the course. *There was no possible way.*

* * *

A whistle blew, and the judge bellowed, "Novice judge's briefing!" Krissy stepped into a real agility ring for the first time, her heart pounding. Over a year's training was on the line. Hours upon countless hours of hard work. All for this sport—for Aslan. Her stomach twisted. Not for the first time today, she wished Honey was there to make her laugh, or for Abby to boost Krissy's morale with her quiet confidence. Mike and Honey weren't ready for competition, but Abby and Jeeves had been entered today. The plan was for the two teams to debut at the same time. However, Abby's great-aunt had died unexpectedly, and she'd had to pull out, leaving Krissy walking into the ring alone and scared.

A herd of around twenty novice handlers gathered in a tight circle around the judge, who stood front and center in the Jumpers with Weaves ring. Krissy glanced at the other handlers. Their faces were pale and their eyes wide. She assumed she looked equally stricken.

The judge introduced himself, reviewed some of the rules, and explained when to enter and where to exit. He seemed kind for a man who'd created such a diabolical course. With her nerves on high alert, her hands repeatedly balled and unballed. Finally, she stuffed them into her jeans pockets to quiet them.

After a quick Q and A session, he said, "You all have eight minutes to walk the course. First dog on the line five minutes after that. Have fun!"

The novice handlers swarmed to the first obstacle, and Krissy joined them. Imagining an invisible Aslan, she walked through the obstacles, giving him cues with her hands and arms, performing her crosses, and saying verbal cues in her head. She stopped to examine dog-path lines and angles between jumps. No one talked, and the tension mushroomed. After she'd walked the course several times, a loud buzzer blew.

"Clear the course!" yelled the judge. "First dog on the line in five minutes!"

CHAPTER 19

The Third Step Continued

October: Seventeen Months Old

Krissy trotted from the ring and rushed to Aslan's crate. Eager to escape, he pushed against the crate's zipper with his nose as she opened it. He bounded out and danced at her feet, eyes sparkling. He looked more alive than she'd ever seen him. In spite of his prancing, she managed to leash him, and turned to face her parents, who had risen from their chairs.

"Go get 'em, Little Mouse," Mom said using her pet name for Krissy and handing her a bag of dog treats before slinging her purse over her shoulder.

"*Mouse?*" Dad repeated in disbelief. "Mouse? She needs a tough sports name, not something like *Go Stomp 'Em, Minuscule Ant* or *Go Squish 'Em, Teensy Fly.*"

Krissy's fingers fumbled to open the treats, her muscles weak with nerves.

"I've got it. *Go Get 'Em, Tough as Nails.*" Dad said, finality in his voice.

Mom groaned. "Tough as Nails? That's your best?" She took the treat bag, opened it for Krissy, returned it, and gave Krissy a hug. "Go get 'em, Little Mouse," she whispered.

After attempting a smile she was sure didn't fool them, Krissy grasped Aslan's leash and led him to the ring's entrance as her parents climbed into the stands. Now she really, *really* wished the other two Musketeers were there to root for her. The area around the entrance gate was crowded with handlers and their dogs preparing to run, but she didn't know any of them. If Abby were there, they'd root each other on and maybe do some good-natured trash talking.

A hand on her shoulder caused her to spin. Basma's encouraging smile warmed her. "Any questions?"

"No," Krissy said. "I have a plan."

"Just make it fun for Aslan," Basma told her. "As long as he doesn't bite the judge, it's all gravy. You have fun, too. Trust me. It won't be long until he has to retire, and you'd give all you own for one more run." Basma's eyes teared up. "My word, it goes by fast. Enjoy the ride."

As she walked away, Krissy looked at Aslan, who was already enjoying the ride, begging without shame for the treats she held in her hands. Three high-pitched barks of frustration rent the air as he asked for cookies.

Another hand patted her shoulder. Judy this time with Daniel right behind her. "Have fun," Judy said in her gentle voice.

"Funny. Basma just said that."

"Yeah. Sage advice," Daniel said. "Follow it. Make this ring Aslan's home. Cheer that talented boy of yours on, regardless of the outcome. Okay?"

"Yes, sir." Krissy performed a sharp salute.

Daniel grinned. "I'm not kidding."

"I know. I'll make it fun for him."

The silver-haired gate steward's baritone voice boomed. "Where is Jewel? Jewel? You're the first dog on the line. After Jewel, we have Apollo on deck and Dorrie in the hole."

"If you have any questions, we'll be right there." Judy gestured to the bottom row of the bleachers. "I'm so proud of you! You've made it!" She gave Krissy a quick hug, and the pair left her alone at the start gate.

Krissy crouched in front of Aslan and whispered, "We can do this, buddy. We can. Even if we fall on our faces out there, we'll have fun."

The words sounded false in her ears. Her heart thumped so hard she could feel it in her chest, and her stomach churned acidic. She gritted her teeth against her body's response to the fear and worked Aslan on some of his puppy class behaviors—sits, drops, and stays. He barked and wagged his tail as he practiced, his eyes full of anticipation, confidence, and, yes, even love.

"We have Prestige on the line," the gate steward yelled. "Last dog this jump height! Then we have Aslan on deck and Tally in the hole."

This is a runner's course. You can't do it. The negative mantra flitted through her head. *You're going to let him down.*

With a numb hand, she patted her left leg to call Aslan to heel position as the corgi ahead of them completed her run to the crowd's cheers. The ring crew sprung from their chairs to raise the bars from eight inches to twelve.

"Next dog on the line, Aslan," yelled the baritone voice. "Then we have Tally on deck and Eddie in the hole."

Krissy maneuvered through the other dogs and handlers to the entrance, feeding Aslan the last treats in her hand as the ring crew returned to their seats.

"You can go in now," the gate steward said. "Have fun!"

Everyone kept telling her that, but she was not having fun. The nerves overwhelmed her, making it hard to breathe—hard to think. Her sneakered feet scuffed up dirt plumes as she shuffled to the start line and commanded Aslan to sit in front of the tunnel, the first obstacle. She faltered unhooking his leash just as she'd done in the mock trial where they'd hit the zone. The zone. She'd found joy there. Aslan's joy. The pretend joy she'd fed him in puppy obedience had grown, multiplied, become real, and returned to her a hundredfold. A lightness spread through her. His

adorable little face sparkled as they locked eyes, and he smiled—
really smiled—at her.

She told him "sit, stay," then tossed the leash beyond the yellow tunnel and turned to its round opening. With a determined
smile of her own, she said, "Okay. Tunnel."

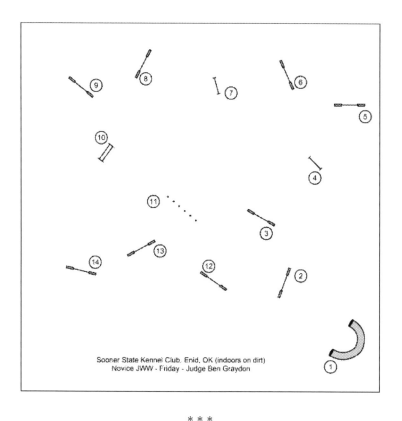

Sooner State Kennel Club, Enid, OK (indoors on dirt)
Novice JWW - Friday - Judge Ben Graydon

* * *

At his Mistress's command, Aslan tore into the tunnel. A thrill
pulsed through him as his paws galloped into the familiar obstacle, and he pushed hard with his legs to build speed. The effort
paid off, and before exiting, he banked the tunnel's ribbed sides
with satisfaction.

Shooting out from its rounded yellow walls into the wide-open ring, he searched for his Mistress. She trotted away from him, pointing at a jump. He ran after her, and at the first jump, he coiled, sprung, and soared over its white bar. Sand grains burst into the air at his push off the ground. As he flew over the bar, she called, "Here." She was late with the command, but as soon as his front feet hit the dirt, he changed direction and took the next jump. He sped past her as she jogged. Although slow, her forward motion moved in a direct line to the jump in front of him, and he greedily ran to it.

A rhythm developed. Aslan would jump, stride, stride, stride, gather, and jump. With the beat in his head, his speed increased. Lagging behind, she yelled, "Back," and pushed in to cross behind him. This push meant to change directions. They'd worked hard on this game, and he'd learned it well. He turned and took the jump ahead of him.

"Straight!" His Mistress's voice changed, sounding loud and high. Was something wrong? He slowed his speed but continued to the jump in front of him. With a quick turn of his head, he spotted her trotting behind, moving toward him as fast as she could, so he took the jump. "Straight!" she yelled. The jump stood before him, but her voice was shrill. Was he going the right way? He turned his head again. Yep. She ran his line. As he took the jump, she yelled, "Out!"

What? Did she want him to take the jump to the right or the jump far to the left? He chose the jump to the right and took two hesitant strides toward it. Unable to see her, he turned to check, but because she was out of his peripheral vision, he had to execute a full spin to find her. Her line confused him. What did she want? He barked his frustration and stepped back to her.

A man standing among the agility equipment raised his hand. Where had that man come from? Sometimes Daniel or Judy stood in the middle of the agility equipment and raised their hands, but Aslan didn't know this guy.

His Mistress called to him, pulling his attention away from the stranger. He ran to her, barking again, trying to communicate his confusion. Where did she want him to go, and who was that man over there?

She trotted forward and motioned to her side. He moved next to her and, turning in the direction she indicated, found a jump right in front of him. With little time to respond, he coiled, sprang open, and tried to float over the bar. One of his back feet hit it, and the bar made a soft *thud* as it fell to the dirt. The man raised one hand and then lowered it only to next raise both. Aslan wanted to look at the man, but his Mistress's voice became insistent.

"Aslan, come!" He ran to her, barking and jumping at her feet. She walked past the jump he'd just taken and pointed again to her side. He obeyed. She turned him around, extended her arm to another jump, and said, "Over!" Understanding, he streaked toward the jump, ready to fly, more obstacles ahead.

* * *

Krissy yelled in excitement as Aslan sailed over the last jump. "Awesome run, Little Man!" He ran to her and barked his agreement. She bent over, circling her arms, and as he jumped into them, she caught him, holding him tight. "That was a blast!" she said. His tail beat a rhythm against her back. "You're such a rock star."

Dipping her hand into a bucket by the ring's exit, she grabbed his leash, which had been retrieved by a volunteer leash runner from its location next to the tunnel, and hastily clipped it to his collar. After exiting the ring, an enthusiastic group of friends and parents embraced her.

"Oh, that was *really* good," Daniel said, a wide grin on his angular face.

"Aslan loved it!" Basma clasped a hand to her chest. "He barked the whole time. Oh, my word, I think I'm gonna have a heart attack."

Judy hugged Krissy and whispered, "That was how a first run is supposed to go. You overcame your nerves and mistakes and made your dog love the ring. You made it his home. That's how it's done!"

Dad gave Aslan's head an awkward pat. "Good job, Little Man," he said, using Krissy's pet name for him.

"Did he qualify?" Mom asked.

"No," Krissy said. "We dropped a bar. It's an automatic NQ."

"But," Daniel said, raising his index finger in the air, "Qs don't matter at the beginning of a career. What matters is making the game fun for the dog. Krissy did just that. Aslan loved being out there. They did what they came to do. They knocked it out of the park."

"And they can find that same success in the Standard class in just a few minutes," Judy said. "Each class is a new start. A new chance for glory—whether that glory comes with a ribbon or not."

Krissy laughed and hugged Aslan. They were both hooked on this odd game of speed and accuracy. At least, she was sure she wanted—no, needed—more.

* * *

On the way home, Aslan, exhausted after his first trial, slept in his crate on the car's backseat next to Krissy. In her hand, she held two ribbons. She rubbed her fingers over them, feeling the silky material. One was green. It said, *Qualifying Score, Sooner State Kennel Club, Enid, Oklahoma, Agility Trial.* The other was yellow and proudly proclaimed, *Third Place, Sooner State Kennel Club, Enid, Oklahoma, Agility Trial.*

The two ribbons came from the Standard class where they'd qualified and won third place. It hadn't been perfect. Aslan had jumped off the pause table early, incurring a table fault, and he'd spun in front of the last obstacle, a tire jump, for a refusal. But it'd been good enough to qualify in Novice. Good enough to earn third place.

In spite of their success in Standard, her mind kept replaying the Jumpers with Weaves run. There had been no zone sequence. No clean run. No ribbons. Yet, the memory seemed so—beautiful, as if they'd achieved something momentous.

Leaning over, she peered through the air holes of Aslan's crate to watch him rest. He raised his head and looked at her with sleepy but contented eyes.

"We did it, Little Man." She mouthed the words so her parents wouldn't hear. "And we'll run again and again and again. I promise."

She set the Standard ribbons aside, understanding for the first time how ribbons could be both precious and unimportant at the same time. They'd failed at Jumpers with Waves and yet still won somehow. She'd always thought winning came with ribbons, but she'd been wrong. Sometimes, just attempting was a win.

She looked out the window at the passing purples of twilight. It hadn't been perfect, but score one for the winners.

CHAPTER 20

Crashes, Kicks, and Other Tragedies

November: Nineteen Months Old

66 *That run was magic! Congrats on your new title! You and Ramsey so deserve this."*

Krissy reread the post before hitting send. Scrolling, she checked for new posts or videos in the Agility Junior Handlers Group. As she worked, Aslan slept nestled in her lap, his bird-like frame warm and light.

At least *he* liked having her home on a Friday night. She ran a hand over the back of her neck and shut her eyes against visual strain—and tears. If it weren't for her online agility friends, she'd have no friends her age at all.

Right now, half of the band was partying at the first-chair saxophone's annual Big Blast Christmas Party, including Violet and Jessica. Word was it was Krissy's kind of thing—no drugs, live music. She longed to go, but once again, she'd been numbered in the uninvited half—the outside half.

So instead of chatting face to face with friends, she slouched at the downstairs computer, reading posts and watching videos from the Agility Junior Handlers Group. She'd made tons of online friends through the group, and her message account had to be wondering if she'd become a cheerleader or something with the increase in mail since she joined. The group included junior handlers from all over the world. Her best online friend, Alyiah, was from Westfield, Massachusetts, and ran a tri-colored sheltie named Zoe. They were in Open, the intermediate class, like Krissy and Aslan now were.

As a dog moved up the ranks in agility, the classes became more difficult. Aslan had earned the three qualifying scores he needed for each of his Novice titles in early November at their second show, which had allowed them to move up to the Open class. When they earned enough Qs for their Open titles, they would move up to Excellent and then Master's. After Master's came the MACH—the title of champions. It was a long way from Novice to MACH, and it took a lot of trial weekends to get there. They'd never earn a championship, but secretly, she hoped they'd get their Master's.

She clicked on a video posted by a friend from Japan. He ran Argo, a beautiful vizsla, and they were stupid-fast. In the video, the brown dog flowed like liquid over the agility equipment. Cheers from the video's audio almost drowned out the ring of the house phone, which she ignored. The video ended—another smoking run from Japan—and she began typing a comment to her friend.

"Andy!" Mom yelled to Dad, who was upstairs in his office. "Get on the phone. Your son's been in another car wreck."

Krissy's heart skipped a beat as she leaped from her chair, toppling Aslan to the floor, and ran into the den where Mom sat on the sofa, face drawn, phone clutched in her left hand. "Is he all right?" Krissy asked.

Mom signaled for her to hush but nodded. Tension that had built in seconds released, and Krissy's whole body relaxed. Holding the phone to her ear, Mom said nothing as she listened to her husband and son converse. Krissy stared at her, willing her to spill clues about the wreck. She could hear Dad's voice from upstairs but couldn't make out any of his words.

Finally, Mom spoke. "And no one on the bus was hurt?"

The bus? Peter, along with Evan, who suspiciously wasn't at the band party with Violet, had gone to check out Laser Foot, a new laser tag/indoor soccer hangout. Peter's car was in the shop, so he'd driven Dad's SUV. How had they gotten on a bus? Good thing they did. Dad would be furious if Peter wrecked the Edge again.

"What bus?" Krissy asked. Mom glared at her and made a shushing motion with her hand while Dad's voice reverberated upstairs. His end of the conversation would divulge far more info. Krissy rushed to the stairs and climbed them as fast as possible.

Dad sounded stern and in control on the phone. "Have the police ticketed anyone yet?"

She stopped outside the fourth bedroom that served as Dad's office where he wrote for a Christian-based blog in his spare time.

"Don't admit fault," Dad said, and after a moment, "No, no. Don't say anything until we arrive. We'll be there in fifteen minutes." More silence. "We'll be there. Wait for us."

He hung up the phone and lifted his eyes to see Krissy listening outside the door.

"Is he okay?" Krissy asked.

"No one is badly injured. You stay here. We'll be back in a while." His jaw muscles flexed as he tried to control his anger. It'd be a bad idea to push him for more information. She turned and almost tripped over Aslan hovering at her heels. She picked him up and scurried downstairs.

In the kitchen, Mom checked the contents of her purse. "Do we have all the insurance information in the car?" she asked as Dad came into the room.

"We should, but I grabbed the insurance file anyway." He held up a manila file folder.

"I can't believe this." Mom sounded furious. "Teenage drivers. I bet he was joyriding again. I told him I didn't like him hanging around with Evan. That boy must have put him up to this. He's going to get our son killed."

Dad pulled the car fob from his pocket and headed to the garage. "They're fine. They're not injured, and it sounds like nobody on the bus was hurt, either."

The bus again. What had happened? Krissy couldn't resist asking. "What bus?"

"He hit a church bus," Mom said, her mouth set in a thin line. "We'll be back later. Lock the house."

If her parents ever needed to be fed happy emotions, it was now. Krissy followed them to the garage. "Don't worry. I'll take care of the house and dogs. Everything here will be just fine."

It wasn't until they'd shut the door that her words played back in her head. How stupid. Of course, everything at home would be fine. Mark up another F for failing to feed the right emotion at the right time.

She really sucked at this "make-the-family-happy" stuff.

* * *

Godzilla roared over Tokyo. He shook his head, and the nose and scales of the rubber monster suit wobbled with the motion. In frustration, he raised his arms and slammed them onto a miniature apartment building, splitting it in two and causing doll furniture to tumble to the ground.

Krissy absently petted Aslan, who sat by her side on the sofa, while Ruffis—not wanting to be far from his sheltie hero—snoozed at her feet. The clatter of the garage door opener blended with Godzilla's shrill screams. She turned off the black-and-white monster flick and hurried to the kitchen, eager to see Peter.

He came in first, Evan right behind. She agreed with Mom about Evan and the sight of him made her frown. The friendship between him and Peter had cooled since last summer, which pleased Krissy. She'd already lost a best friend to Evan's manipulations, and she'd worried he would drag Peter down to his low-level burnout status, too. When Peter said he and Evan were headed to Laser Foot earlier that evening, she'd been disappointed. Peter had lots of other good friends. He didn't need Evan.

She leaned on the counter by the kitchen sink and stared at the boys as they walked by. Peter looked sullen and a bit panicky, but he didn't seem injured. Evan, on the other hand, sauntered by her with a wink, his mouth twisted into his trademark Elvis smirk again.

"Peter, a word." Dad motioned for Peter to stay in the kitchen. "Evan, you can wait in the den with Krissy until your parents come to pick you up."

"Would you like something to drink?" Mom asked him. The zombie apocalypse could be raging, but Mom never forgot her manners.

"Nah," Evan said with a dismissive wave. "Thanks, though."

Krissy went into the den with Evan and took a seat on the recliner angled next to the sofa. After sitting, Evan leaned back into the sofa and rested an ankle on the opposite knee. He looked at ease, even though Krissy's father, mother, and brother were arguing with low hisses in the kitchen.

"Are you guys okay?" she asked.

"We're fine. It was no big deal. Your parents are freaking out over nothing." He leaned his head against the cushions and closed his eyes.

"What happened?"

"A church bus pulled out right in front of us. The roads were wet from the rain, of course, and Peter hydroplaned into it. Nothing could be done. The bus got a light bump, although your dad's car looks sprung. The police think it's totaled. Really, it's much ado about nothing. Your folks need to glide."

"The car is totaled?" she asked, aghast.

"Probably." He rubbed the top of his right hand.

"Your hand hurt?" She leaned forward to peer at it.

He opened his eyes and, without moving his head from the back of the sofa, glared at her. "Shut up. It's fine. Just a bump. You wanna see your parents really go off?"

Krissy bit back a retort. Why had Evan chosen to hang out with Peter tonight, anyway? He should have been with Violet, unless something had happened. Krissy and Violet hadn't talked much lately, what with Violet spending so much time with Evan and her new friends. It put Krissy further out of the loop—any loop—and if Evan and Violet had broken up, Krissy might get her friend back. "Why weren't you at Josh's party?" The question that had bugged her all night slipped out.

"You're nosy, aren't you?" he said, lifting his head to level his gaze at her.

"Things not so hot with Violet, huh?" She tried to hide her smile but failed.

"You're such a zero." Something ugly replaced his Elvis sneer. "Why don't you go play with your doggie? Here poochie, poochie." He sat forward, reaching for Aslan, who'd positioned himself protectively by her leg. Aslan stiffened, his ears plastered back against his head.

"Leave him alone," she said, voice icy.

"He's no athlete. He's a runt—a purse toy."

Reacting on instinct to Evan's dark mood, Krissy extended her right leg and with gentle pressure pushed Aslan away from him and toward the other side of her chair. At the same time, Evan kicked half-heartedly at Aslan, missing his mark due to her protective push and clipping Krissy's ankle instead. It forced her leg sharply to the left into Aslan, who tumbled to his side. She gasped and snatched Aslan into her arms before limping several steps away from Evan, who held his ugly smirk.

"It's no wonder you're a zero," he said.

Stunned by the sudden violence, she couldn't think of a come-back. A rumble erupted deep within Aslan, and his body vibrated in her arms. Was that a growl? He'd never growled before. Evan must have heard it, too, because he leaned away from the "purse toy" in her arms.

The doorbell rang, and Mom appeared in the kitchen doorway. "That'll probably be your folks," Mom told Evan. "Please let us know how you're doing tomorrow. If you're sore or have a headache or anything, we want to hear about it."

He flashed a warm smile as he rose, the sneer a dark memory. "I'm great, Mrs. Johnson. It was just a fender bender."

"Cars aren't totaled in fender benders, Evan." Mom ushered him to the door. They couldn't get there fast enough for Krissy.

As he left the room, Ruffis followed, legs stiff, hackles raised. Krissy cocked her head. Had old Ruffis been ready to fall on the sword for his hero? She put the old dog's hero on the ground, and the collie rushed to nose the sheltie, checking for injuries.

As the door closed behind Evan, the volume of the argument in the kitchen increased. "It wasn't like that!" Peter sounded furious.

Dad's voice escalated in response. "It was your inexperience and inattention that caused this. My car is totaled. I trusted you with it, and for the second time, you broke that—"

"This was different." Peter looked exasperated. "I was driving the speed limit. I paid attention. The bus pulled out in front of me. What did you want me to do? Swerve into oncoming traffic? Hit cars head-on?"

Krissy and Mom walked into the kitchen but both remained silent as the argument persisted.

"I received a full description of the wreck," Dad said. "I have no doubt you could have avoided it. Your—"

"Even the pastor said it was his fault, and that I had no other choice but to clip the bus! He got the ticket."

"Clip? My car is totaled. It wasn't a 'clip.'"

"This is so unfair! I didn't do anything wrong!" Peter's voice climbed to a scream. "You're always accusing me of doing things

I didn't do." He gestured at Krissy. "If she'd had a car wreck, you'd be all, 'Are you okay, sweetie? Are you hurt?' With me, it's nothing but blame!"

Krissy stared at him in disbelief. How did she get dragged into this? She'd been on Peter's side until that comment. How was this her fault? Heat flooded her face, and she opened her mouth to defend herself. Then closed it. Her family needed calming emotions. Peaceful emotions.

No, forget that. That stupid concept hadn't helped so far, had it?

Mom turned to Krissy, "Go upstairs."

"But I didn't do anything wrong." Her anger at Peter came out in Krissy's tone.

"Now!" Mom ordered.

With a huff, Krissy marched from the room but took her time climbing the stairs, while the argument raged on.

CHAPTER 21

Agile Iron

November: Nineteen Months Old

Aslan stood rigid in the kitchen doorway, Ruffis close behind. Aslan had never seen the pack fight like this. There'd been brief dust ups, but nothing so serious. Based on the noise, facial expressions, and body posture, this was dire.

He looked from person to person, reading non-verbal cues. Dad, and, to a degree, Mom, challenged Peter. While incensed, Peter hadn't directly challenged back—yet. Wise decision. Instead, he showed signs of angry yet baffled submission.

As it went on, the fighting became louder and more intense. With the increased volume, Aslan's feet shuffled in place, and behind him Ruffis stress-panted. The threat ratcheted up when Peter raised his head, increased his height, and pulled his back up straight. Dad matched and beat that increase. An explosion was imminent. Dad took a small step forward and tilted his head, fixing a hard glare on Peter. Peter held his ground. Mom stepped back at Dad's subtle shift in body posture and let him take the battle.

Aslan hoped it wouldn't turn violent. The boy with the light-colored hair had already kicked at his Mistress tonight. It'd taken all of Aslan's training to keep from lunging at the boy's calf. For a brief instant, the thought of sinking his teeth into the meaty flesh had been so very, very tempting, and he might have done it if his Mistress hadn't picked him up. Maybe Peter and Dad were thinking similar thoughts right now.

Dad growled something low and potent. For a horrifying moment, no one moved. Then, Peter shifted his weight backwards. It was slight, but it was there. Peter had lost.

Dad stormed out of the kitchen. Peter frowned at Mom, who glowered back. Without a word, she, too, left the room and climbed the stairs. With both parents out of the room, Peter's shoulders slumped. Head down, he slunk like an admonished pup into the den and sat, bent over, on the sofa.

Aslan joined him. Disagreements in the pack weren't uncommon, but he had never seen such a fierce battle between Peter and Dad.

Peter remained on the sofa for quite some time. Then he breathed a small whine and gasped. It sounded like Ruffis's whines when he'd hung from the fence. Aslan crept closer to Peter and gazed at him. There was no distress. No difficulty breathing. Just a wet face and an overwhelming sadness.

Peter reached down and placed Aslan in his lap. Aslan let him. Most times, he squirmed when held by anyone other than his Mistress, but he remained motionless as Peter hugged him tight and cried into his furry neck. A good dog needs to know when to sit still and just be a warm shoulder.

* * *

Krissy woke. The alarm clock read 3:04 a.m. She extended a hand and swept it over the bed, expecting to find a pile of warm, soft fur. Cool sheets met her reach.

Ah, yes. Peter had wrecked Dad's car, and she'd been banned to her room. She'd changed into her oversized sweatshirt and thrown herself on the bed, livid about Peter's accusation that *her* illness had somehow caused *his* problems. Wrapped up in her anger at the persecution, she'd forgotten Aslan and had fallen asleep. Was he stuck outside like that night he'd chewed Ruffis's collar? It could've happened in all the chaos, and it was November. If he were outside, he'd get downright cold.

She jumped out of bed and rushed from her room, bare feet silent on the carpet. This was her fault. In puppy obedience class, Shelly had said to protect Aslan from arguments and family stress. Krissy hadn't even thought about it until now, but what if Aslan were to suffer emotional issues from the horrible fight and took them into the agility ring? Could that happen? Shelly had said it could, and last night, Krissy had been too interested in the argument and then too angry at Peter to think about keeping Aslan safe from the friction. They were doing so well with their training. What if she'd blown it?

The upstairs hallway overlooking the front entry was empty. No dog. She passed Peter's room. Light from his nightstand lamp leaked around the cracks of the door, which rested ajar. Maybe Peter was still awake and Aslan was with him? A gentle push opened the door a few more inches, and she stuck her head into the room.

Peter lay asleep on the bed, Aslan resting in the crook of his arm. Aslan raised his head at her appearance, and their eyes met. The tip of his tail lifted and lowered once in greeting, but he made no move to leave. He lowered his head back onto Peter's shoulder, making his intentions to stay with Peter clear.

She went back to bed alone. Tonight, Aslan was on teddy dog duty for another master. She slid under her covers, unsure how she felt about that.

* * *

Two days later, Krissy put down her book and rubbed her burning eyes. Reaching to her side to pet Aslan, who had been resting next to her as she sat on the bedroom floor, her hand found only carpet. A hasty look around her bedroom confirmed it. Aslan had snuck off just like the night of Peter's accident. This was getting old.

Where had her dog disappeared to this time? She unfolded her legs, stretched, and, using her hands to push off the floor, stood. Her joints creaked in protest. Stupid useless body. She was only fifteen. Working out the stiffness, she hobbled from her room and through the hall.

Voices ascended from the den. On cat's paws, she crept halfway down the stairs and stopped before she would be visible from the den. Since Peter's accident the other night, the strain in the house had been palpable—like an overfilled water balloon, latex stretched tight and shiny—and she didn't want to walk into another argument.

"So, I may have overreacted a bit," Dad was saying. "I don't think you were speeding or distracted. You're just young."

For a few moments, no one spoke. Krissy almost exposed herself by proceeding down the staircase, when Peter said, "But you didn't believe me. I told you that, and you didn't believe me."

"You'd set a precedent," Dad said. "The first accident, you were speeding and crashed my car into that pole. What did you expect me to think this time?"

"I admitted what I did the first time! I was honest. I expected you to believe me this time, too."

"Trust is earned, Peter."

"I thought my honesty would've earned that trust. If it'd been Krissy, you'd have worried about her kidney and then given her a dog or something. With me, you always assume the worst."

"This has nothing to do with your sister. It has to do with your driving record."

"Does it? It seems to me that a lot in this house has to do with Krissy."

"This family is doing the best it can under difficult circumstances," Dad said, sternly. "The wreck and the fallout from it have nothing to do with your sister's illness. That's unfair to me, your mom, and Krissy. . .My apology for overreacting was sincere. Your response should be to accept that apology, not to rekindle the same old argument."

Krissy's nails bit into her palms, and her heart quickened. Peter had done it again! How could he? She hadn't asked to lose her kidneys! How dare he blame her for their parents' reactions? She'd figured his rude comment the night of the fight had just been rash, the result of overwrought emotions, and she'd decided to ignore it. But here it was again. *A lot in this house has to do with Krissy.* Seriously?

Gritting her teeth, she turned to tiptoe back to her room. With the conversation turning to her, if she got caught eavesdropping now, she could get into serious trouble.

"How's Evan?" Dad asked. "Any signs of pain in his back or neck?"

Krissy stopped, unable to keep from listening.

"He's fine." After a moment, Peter added, "I'm thinking about not hanging around him as much anymore."

Dad gave a soft chuckle.

Peter continued. "I mean, he didn't do anything to cause the accident. He didn't distract me or anything. It's just—he's acting kind of strange. Today, when I asked how he was, he said he was fine. Then out of the blue he said something like, 'Your sister's stupid dog needs to disappear. You should do something about that, like forget to close the gate.' It was creepy. What's wrong with Aslan? Who could hate that little guy?"

A jolt ran along Krissy's spine. Did Evan want Peter to hurt Aslan? Why? Because Aslan had growled at him? Krissy wanted to bend down and peek into the den to see Dad's reaction, but if she got caught. . .

"You know, Evan's dad is an alcoholic. And. . .as we get older, he occasionally reminds me of his dad," Peter said. "I worry about him hanging around here with Aslan."

"It's probably a good idea to limit Evan's exposure to Aslan." After a pause, Dad added, "In Proverbs it says, 'As iron sharpens iron, so one person sharpens another.' Our friends help form who we are. Surrounding ourselves with loyal, intelligent friends keeps us sharp and growing in the direction we want to grow. Will Evan sharpen or dull you?"

When Peter didn't answer, Dad said, "You can remain friends, staying in touch through school, and you can be there for him. But maybe your closest friends should be young people who will help you become sharper and stronger—like iron."

"Yeah. I guess so." Peter sounded hesitant, confused. Logical advice, but after their big blow up, would Peter listen?

Dad's chair creaked. Braving a peek, Krissy leaned over the stairs. Her viewpoint allowed her to see Dad's feet walk into the kitchen, but she also had a full view of Peter in the recliner, Aslan curled in his lap.

Before she pulled back behind the stairwell wall, Peter hugged Aslan and bent his head to kiss the sheltie on the top of his long noble nose.

Krissy snuck up the stairs, careful to avoid the boards that creaked. Her head whirled. So, Evan had told Peter to get rid of Aslan? She put a hand on her stomach and swallowed against a wave of nausea. What a hideous thought. Peter was smart to not want Evan around the house, around Aslan, but would Peter continue to hang out with him at school? How could he? And what of Violet? If Evan spun out of control, Violet could be pulled into his vortex. At least Peter was thinking of pulling away, but was Violet?

And how could Peter say that everything rotated around her? That was flat unfair. Yeah, her parents had to give her extra attention because of her medications and doctors' appointments, but none of that was her fault. She didn't want this stupid disease. He could have it if he wanted attention that much. She'd be overjoyed to give it to him.

She pictured Peter hooked to a dialysis machine. Bile from her stomach flared into her throat. No. What a horrible thing to think. No way would she wish this on Peter. Never.

With no awareness of where she was, she tiptoed toward her room. *"This family is doing the best it can under difficult circumstances,"* Dad had said. And, she, too, had done her best to make everyone happy, but it hadn't been good enough. She'd failed. Again. FAILED with all caps. For months, she'd eaten words and shown support and happiness in an attempt to ease the tension. And for what? To discover Dad's continued mistrust and Peter's frustration? And worse, to hear that, after all she'd done, she was still the cause of the family's turmoil? What more could she do?

A strong desire to grab Aslan from Peter's lap and whisk him into the backyard where she could escape her illness through agility overtook her. She wanted to push her weak body—the same body that caused her family so much strife—to its limits, and there, within the pain of her stilted movement, she could reach out to Aslan, join his strength, and find freedom from herself.

She half-turned to reclaim her dog but stopped. Aslan was working. He was sitting on Peter's lap offering consolation. Aslan had snuggled next to Peter the night of the accident, too. Teddy-dog work.

But she needed her dog. She needed his comfort. She needed agility. She needed to feel normal. Free. She wiped at tears threatening to overflow onto her cheeks. Overwhelmed and more alone than ever, she crept to her room and closed the door.

CHAPTER 22

Shirking Duties

February: Twenty-Two Months Old

Aside from actually running agility, this was Krissy's favorite part about agility trials. All *four* Musketeers—their numbers had increased by one when Alonzo had joined their informal group—sat and chatted in a wide circle of camp chairs with Daniel, Judy, and Estelle, a City Dogger in her seventies, who ran a beautiful, blue-merle border collie named Alex. Their dogs lounged in their laps or next to their chairs on woven mats covering the horse arena's dirt floor.

"I wish we'd caught that on video," Abby said, referring to Aslan's last run. "It was so classic."

"Next time, I'm going to insist Dad stays to video," Krissy said. "You never know what's gonna happen out there."

Daniel shook his head, smiling. "Yeah. Aslan must've stood on the apex of the A-frame barking at that photographer for fifteen seconds, yet, that pup's so fast, you easily made time. We'll need to run him at practice while someone takes pictures with a noisy camera to get him used to it. He'd better not do that at Nationals next year. There'll be lots of photographers there."

"Nationals?" Krissy snorted. "We could never make Nationals. You gotta be iconic to get there."

"You're on track," Daniel said. When Krissy gaped at him, he nodded. "You are. Now that you're in Master's, you can start qualifying. You have until November 30th—almost eleven months. If you keep working as hard as you have been, I think you've got a chance. Granted, it's an uphill climb with a baby dog, but it's doable."

"Me? Do people like me make Nationals?"

"People like you?" Judy asked. "Do you have spikes growing from your head? Do you speak Klingon? You're just *people*, and yes, people who can't run fast make Nationals every year."

"I saw someone handling from a wheelchair when Alex and I went to Nationals a few years ago," Estelle said in her wispy-sweet voice. "She ran a whippet. That was one well-trained dog."

Judy nodded. "While there aren't a lot of disabled handlers around here, there are several across the nation. Even if you don't qualify, you should go to Nationals to volunteer. You will see you're not alone."

"I don't think my folks would take me out of school just to volunteer. Where's it held?"

"You haven't heard?" Mike asked. "It's in Tulsa this year, just two hours from home. You can drop by for the weekend."

"Here in Oklahoma?" Krissy asked, astonished.

"See. Now you gotta try and qualify," Daniel said. "If you're interested, I'll talk to your dad. Yeah. We'll see if we can't get you to a few more shows, so you can rack up the needed points and Qs to qualify."

"I'm gonna try," Abby told Krissy. "I've already scheduled extra shows this spring. Maybe we could go together to a few of them?"

"We won the Oklahoma Cup the year we went," Estelle said in a rare brag. "And Daniel and Judy have both won before, right?"

"Daniel and Q won twice," Judy said. "I won with my old girl, Emma."

"What's the Oklahoma Cup?" Abby asked.

"It's a trophy the Oklahoma agility community hands out each year to the team from Oklahoma who places highest in the three rounds at Nationals," Judy said. "It's unofficial. The AKC doesn't give out state cups. It's just the Okies honoring our best. A bragging rights thing."

"Qualifying for Nationals is a great journey. Even if you never make the destination, you'll have a fantastic yearlong trip with your teammate. If you qualify, it's a bonus." Daniel fingered the hem of his long-sleeved T-shirt. His next words sounded measured. "But, if you decide to go on this trip, enjoy what happens—both the good and bad. Soon enough, you'll look back, and it'll be over. They never live long enough." His voice broke. Were those tears in his eyes?

Judy reached for Autumn, who lay next to her, and patted the golden's head. An uncomfortable silence fell over the group. What was up? Krissy must have missed something. Even staid Alonzo fidgeted.

Breaking the awkward moment, Judy stood and called Autumn to her side. "I think the judge is about to brief the Standard ring. Anybody up to attending with me?"

"I'd go," Mike said, "but we're in Novice. For now and forever."

Judy gave a tense chuckle. "Then come root us on as we listen to the rules for the thousandth time." A weak joke.

The group put their dogs in their crates and headed for the Standard ring. Krissy glanced back at Daniel. He combed his fingers through his hair, head turned away as he watched Mia walk past with Cool off lead. Something was definitely going on. What were they keeping from her?

* * *

"You took it to the house!" Krissy told Aslan, a couple of hours later. Aslan pranced at her side, tail waving, eyes dancing. His face lit with the thrill of the game. They'd qualified on the Standard course, and, after he'd inhaled a boatload of treats, they'd headed out for their post-run cool down. It'd become their ritual. After each run, they'd walk and let their heart rates and muscles relax from the sprint through the equipment. Peppered in between the walking, they'd stop and stretch, and always, they'd share a detailed conversation about how the run had gone. Granted, she did most of the chattering.

"You held that A-frame contact forever. Because of that, I was able to get into position for that pushback. And your start-line stay? Ah-may-zing!" Aslan huffed with happiness as she opened the seldom-used side door of the arena and stepped into the winter sunshine.

Once outside, his nose dropped to the ground like a stone, and he sniffed aimlessly as she breathed in the brisk air. Several steps later, she rounded a corner of the building where two dirty beige concrete walls jutted out to create a washing stall for livestock. As she passed the open side of the walls, Mia, coatless in the winter breeze, was standing in the stall with Cool.

"You're despicable." Mia jerked hard on Cool's leash, her back to Krissy. Cool held his head low, tail tucked. "I said 'here.' You *know* to listen. You worthless. . ." Mia slapped him on the side of his head. His body twisted from the blow, and he pulled in vain on the leash to escape.

Stunned, Krissy stared for several seconds. Had she really seen that? She balled her fists until her fingernails dug into her palms. "Hey" she yelled. "What are you doing?"

Mia's head shot up, eyes wide. "It's none of your business," she said evenly. "I'm training my dog."

"You call that training?" Krissy retorted, anger rising. "You never hit a dog. Ever. What are you thinking?"

"Shut up." Mia's eyes narrowed. "What do you know about training, newbie? We beat your time on every run. Maybe if you disciplined that runt every now and then, he'd. . .I don't know. . .run? You wish your dog were as good as Cool."

Krissy looked at Cool, who cowered at the end of the leash, his small white body quivering, tan ears plastered to his head. "I can see your methods are developing a great relationship. He's scared to death of you. How could—"

"You're such a loser—in the real sense. I've heard people make fun of you ringside. You waddle instead of run. What an embarrassment."

The words stung. Krissy knew well what she looked like when she ran. But no one had ever said a thing about her weird sort of side-to-side trot. At least, not to her face. Surely Mia was lying.

Mia continued, "I don't know an agility competitor who doesn't punish their dog for disobeying in the ring. Well, except for losers like you. It's why we're gonna continue to beat the snot out of you and Aslan. I know how to train, and I can run. You? Maybe you should take up knitting."

"There must be a rule that says you can't hit your dog." Krissy hated how unsure she sounded.

"I didn't *hit* him. It were a small training slap." Mia's eyes blazed. "He's a terrier. It's how you train stubborn terriers. Go tell if you want. No one will care. Shoot, I'll go tell them now myself. They all do it, too."

"Like who?" Krissy asked, a numbness creeping over her body and brain.

"Look. Just go away and leave us alone. You and your hand-me-down parts make me want to hurl." Mia yanked on Cool's lead, forcing him to follow, and stomped to the arena's side door.

Krissy remained frozen, unsure what to do. Emotions—confusion, rage, shame, pity—warred within, none pushing to the forefront to propel her to action. If Mia would cop to the slap, why tell?

Saying nothing, doing nothing, Krissy turned and walked away. But Mia's last words rang in her ears.

Before Cool, Mia had run Charlotte's border collies and had even earned a MACH with one. She wasn't a newbie to dog training and dog sports. She knew how it was done. Yet, hitting a dog for misbehaving in the ring had to be wrong. Hitting a dog was always wrong. But was it really a hit or just a training slap? Did it matter? Mia had said other agility competitors did it all the time. Krissy was new to the sport. What did she know? Did the Furutas slap their dogs in private? She couldn't imagine it. No. No, they would never do that.

Her head spun. Maybe she should tell Daniel, but what could he do? He had no control over Mia. All he could do was tell Charlotte, who may have sent Mia outside to "train" Cool. Daniel had mentioned that training philosophies ran along a spectrum from punishment-based methods to positive reinforcement methods. Hitting would be punishment-based, but didn't this go too far? Was it even legal?

And, if she told, who would believe her? Mia might say Krissy had made it up, or that Krissy didn't know the difference between a hit and a training slap, whatever that was. Mia had been in the sport for years. Everyone knew her. Like she'd said, Krissy was a nobody and, doubtless, even a bit of a joke. It would be the word of a respected teen competitor who usually won against the word of an unknown teen who usually lagged behind. People would think Krissy had lied out of jealousy.

Yet, the image of Cool's little shaking body crouched and pulling against the leash seared into her. He'd been slapped for what? Not coming when Mia called *here* on course?

Crazy. Wrong.

But—what could she do about it?

"Krissy!" Dad waved to her from across the parking lot. She realized she was seated, slumped on the curb of the arena's main lot. How had she gotten here? "The gear's loaded. Let's go!"

Aslan stood in front of her, searching her eyes with concern. He touched his cold nose to her hand, which had clenched into a tight fist and rested on one knee.

There was nothing she could do about it.

So, she walked away from the unbidden turmoil and an unfinished duty toward home.

Chapter 23

Graduation

May: Two Years Old

W rapping paper lay in colorful crumpled heaps around Peter's feet. In his hands, he held a desk lamp. Two blue plaid suitcases—one large, one small—leaned against the sofa where he sat, a couple remnants of bright paper still stuck with clear tape to their sides. Krissy grabbed one of the clumps of graduation-themed gift wrap and stuffed it into a trash bag.

"Come into the kitchen, everyone," Mom announced from the den's doorway. "There's cake, ice cream, and iced tea."

The entourage of Krissy, Dad, Grandma Johnson, Peter, Aslan, and Ruffis moved like a hungry amoeba toward the kitchen and cake.

"I'm so proud of you, Peter." Everything about Grandma Johnson was grandmotherly, even her quavering voice. Well, except her size. In spite of her drooping shoulders caused by eighty years of relentless gravity, she managed to tower a few inches above Peter. "You're going to do so well in college." She gave him a small hug, and he reached up to return it.

"I couldn't pass up this wonderful mortarboard candle. It was on sale." Mom lit the wax hat perched on the cake. "Come sit here, Peter, so I can snap a picture before the hat melts." Peter took a seat next to the cake on the kitchen table, smiling for the camera like a victorious Superman.

"It won't be long before it's your turn, Krissy," Grandma said as she pulled a chair out from the table and eased herself onto it.

"Two more years." High school would have an end. Hallelujah.

Peter blew out the candle, and Mom cut the lemon cake. Soon, the five humans were situated around the kitchen table eating Peter's just desserts.

"When will I get to take possession?" Krissy asked. She offered no further explanation. There was no need.

"Two weeks." Peter emphasized each word. "Two weeks. I said that before."

"Maybe it'll come in sooner."

"Two weeks. I'll give you the keys then."

"Will your new Mustang be red like the old one?" Grandma shoveled a large bite of cake into her mouth. She wasn't dainty, but she was sweet.

"I decided to go with blue," Peter said. "It's got an ebony interior. It's gonna be sleek."

With Peter getting a new car for graduation, Krissy would be inheriting the 'Tang. She'd had her driver's license for a month, so the timing couldn't be more perfect. Well, if she didn't have to wait two weeks, it'd be more perfect. She was thrilled with the auto hand-me-down, although Peter had been wrong. The 'Tang had never been a woman. He was a man, and Krissy was gonna treat him like the high-class man he was. Not that she knew anything about high-class men. But still.

"Are you thinking of going into the ministry?" Grandma asked Peter, her expression hopeful. "Your dad said it was something you were considering."

Dad averted his eyes when Peter glanced at him. This was a touchy subject. Peter had once mentioned in passing that he might someday consider becoming a pastor. Dad had told a few extended family members, and now, Peter couldn't escape the subject.

"Not really," Peter said. "I haven't felt God's call to pastoral ministry. I'm looking at getting a business degree. If someday God calls me to ministry, then a business degree will give me a good background for church administration, but I'm really leaning more toward law school. It's all a long way off. My main focus is getting enrolled and into my freshman year."

"I'll pray you follow in your Grandpa Johnson's footsteps into ministry," Grandma said. "He'd be so proud."

As Peter and Grandma chatted about his college plans, Krissy chased mini chocolate chips through the melted remains of her ice cream with her spoon and kept an eye on the oven's digital clock. The family would be leaving in a few hours for Peter's graduation ceremony. Krissy would watch it from the vantage point of the school band, which had to be on hand to play "Pomp and Circumstance" about a thousand times. As class president, Peter would deliver a small speech he'd been working on for weeks. He'd practiced it over and over in his room: "Fellow classmates, faculty, parents, and family. . ."

After the ceremony, the real fun would begin. Violet's church, trendy with kids in their school, planned to host a post-graduation party at the barn of one of its members. She'd asked Krissy and Jessica to go. It'd been ages since Krissy had hung out with the girls. With Evan graduating and heading for college, he and Violet had cooled, which made Krissy all sorts of shades of happy. It was good to have her friend back, although it wasn't exactly like old times. Violet found herself pulled in two directions, spending her free time with either Jessica or Krissy, but never both. Jessica would clam up or walk away whenever Krissy was around.

Krissy missed the days when the trio had hung out together and hoped tonight would help mend things, although she had no clue what had torn.

Grandma told Peter, "Make sure you send me your address at college. I want to mail you a few care packages."

"That would be great," he said with genuine enthusiasm. "Too bad you can't ship your fried chicken."

"I bet I can figure out how to do that," Grandma said. "Don't be shocked if it shows up."

"It wouldn't last long," Dad said. "College boys would rip through your chicken like combines though ripe wheat."

"You're going to love St. John's," Grandma told Peter. "It's such a nice school."

A nice school. Krissy stopped herself from an eye roll. Would this afternoon never end? Maybe she could sneak to the backyard to train. She glanced at Aslan, lying by her feet. He looked so content. She wasn't. She hadn't been since Peter's car wreck months ago. The cracks in the family seemed to have smoothed over, but each time she replayed the conversation she'd overheard between Peter and Dad, her frustration and—she might as well admit it—anger increased.

She'd given up on the "being kind" stuff. It hadn't worked. With no more reason to pretend to be happy, she'd become moody. Her grouchy attitude should have had everyone at each other's throats, but instead, they all seemed happier. Maybe she should've fed them "moody teenager" all along.

Krissy rubbed her eyes. The desire to escape and run Aslan pulled at her. She'd been fleeing to the backyard a lot lately, and, since she was being honest, she might as well admit that, too: it was escape. The thrill she found in those moments when it all came together freed her. When she trained, the only things that mattered were her bond with Aslan, her timing, her vocal cues, and the challenge presented by the current sequence. Everything else—school, family, medication—disappeared. And, with that disappearance came release.

The need to escape, that desire for liberation, called often. It was calling her now. Krissy tossed her paper plate into the garbage. "I'm going out to the yard to practice."

"Again?" Mom sounded exasperated. "How often do you get to celebrate your brother's graduation? Aslan could use a break, too."

"We've got to train if we're going to make it to Nationals," Krissy said. "Only the best go."

Grandma smiled at Krissy. "She should go train. Dreams as big as going to Nationals require lots of work. Besides, I so enjoy watching her train her beautiful dog."

Mom frowned. "Don't get all sweaty, Krissy. It's only two hours until you leave for band."

Without answering, Krissy left the cool kitchen, Aslan at her heels, and found sweet freedom in the backyard and the May afternoon sun.

* * *

Two hours later, Krissy, flute case in one hand and black concert-band blazer in the other, slid into the backseat of Violet's blue Focus.

Riding shotgun, Jessica pointed at Krissy's blazer. "We're gonna melt like butter on Satan's all-you-can-eat breakfast buffet in these stupid coats. Why do we have to wear them in this heat? The band's already dressed in black pants and white shirts. That should be good enough. But, no! We have to sweat in these colorless coordinated coats, or we won't sound like a band or something. We don't have to wear uniforms to sound uniform."

Krissy smiled and laid the heavy blazer on her lap.

Jessica swiveled and, with a pinky extended, plucked one of Aslan's hairs off the blazer's sleeve. "Eww." She flicked the hair to the car's floor.

Krissy lifted another hair from the jacket. She held it between her fingers, unsure what to do. Jessica had just dropped hers, but wasn't that rude? Violet would have to vacuum it up later. Instead, Krissy put it back on the jacket. "I forgot to roll it before I left. I bet my pants are furry, too."

"Gross." Jessica turned around. "You're like an old weird cat lady, only it's dogs, and you're a hundred years short of old."

"Your math is a little off," Krissy said.

"You know what I mean," Jessica said.

Violet grinned at Krissy in the rearview mirror.

"At least I won't be wearing this hairy stuff to the party tonight," Krissy said. "We're going home to change first, right? It'd be nerdy to go to a party in our concert uniforms."

"Party?" Violet's smile faded, and she stole a quick glare at Jessica.

Krissy leaned forward. "The after-graduation party at the barn. The one your church is having. If y'all brought your clothes to change into, I can have Mom bring mine to graduation tonight."

"Jessica." Violet's voice held a chill. "Did you forget?"

Krissy glanced from Violet to Jessica. Now what?

"Oh, yeah!" Jessica swiveled in her seat again. "I was supposed to tell you. We're not going to that party. Sarah said she'd be happy to take you to the church wingding, though. I completely forgot with all of the graduation stuff going on. Sorry."

She didn't sound sorry. How long had they known this? Krissy's throat tightened.

"Where are you all going?"

"Dahlia's." Jessica waved as if the change in plans were no big deal. "She's invited a few people over for a small party. We know you aren't a big fan of hers, so we set it up for you to go with Sarah and her crew to that church thingy."

Krissy slouched against her seat. Violet drove in stony silence.

Abandoned for the cool kids. Again. Stunned, Krissy couldn't react. Conflicting emotions from anger to detachment kept her silent.

"Evan really wanted us to go to Dahlia's," Violet said at last. "Since it's his graduation, we couldn't refuse. Sarah is fine with you joining her."

Pressure built in Krissy's head. "I don't really know Sarah or her friends."

"She's a sweetie," Jessica said. "Just get a spine for once and go."

"Jessica!" Violet shot her another glare.

"Well, it's not a big deal. She wants to go to the church-whatever, so go. Or she could come drink with us."

"No!" Violet said. "She can't come with us. She wouldn't like it. She'd be happier at the church party."

"How about if I decide what I'd like?" Anger won the battle for emotional supremacy, and Krissy's voice amplified. "How about if I decide what I want to do tonight?"

"Whatever." Jessica crossed her arms and stared ahead. "Just trying to help. Sit at home and play with your dog. Get your clothes nice and hairy. Like I care."

"Stop it!" Violet slammed the car's brakes. Unbuckled, Krissy's knees smacked the back of the driver's seat. Krissy stared at her friend in shock.

"Jessica was supposed to tell you days ago." Violet's soft voice had a rare sharp edge. "But if you don't want to go to the church party, I'd be happy to take you home after graduation."

"No, it's fine." Krissy's tone matched Violet's. "I'll get a ride home with the folks."

Violet nodded, her face tight and inscrutable in the reflection of the rearview mirror. In contrast, Krissy was pretty sure her face was as readable as the big *E* on an eye chart. What was up with them? Why did they always do this to her? The three of them had made plans. Krissy had been excited about the party, talking about it for days, and they knew it. She didn't understand Violet anymore. Not at all. Maybe Evan and Violet were a thing again? Maybe he'd told Violet to stay away from her? If Krissy had two brain cells to rub together, she'd look for another best friend. But it was Violet, her bestie since first grade. Loyal, desk-kicking Violet.

She crossed her arms and stared out the window. No one talked as Violet accelerated toward school.

* * *

Later that night, Krissy opened the messaging app on the downstairs computer. While she waited for it to load on the antiquated machine, Aslan hopped into her lap and curled into a sleepy ball.

She'd already checked the junior handlers' group. It'd been quiet, as expected. They were all probably at trials or busy with friends.

Her real-life friends were busy, too—with other friends. It'd hurt to watch everyone head out after graduation, the air thick with excitement over the evening parties. She'd slunk off to Dad's car, listening to the cheers and celebratory laughter. It'd sounded fun, but she wasn't part of it. As soon as Dad had unlocked the car, she'd hopped in and closed the door against the buzz.

Now, she sat at home, alone. Well, not totally alone. She had Aslan. And maybe Abby would be online to chat. They'd become good friends, in spite of their difference in age. They'd traveled to several shows over the last few months in their race to qualify for Nationals. It turned out that quiet Abby was a "hoot-n-a-holler," as Basma would say.

Krissy wasn't friendless. She had Aslan, and he'd led her to her agility friends. Her fingers tapped on the keyboard.

Krissy Johnson:

Hey. Are you there? 10:04 p.m.

Abby Weber:
Just watching some vids. Agility, of course. What's up? 10:09
p.m.

Krissy Johnson:
*Bored. I was supposed to go to a party tonight but lost my ride.
I'm bummed. I wish we were at a trial this weekend.* 10:11 p.m.

Abby Weber:
*Bored here, too. Alonzo is still at his folks'. He'll be home Tuesday.
Did you get entered in the Wichita Falls trial?* 10:13 p.m.

Krissy Johnson:
*Yeppers. Mom booked a room at the hotel you mentioned. Hoping
we knock out some Qs that weekend.* 10:14 p.m.

Abby Weber:
*I heard that Mia and Cool are well on their way to qualifying for
Nationals. She and her mom have trialed almost every weekend for
the last two months. How do they afford it? Mia's dad must make the
bucks.* 10:16 p.m.

Little Cool. Every time Krissy heard his name, her abdomen
clenched. She couldn't erase the image of Cool cowering in the
outdoor washing stall. How could she have walked away from
that poor dog? She was as guilty as Mia. But if she said something
now—three months later—who would believe her? She swallowed against the lump in her throat. Was Cool okay tonight?
Was he scared?

Krissy Johnson:
*Her dad owns a siding company or something. He built Mia that
fantastic training barn and field. Have you been there?* 10:18 p.m.

Abby Weber:
*No. I've heard it's nice though. Did you hear a judge nailed Mia
for being mean to Cool?* 10:19 p.m.

Krissy Johnson:
Really?! 10:20 p.m.

Finally. Maybe someone else had done what Krissy had been
too chicken to do? No one would doubt a judge.

Abby Weber:

Word is Mia cued Cool way too early and pulled him off a jump in JWW. Then, Mia apparently threw a hissy fit right there in the ring and yelled at Cool for her mistake. As she picked him up to leave the ring, the judge walked over to her and said the mistake had been Mia's, not her dog's, and that the judge had better never see Mia talk to her dog like that again. 10:23 p.m.

That's all? A verbal slap on the hand? How could Mia get away with such mean behavior time after time? Because people like me don't speak up, Krissy thought.

Krissy Johnson:

I wish the judge had arrested her for dog abuse or something. 10:24 p.m.

Abby Weber:

LOL!! That's hilarious. I can see the headlines on the ten o'clock news now. "Dog Agility Competitor Arrested for Accusing Dog of Competitor's Own Mistake." They'd have film of police loading a handcuffed Mia into a cruiser while Charlotte cries in the background. "We'll get you out, Mia! I'll start a funding campaign for your bail!" 10:27 p.m.

Krissy rubbed a hand over her eyes. Abby wouldn't be joking about this if she knew the truth—if, like Jessica had said, Krissy grew a spine and told. And here, right now, was another chance to speak out. To come clean.

Should she?

She continued typing. *There may be more to this story.*

She pressed the delete key several times, removing the sentence. She tried again. *There's more to this story. Three months ago, I saw Mia slap Cool.*

Again, she punched the delete key, erasing the words Cool and slap. Was it a slap or a hit? How should she phrase it?

Abby Weber:

Alonzo is calling. I'll call you tomorrow. Maybe we can go to the City Dogs' field to train. 10:32 p.m.

Blowing out a breath, Krissy deleted the reply she'd been working on and sent another.

Krissy Johnson:

Sounds good. Talk at u tomorrow. 10:34 p.m.

Would she ever grow a backbone? Shoot, would she ever grow any bone, like even a pinky or something? She turned off the computer and hugged Aslan. Aslan could have been sold to a person who hit him. He could have wound up like Cool. She should have said something months ago.

Chapter 24

Dichotomies

November: Two Years Old

With a camp chair slung over one shoulder and Aslan's soft-sided crate clutched in her hand, Krissy entered yet another horse arena. This one was in Hutchinson, Kansas. Two weekends ago, it was a horse arena in Wichita Falls, Texas. Before that—an arena in Carthage, Missouri. There was always another horse arena.

She followed Abby to the crating area, where they staked a suitable claim to set up their crates for the weekend. This trial was their last shot to meet the requirements for Nationals. Krissy wasn't entered in any more shows before the November thirtieth deadline, and she and Aslan were still shy by two Qs.

Abby threw down a floor mat, and they arranged crates and chairs. The facility was similar to others they'd competed in with a large dirt arena, bleachers rising on one side, a concrete apron edging the walls, and a concession stand. Two rings filled with agility equipment graced center stage. The sight made her heart pound in anticipation, and the pressure of earning those last two Qs tightened her shoulder muscles.

Getting two Qs in two days wasn't hard. The difficulty was the Nationals' Qs had to come in the Jumpers With Weaves and Standard classes on the same day. Called a Double Q, it required accuracy to pull it off, and there were only two days—two chances—left. The odds were not in their favor.

Abby and Jeeves hadn't met the requirements for Nationals yet, either, but while Krissy and Aslan lacked the Double Q, Abby and Jeeves lacked speed points. There were two components to qualifying for Nationals—speed points and Double Qs. Slower, more accurate dogs struggled to accumulate the speed points. Fast dogs had lots of speed points, but often lacked accuracy to get the Double Qs. Every team had their own strengths and weaknesses.

Krissy hoped Team Jeeves would have a good weekend. Nationals would somehow seem less, well, everything if Jeeves and Abby weren't there.

There was a lot riding on this weekend for the Okies.

Soon, Krissy and Abby found themselves lounging in their chairs studying their course maps.

"Judy said this judge designs flowy courses." Abby's finger traced the dog's path on her map. "She was right. They look nice and fast. That bodes well for both of us."

Krissy nodded. "Wide open. No hard, technical sequences. We don't need technical, especially this weekend."

It was good news for Jeeves and Aslan, both of whom had been competing only for a little over a year. And what a year it had been! If she discounted high school and its constant drama—which, granted, would be a lot to discount—this had been the best year of Krissy's life. She'd traveled all over with Aslan, developed a relationship with him that went far beyond her dreams, made countless new friends—it was weird, but most of them were adults—and had grown as a person. Agility taught so many life lessons.

Abby pulled her chair closer to Krissy, and, heads together over the maps, the two discussed handling strategies.

* * *

Aslan's paws continued their running pattern even though Krissy held him in her arms as they exited the Jumpers With Weaves ring. Their first qualifying score of the day was in the books. With it, they had a chance to get the Standard Q, earn the Double Q, and qualify for Nationals! Laughing through her gasping breaths, she leashed him while he barked in her arms, his dangling feet quieting. "Good job, Little Man!" she said. "Oh, yeah. There'll be treaties. Where are they? Find the treaties!"

Four paws back on the ground, Aslan pulled on the leash in a beeline to the ribbon table where she'd left his treat bag, his high-pitched bark requesting his reward. They stopped in front of the table, where he bounced up and down.

Estelle jogged up, clapping her hands like a proud grandma whose baby granddaughter had just spoken her first word. "That was a beautiful run! I'm so excited for you. One more!"

Aslan barked his ecstatic reply. "I don't want to think about it." Krissy doled out treats to her peppy pup. "I need to stay focused. In the moment. My head game is so weak."

"Are you kidding?" Estelle asked. "Do you know how few teams go from their first trial to making it to Nationals in barely over a year? You two are inspiring! I have to say, when it comes to agility, kids always do better than adults."

"Don't jinx us! We haven't made it yet. We have to Q in Standard."

"Yes, but if you don't get the Double Q today, you still have tomorrow."

From the ring, Abby called Jeeves, overpowering Estelle's wispy voice, and Krissy and Estelle sidestepped through the crowded ringside to get a better view of their run. Jeeves wasn't blazing fast, but he was as accurate as always. Abby ran ahead of him, blind-crossing here, front-crossing there, encouraging every split second of speed from him she could. Halfway through their run, they were clean.

Krissy glanced at the time clock. Abby had said course time was forty-one seconds. For every second they came in under course time, Jeeves would get a speed point. He and Abby needed another twenty-two points for Nationals.

Three jumps before the finish, a dog barked outside the ring. Jeeves slowed, head angled toward the hubbub. Abby called, urging him back to task. After a few tentative steps, he finished the run clean. He'd qualified but lost several precious seconds due to the distraction. Abby, Krissy, and Estelle all looked at the time clock as he crossed the final jump. Six seconds under course time. Team Jeeves needed sixteen more speed points to make it to Nationals.

Estelle ran to Abby as she and a happy Jeeves left the ring. "Great job! You shaved off six points."

Abby nodded. "We could have gotten more if he hadn't slowed. What bothered him?"

"A dog barked," Estelle said.

Krissy handed Abby some treats for Jeeves, who wagged his tail in expectation.

"Three runs left this weekend," Abby said. "We'd have to qualify on every single run at five or six points each. I don't know. This is so stressful."

Estelle said, "Don't get all wrapped up in that. Even if you don't make it, when you look back, you'll remember the journey."

"You sound like Daniel. I want to compete at Nationals. That's what I want. This—" Abby gestured at the agility ring, "—is a means to an end."

Estelle's normally bright, grandmotherly face fell. "When Jeeves gets older and you're winding down his agility career, you'll understand. The journey stuff is real. Nationals is nice, but it's the practices, the trials, the mountaintops, the tribulations that you'll remember. When he retires and passes, you'll give all your ribbons for one more run. One more every-day-trial kinda run."

* * *

"Your weaves were to die for," Krissy said as she walked with Aslan during their post-run ritual. It was rainy outside, so they wandered around the crating area's long circular aisle after their successful Jumpers With Weaves run. He pranced, tail up, head high, a big smile on his face. "And that serpentine jump combo was tight, tight, tight."

Out of the corner of her eye, she spotted Cool resting in his crate. She paused and glanced around. Neither Mia nor Charlotte was in sight. Taking a small step toward him, she cooed. "How are you, little buddy?" He stood and wagged his stub of a tail in greeting.

She hadn't told anyone about Mia hitting Cool at the trial ten months ago, and she'd never seen her hit him again. Even so, everyone knew Mia was hard on the dog, calling him a "typical stubborn terrier" and fingering him for her handling mistakes. Most people disliked her turning the blame on him, yet on the other hand they respected her athletic handling. But there had been no more signs of physical abuse.

Taking a few steps closer, Krissy bent toward Cool's crate. His stumpy tail went into overdrive, causing his entire butt to wag.

"You doing okay, Cool?" He whined in response. "Everyone treating you well?" His black nose pressed through the wires of the crate, and she petted it with a finger.

"Are you feeding him?" an angry voice yelled from behind. Krissy wheeled to find Charlotte storming up. "Get away from him! What do you think you're doing? What do you have in your hand?"

Shocked, Krissy showed Charlotte her hand, finger still pointed. "I was talking to him. I wasn't feeding him anything."

"Get away from here, or I'll bring you up before trial chair for trying to poison him."

"What?" Stricken and horrified, Krissy backed away from Cool's crate. His tail had stopped wagging. "That's crazy. I would never—"

"Of course, you would," Charlotte hissed. "Maybe nothing to kill him, but you'd give him something to upset his stomach and keep him from earning the requirements for Nationals. Mia told me what you said about her and Cool."

"I haven't said anything about Mia and Cool. I didn't even know she hadn't made it into Nationals, yet. I was visiting—"

"You think no one knows what a snake you are, but they do. You think you'll have the Oklahoma Cup all wrapped up if Cool doesn't qualify for Nationals, but there are lots of other great Oklahoma teams to beat. You'd have to outrun all the dogs in all the jump heights, you know."

Krissy gaped, eyes wide. She was really confused. Where was all of this coming from? "I have no idea what you're talking about. You guys are nuts." She hadn't meant for the last part to come out, but there it was. She spun to leave, Aslan close to her feet, ears back.

"Stay away from our dogs and my daughter," Charlotte spat as Krissy darted away.

* * *

Daniel and Judy listened with concerned, intent faces as Krissy slumped in her chair and described her encounter with Charlotte. "She threatened a misconduct hearing because you spoke to Cool?" Daniel's eyes flashed. "Yeah. She's a piece of work."

"I want you to avoid Charlotte, Mia, and their dogs at all costs." Judy put her hand on Krissy's shoulder. "They're going too far, trying to get into your head. A misconduct hearing!"

"What's a misconduct hearing?" Krissy asked.

"It's when someone does something bad like abuse their dog—the trial chair calls a misconduct hearing," Daniel said. "The club's event committee meets, hears evidence, and decides if misconduct has occurred or not. If misconduct is proved, the accused is suspended from the AKC. These are never good."

Krissy stiffened. "You mean, if someone hits their dog, they can be kicked out of competition?"

"Yep. It's rare, but everyone wants the dogs protected," Daniel said. "Suspension is a powerful tool. But you have nothing to worry about. Charlotte would have to prove you had poison. It's ludicrous."

Krissy stared at her hands in her lap. After several seconds of silence, Judy asked in her soft, comforting counselor's voice, "What is it, Krissy?"

"Last January, at the Red Dirt show, I saw Mia wallop Cool on the side of his head after a run," Krissy said. "She'd taken him out behind the arena where the livestock washing stalls are. She didn't see us, and as we came around the corner, she hit him. I didn't tell anyone. I didn't think anyone could do anything about it, and Mia said everyone did it. She called it a training slap." Krissy's eyes burned. "I thought it would be her word against mine, and no one would believe me. Mia said everyone thought I was a loser."

Her words sounded hollow, insubstantial.

"I wish you'd talked to us." Daniel ran his fingers through his dark hair. "Mia convinced you not to tell—not to ask for a misconduct hearing. So that's where all this with Charlotte is coming from."

He turned to Judy. "Do you think she knows Mia hit Cool?"

Judy shrugged. "It's possible. Now, more than ever, Krissy, stay away from them. Let Daniel and me handle this."

"What are you going to do? Can we call a hearing?" Krissy asked.

Daniel shook his head. "Not now. It would have to been done at the show in January."

"But what if she's still hitting Cool?" Krissy asked. "I've felt so guilty about not telling."

"All we can do is watch." Judy put a gentle hand on Krissy's arm. "We'll keep an eye out for abuse. If we see something, we'll report it. You, however, need to stay away. Daniel and I will discuss what other options are available to us. We want you to relax and enjoy your time here with Aslan. Try to refocus. You have a big run coming up."

Daniel nodded. "I agree. Let it go and let us handle it. Conflict resolution is smack-dab in Judy's wheelhouse."

Krissy glanced at Aslan, who was resting on a pile of soft cushions in his crate. "Who could do that to a dog?"

Daniel's jaw muscles tensed. "Charlotte puts a lot of pressure on Mia. She's like a stage mom. She expects Mia and Cool to challenge for the USA World Team. It's crazy pressure, and obviously Mia isn't holding up well under it. But that's not your fault. Your only goal today is to focus on your Standard run." Then he hugged Krissy. "You're a good kid. Everyone thinks so. I'm proud to call you a City Dogger."

Krissy gave a weak smile, but her stomach churned and her head hurt. She'd let fear and shame silence her. The moment had passed, and Mia remained unpunished. Because of fear, she'd failed Whickery, and now a different kind of fear—one of conflict and insecurity—had failed Cool.

* * *

Krissy tossed the small blue tennis ball up in the air and reached out to snag it. Instead, it bounced at her feet on the sidewalk and rolled several feet. Aslan lunged after it, and she had to take three fast steps forward to keep his leash from going taut and accidentally collar-popping him. She was a terrible catcher.

Walking, tossing, and catching a ball all at the same time were well beyond her "pay grade."

She should be over the moon. In spite of the drama hours earlier, they'd qualified in Standard. They were on their way to Nationals in Tulsa in four short months, yet the Cool incident had pulled the party hat straight off her head. After receiving multiple congratulations from City Doggers and other friends, she'd snuck away, deciding to celebrate alone with Aslan and a rousing game of fetch in the covered open-air ring across the alleyway from the trial site.

As she neared the ring, a dog barked. Someone was already out there, exercising their dog. She peeked around the corner. It was Mia and Cool. She almost ran like a frightened puppy back to the safety of the agility arena, but instead, she pulled Aslan behind the building's corner and spied.

Mia, giggling, skipped in a tight circle and then, like a flitting hummingbird, switched directions in a flash. Cool chased her erratic line, barking and wagging his stump. Mia held a floppy toy that looked like a dead rodent. Cool jumped, and his jaws snapped at it in zeal. Finally catching it, he mock-growled and threw his head this way and that in an attempt to jerk the toy from her grasp.

"You can't!" Mia laughed and jerked the toy herself. "It's mine! All mine, you little *terrierist*!" After pulling the toy free, she ran away—Cool, the tenacious terrier that he was, in heavy pursuit. Her laughter mixed with his barks and echoed off the nearby buildings.

Krissy pulled back from the view. How could someone hit a dog and so clearly love that dog? Heeding Judy's advice, she headed back to the agility building feeling a bit better—yet also worse.

Chapter 25

The Road to Nowhere

February: Two Years Old

S tiff winter grass crunched under Krissy's feet as she did her wonky trot past a jump in the backyard.

"Turn!" She wrenched her body a sharp one hundred degrees to the left, pulling her right hand across her stomach, forcing her right shoulder to turn with it. Her left arm, positioned across her lower abdomen, lifted somewhat. She pointed her left index finger, cuing a tight turn. Aslan read it, adjusted his line, and took the jump. As he accelerated for the next jump, she put on the afterburners—well, what sufficed as afterburners for her—and, teeth gritted against the pain, funky-trotted down the almost-straight line of four jumps. Another Third Vault Veto.

"Straight!" she called, raising her voice, urging him to greater extension and speed. As he passed her, he read her motion and her verbal cue, tore over the jump, and headed straight for the second jump in the cursed line. In a blink, she was half a jump directly behind him and out of his peripheral vision. From here to the end, Aslan was working on voice cues alone.

He approached the second jump as she again yelled, "Straight!" Her voice rang loud, strong—demanding. He locked on to the third jump even before taking the second. Back between Jumps One and Two, she hobbled as fast as she could, her forward motion and entire body pushing him on toward that dratted third jump.

Although he couldn't see her, he ran without hesitation toward Jump Three. Her heart soared with him. He was going to take the third jump! "Straight!" she yelled again. He vaulted over it. But upon landing, his stride shortened. He slowed instead of moving with confidence to the fourth and final jump.

"Straight!" she repeated, trying to reinforce the command. As he reached the final jump, he spun to visually connect with her. He saw her move past Jump Two as fast as she could straight along the line of jumps. Satisfied the fourth jump was what she wanted, he turned and took it.

It didn't matter. The spin had caused a refusal. If the course had been real, they'd have gotten a NQ. She called him to her and asked for a sit and then a drop, both of which he performed beautifully. From her pocket, she pulled a small plush squirrel that held a treat in a pouch on its belly and threw it to reward the sit and drop and keep his confidence high. As Aslan chased the toy, she collapsed onto the dry bristle-brush Bermuda grass. Lying on her back, her breath puffed in white wisps. With gloved fingers, she pushed her hair off her sweaty brow. How many years would she need to train this sequence until they got it right? Her jaw muscles flexed as she ground her teeth. Aslan could do all sorts of fancy moves—threadles, pushbacks, forced fronts, reverse spins—but ask for three or four jumps in a simple row with her out of view and no go.

He trotted up, the squirrel disemboweled and the treat gone. He dropped the slobbery toy on her upturned face. "Fill it and go again!" He might as well have spoken in plain English. His eyes danced, and his narrow pink tongue curled at the tip as he panted in spite of the brisk winter air.

"Okay." She picked herself up off the ground using her hands instead of her aching knees. "Let's try again. We'll back-chain the ending."

She called Aslan to her side, ready to send him over the last two jumps, when the backyard's gate rattled. Violet came in dressed in a brown coat, black gloves, and a red knitted beanie with *Northland Heights Lions* in bold black letters on the front.

This was a surprise. Violet's on-again, off-again relationship with Evan was on again, or at least Krissy thought so. It had been several weeks since she and Violet had spent much time together or even really talked.

"Hey," Krissy called, smiling. Aslan ran to Violet and bounced in front of her, barking a similar welcome.

"I saw you practicing from my window." Violet nodded toward her house. "I thought I'd drop by and say hi."

"Good timing," Krissy said. "Aslan and I could use a break. Do you want something to drink? I can get you a Coke."

"Nah. I can only stay a second."

Leading Violet to the patio, Krissy motioned for her to take a seat on the redwood settee. Krissy grabbed her water bottle and took several long, drenching gulps as she sat on the edge of the chaise lounge. One of the golden rules of kidney transplant care was to never get dehydrated. The doctors wanted her to drink at least two liters a day. Although the kidney was super healthy now, she downed a few more swallows just to be safe.

"Are you practicing for Nationals?" Violet's drawl sounded thicker than usual.

Krissy screwed the lid back on the bottle. "Yeppers. Just a few months to go."

"I think Team Aslan will do great." Violet slurred the words.

Krissy stared into her eyes. They were unfocused, rims red and swollen. "Are you sick?"

"I'm fighting a cold or something." She spoke each word with care, trying to enunciate, but falling short. "I probably shouldn't have come over. I don't want to give you anything, what with your immune system being low from the transplant meds. Maybe I should go."

"I'm okay. We're outside. It's harder to catch germs outside."

Violet might be on some pretty stiff cold medication, but her nose didn't seem stuffy. A tingling danced along Krissy's skin. She'd never seen Violet altered by drugs or alcohol. Was she now? A rare, uncomfortable silence fell between them. . ."Is everything okay with you? Are you high?" Krissy hadn't intended to say that last bit, and "high" came out staccato.

"Nah. I'm fine. It's a cold." Violet hesitated, her eyes raised as if searching for the right words. "What I mean is, you shouldn't be hanging around me. Not just because of the cold, but for real, that is." Violet paused a second time, then, looking straight into Krissy's eyes, said cryptically, "You're a good person. And I think you're cool with your dog stuff and all. It's just. . .I think I'm going places you shouldn't go, and I don't want you to follow, you know? You've got enough on your plate without being dragged down by me. I'm not mad or anything. I'm not. I just wanted you to know." She rose and walked toward the gate.

Krissy sat stunned for a moment, brows creased. "Wait!" she said, following. "What do you mean? Stay and talk to me. Why do you think you're being dragged down?" When Violet refused to look at her, she added, "Look, I'm not worried about your cold. You can stay and run Aslan over a few obstacles, and we can talk."

"I need to get back." Violet opened the gate. "I just came over to tell you."

"But I don't understand."

Violet fumbled with the latch and, after stumbling through, closed the gate behind her.

* * *

That evening, the muscles in Krissy's upper thighs complained as she eased onto a kitchen chair, phone in hand. Oklahoma winters were great for agility training, offering many days passable enough for outdoor practice. Today had been one of those days.

After an ice storm had made practice impossible for a week, she and Aslan had taken advantage of a melt, working hard, honing their skills in anticipation of Nationals only eight weeks away. But the inconsistent training came at an achy price.

She groaned and dialed Violet's number. "Hey," she said when Violet answered. "I was wondering, would you like to come to Nationals? I could use the moral support. It'll be a lot of dogs and stuff, but I'll have tons of downtime when we can shop the vendors and watch the other events."

After a moment of silence, Violet replied coolly, "My folks would never let me go. You guys go rock it though, okay?" A male voice spoke in the background, and Violet made a shushing noise.

"Is Evan there?" Krissy asked.

"Yeah. We're watching a movie."

So Evan and Violet were dating again. Tracking their on-again, off-again relationship was like staring into the lights of a strobe.

"Okay. I'll let you go. Say hi to him for me." Not that she really wanted to say anything to Evan.

"I'll see you in school Monday." Violet hung up.

Her odd words from earlier that afternoon replayed in Krissy's head. *I'm going places you shouldn't go.* What was up with her? What did she mean?

Krissy ran her fingers through her hair. The answer was obvious. She could pretend she didn't understand, but she did.

Violet had decided to head down the exact same road Dad had discussed with Peter after the car wreck. Instead of dragging Peter down it, Evan had lured Violet there. It was a road Krissy didn't want her best friend traveling.

She leaned her head back and winced at the movement. Aslan jumped unbidden into her lap. In his best teddy-bear imitation, he pushed against her and gazed into her eyes, offering consolation. How did dogs know to do that? She held him close and pressed her face into his warm fur. Somewhere along the journey, her serious puppy had morphed into an adorable, talented, and sympathetic dog.

"God always brings the right dog at the right time" was the well-known saying. God had done that with Aslan. He had brought her companionship, the friendship of others, a feeling of belonging, a sport, travel, adventures, and a life away from school.

He was iron to her iron, sharpening her—changing her.

Like a good friend, Violet had always been iron to her iron, too. But Evan's influence over Violet scared Krissy. What if Krissy had to make the same decision about Violet that Peter had been forced to make about Evan? If Violet stayed on the wrong road and her iron continued to dull, would Krissy be forced to abandon their friendship?

And, if Violet was headed down the wrong road, who would meet her there to offer their iron as a sharpening agent for hers?

CHAPTER 26

The Big Dance

March: Two Years Old

Stepping back, Krissy admired her creation.

"It looks great!" Basma said, peering out through the metal bars of the horse stall. "I love the shark on top."

Krissy smiled at the silvery-gray blow-up shark balanced precariously on the top railing of the stall's front right corner. In turn, it flashed a fiendish, sharp-toothed grin at her. They'd dubbed him the infamous Oklahoma land shark.

The front rails of the stall were plastered with three posters announcing with unabashed pride the names of the three dogs crated within. Each displayed a large photo of the dog with the dog's name above it. Below each photo were the words *Team Oklahoma, AKC Agility National Championship, Tulsa, OK.*

On one poster, Aslan weaved through the poles, his tail whipping behind him, sand grains flying from beneath his paws. Another poster was of Jeeves, gray fur shining and large hangdog ears flapping from his head like rubbery plane wings as he landed a jump.

After traveling most of last year with Abby and Jeeves, things wouldn't have felt right if they hadn't been here to share this weekend with Krissy. She was so glad they'd qualified.

On the last poster, a mahogany sable sheltie sailed over the apex of the A-frame. It was Basma's Tango—a legend. This was his seventh and last Nationals.

Abby, normally quiet and subdued, hadn't stopped chattering since arriving that morning. "Do you think we need more crepe paper on top?" she asked from inside the stall.

Studying the top rails, Krissy couldn't imagine where any more sky-blue-and-white crepe paper could be attached.

"It's perfect," Basma said. "I think you two have done a great job with the decorations."

From top to bottom, the stall was a blue-and-white mishmash, including the large—very large—sky-blue Oklahoma state flag that covered the south side of the corner stall. No doubt, every-one would know the home team was present and accounted for.

"Ladies." The stall door behind Krissy clanged shut, and Daniel entered the aisle. Almost the entire Oklahoma contingent had reserved adjacent crating stalls on row C, with the notable exception of Charlotte and Mia, who were crated with friends from another state. "You guys look like a giant Oklahoma state flag."

"Then our work here is done," Basma said, picking up crepe paper remnants from the floor. Krissy peered inside the stall. Dog crates, camp chairs, and trial gear covered the floor from wall to wall. Regular trials rarely allowed crating in horse stalls, but Nationals was a fun exception. It gave the dogs a peaceful space to rest during the ample time between runs.

"Walk with me and let's look at the decorations." Daniel put an arm around Krissy's shoulders and steered her away. "We'll be back in a few, ladies."

"No rush," Basma said. "I've got some unloading to do."

Krissy glanced back in surprise. Unloading? Where would they put any more stuff?

Daniel led her along the main corridor of the barn. Aisle after aisle of stalls led off to the left and right. Many were decorated—some in dramatic, colorful style, others with a lone banner or a little crepe paper. Posters from Alaska, Maine, Texas, and, well, basically everywhere hung on stall doors. The stalls stretched on and on—perhaps hundreds of them. It would make sense. With thousands of dogs entered in this weekend's agility, rally, and obedience competitions, there would need to be plenty of crating space.

Daniel turned her to the left and headed toward a door to the outside. "I wanted to talk with you before the hubbub starts tomorrow."

Krissy dodged around two ladies, one of whom tottered on a camp chair as she hung an elaborate poster. Krissy glimpsed the words *New York* as she passed. "Looks like the hubbub has already started. I wasn't expecting the party-streamer vibe."

"Yeah. Nationals isn't just a competition. It's also a big party." Daniel opened the door and walked toward a quiet alcove formed by the enormous brick barn building. "That's kinda part of what I want to say."

She nodded and waited for him to continue. "Most people came here because their team was skilled enough to earn the invitation to the Big Dance, so they're here to dance and play," Daniel said. "They'll have the incredible honor of stepping to the start line at Nationals with their best teammate. At the end of the weekend, they'll go home, happy and content with memories of a special weekend with their dog. Some, though, came here to win. Yeah, a few will get all wrapped up in that. I've seen normally pleasant people become testy and rude because of the pressure they put on themselves. You sometimes hear them talking trash or acting out after a bad run."

Then his tone softened and deepened, adding meaning to his next words. "Don't let the competition get to you, or you'll miss what's important here. This is your first Nationals. Soak it up, enjoy the ride, and walk away with lots of pictures and videos.

You'll get only so many Nationals runs with Aslan. Don't waste them. *Live* them."

His eyes became dark and shiny, and his brow furrowed. She could tell there was more behind this speech, and she almost said something light and dismissive to break the mood. Instead, she said, "Okay. I'll try not to get wrapped up in any uber-competitiveness."

"That's my kid." Daniel smiled, but his eyes looked—haunted. "Yeah. Let's grab the other City Doggers and go register. You're gonna want your exhibitor's T-shirt."

* * *

Krissy scanned the hundreds of handlers who remained in line, some with their dogs. She fingered her registration envelope, glad to be out of the crowded cattle call. After receiving their exhibitor number, event bag, and T-shirt, the handlers were herded to the souvenir tables. There, pre-ordered tees, hats, coats, vests, and hoodies emblazoned with this year's Nationals logo could be picked up. Volunteers scurried back and forth, filling orders and ushering competitors through the lines. Most of the volunteers were fellow agility competitors from Oklahoma and neighboring states, so Krissy knew a lot of them. As she'd gone through the line, they'd greeted her with sincere smiles and well-wishes. Their unwavering support eased her building nerves.

In the exhibition hall behind her, vendors selling everything from canine chiropractic care to agility clothes, gear, and equipment displayed their goods and services. She couldn't wait to visit the jewelry vendor, who was offering a special Nationals charm. A competitor from Utah had shown hers to Basma while they'd waited in the registration line. Krissy waved at Basma, but she stood oblivious at the end of the souvenir table, gesturing and laughing with a friend from somewhere on the East Coast. Abby and Daniel had returned to the stalls to help Estelle, who'd just arrived, get situated. That left Basma and Krissy to shop, but Basma was more interested in chatting. Anxious to find the charm, Krissy turned to the vendors and left her behind.

Let the shopping begin. The colorful array of products, services, clothes, and dog supplies were displayed in four long rows of vendor booths. Each booth targeted her wallet. She wanted all of it. The cutest pair of black warm-up pants with a white-and-black paw-print stripe down the side caught her eye. After pulling a size small from the rack, she walked to the vendor's full-length mirror and held the pants up to her legs. They didn't seem too long. She checked the price before holding them up for a second inspection.

A figure standing behind her reflected in the mirror. Charlotte. Her eyes shot daggers at Krissy's back, unaware that the mirror's angle caught her hostile glare. Krissy shivered. She'd never been the victim of such venom. She spun to expose the hatred, but Charlotte had turned away. Mia, whose back was to Krissy, held a leash out, waiting for her mom's opinion. Cool stood by Mia's side, head and tail down. The playful dog barking with his girl in the empty exercise ring was gone, replaced with a tired terrier.

Disturbed by the reflected encounter, Krissy returned the pants to their rack and, moving away from Charlotte and Mia, sought the safety of Basma's chatter.

* * *

The Nationals charm was feather-light in its translucent plastic bag. Krissy lifted it to catch the light, entranced by the sparkling silver as she walked with Basma through the main arena on their way back to the horse stalls.

"This is where most of the action will be." Basma pulled Krissy to the concourse rail that overlooked the facility. Below on the dirt floor were three agility rings with the bright-blue, yellow, and white agility equipment already arranged in ardent

246 • KRISTIN KALDAHL

readiness. The rings looked like rare identical triplets. The following day's warm-up course was laid out and copied from ring to ring. Krissy's skin tingled.

"On Sunday, this is where the challengers and finals rounds will be held," Basma said. "For warm-up day and the first three rounds of Nationals, these will be Rings One, Two, and Three of the six total rings. There'll be lots of noise when these seats fill." The rings below served as the bottom of a large oblong bowl flanked by hundreds of blue stadium seats. "It gets so loud in here," Basma continued. "The sound flows down from the spectators to the arena floor where it kind of bounces around. It makes it all the more exciting."

An expectant silence filled the vast empty bowl. Krissy hugged herself. They'd made it. They were here. As proof, she held a large envelope with an exhibitor's number. How had this even happened? She—physically broken. Aslan—a serious runt. As her eyes began to moisten, she pushed away from the rail and let Basma lead the way to the awards table.

"Hello gals," Basma called to two volunteers who arranged jeweled-colored ribbons on an artful, lattice-board display. "My word, it's looking bea-u-ti-ful!"

Krissy recognized the volunteers as fellow agility competitors from Tulsa.

"I swear. I'm never doing this again." The shorter lady, Kelly, wiped sweat from the sides of her round cheeks. Strands of graying hair escaped her tight ponytail. "I say that every Nationals, but this time I mean it. When Nationals comes back in three years, I'm done."

"Well, your hard work is paying off," Basma said. "The awards table looks better than ever."

"Did you see this year's Oklahoma Cup?" Kelly reached across several glittering trophies to lift a silver cup from the display of awards. It was a traditional one-foot cup with filigreed handles. A plate on its black marble base was half-engraved with the words

Oklahoma Cup. Her chubby fingers held it out for Basma's approval. "I hope you win it. No, wait. I hope Krissy wins it." Kelly nodded in Krissy's direction. "It would be great to have a junior handler win for once."

"Mia's got a chance, too," Robin, the other, younger volunteer said from underneath a table where she rummaged through boxes for more ribbons.

"That's true," Kelly said, "but if a junior's gonna win, I'd rather it be Krissy. Don't y'all tell anyone I said that, though. I don't want Charlotte on my case."

"No, you don't," Basma agreed. "The cup is lovely. Whoever wins this year will have a beautiful trophy to take home."

"We're sneaking it onto the awards display, even though it's not AKC-sanctioned." Kelly replaced the cup with care. "That's another thing not to tell anyone."

Basma laughed. "So many secrets to keep. My word, with my chatty nature, this is gonna be a trial."

"No, *that's* a trial." Robin pushed back from the table's underside and pointed at the agility rings on the arena's floor. "I wish I could join y'all down there again this year. Nattie is almost through her knee rehab, so maybe next year we can qualify."

"You'll be back at it soon," Basma said. "In the meantime, we so appreciate you ladies volunteering."

"We really do," Krissy said. "Everything looks so inspiring."

"Thank you, dear," Kelly said. "Come and visit us during the trial. We'll be cheering for you from here."

Heading across the concourse, Krissy looked at the silent rings on the arena floor again. Goosebumps prickled on her arms. Over fifteen hundred teams. A huge crowded venue. Beautiful National Championship trophies and ribbons. The shiny Oklahoma Cup. No wonder people got wrapped up in the competition.

She inhaled, taking a mental video of not just the rings, but the smell, the quiet pre-storm calm of the coliseum, and the awards table in the corner manned by friends. She hoped that image would forever stick in her memory, so she could revisit it in her old age.

Soak it up and enjoy the ride, Daniel had said.

Suddenly, she longed to get to the stall and give Aslan a big thank-you hug.

CHAPTER 27

Sticky Birds

March: Two Years Old

An impatient herd of handlers fidgeted at the ring gate. In the ring, another herd of sixty-plus handlers roamed through the agility equipment. The only obstacles in this ring were jumps and weave poles. It was Saturday, and Krissy was about to step onto her first-ever Nationals course.

She, yes, *she* stood waiting with the best handlers in the nation. Unbelievable.

Walk-throughs at Nationals were a timed dance. Teams were sorted into walk-through groups of over sixty handlers, and with 324 twelve-inch dogs competing, that created five groups. For Jumpers with Weaves, Krissy and Aslan were Team 148 in the running order, putting them in walk-through Group Three.

Group Two milled around the ring in utter silence. With foreheads scrunched, each handler focused on strategy, checking and rechecking lines and angles, miming different handling maneuvers on the more technical sections. Krissy noticed a clog of people around Jumps Four through Nine. Frustrated handlers jockeyed for position in an attempt to get the spatial feel for the difficult sequence. It was hard with so many bodies jostling for the limited space.

A loud buzzer blew. Like a well-rehearsed marching band, the handlers from Group Two exited the ring to the right while the handlers from Group Three entered from the left. Shivers crawled up Krissy's back as she stepped onto the big stage for the first time. She remembered her guilt over rehoming Whickery and the stabbing fear that she'd repeat that failure with Aslan. That frightened monkey was off her back, banished forever. Aslan would soon shine in his first run at a national agility event.

She had to stop this sentimental horse hooey. Eight minutes were all she had to get this course and her handling moves memorized. Centering her mind, she walked, checking her dog's path, studying her own path, figuring out what moves to put where. "Here!"..."Back around!"..."Back around!"..."Around!"..."Around!"..."Dig, dig, dig, dig!" Each verbal cue and the multiple physical cues that accompanied it were executed in order and in slow motion. She spent most of the eight minutes stressing over the last three obstacles, which combined into a vile Third Vault Veto. To make matters worse, the final obstacle was set a hair far enough to the left to create a subtle and difficult change of direction. She hadn't yet finished developing a plan when the eight-minute buzzer sounded. Head down and mind whirling, she shuffled from the ring with the other handlers.

The Third Vault Veto. Of course, there had to be one in the first round. How was she going to get Aslan from the wrap at sixteen to the last jump? She would be out of his peripheral vision and unable to give physical cues for the final, slight angle.

Unaware of the handlers and dogs hurrying to and from the rings, she wandered to the crating barn in deep concentration, different handling options playing in her head. Nearing her stall, she was jarred from her thoughts by a yell.

"There she is!" Mom and Dad rushed to her, Dad's arms open. "Basma told us about your great warm-up yesterday." Dad folded her into a rare bear hug. His hug warmed her, and her muscles, tight since the course walk-through, relaxed.

Mom gestured at the myriad stalls humming with activity. "This is impressive."

Krissy nodded, glad to share the event with her folks. "Yeah. It's a big deal."

In the background, someone stepped from behind the stall's corner. Krissy froze. Violet stood there, her arms folded across her body, a sheepish grin on her face. Violet? This was a shocker. Violet had said her parents wouldn't let her come, and she'd barely talked to Krissy since that weird conversation in her backyard weeks ago. So, why was she here? Were they friends again? "I—I thought you couldn't come," Krissy stammered.

"Change of plans." Violet walked up and hugged her. "You didn't think I'd miss this, did you?"

Krissy didn't answer, but, yeah, she had.

"And there's more!" Peter hopped out from behind the stall, one arm held wide in a *ta-da* stance, the other clutching Aslan.

"Peter! How'd you get away from school?" Krissy grinned, her eyes scanning the circle of supportive, smiling faces. "Wow! Everyone's here! How'd you all plan this?"

"Lots of text messages," Mom said. "None of us wanted to miss Aslan's Nationals debut."

"Prince sent out a Royal Decree." Peter ruffled Aslan's ears. "He said his loyal subjects must attend the tournament and watch him defeat his foes."

"Talk about pressure," Krissy said. "What if I bomb?"

Dad shrugged. "It's your first Nationals. If you bomb, it's okay. It's about the journey. Right, Tough as Nails?"

"The journey," Krissy agreed with a half-smile. Dad had learned a lot sitting on the sidelines at agility practice.

"When do you show?" Peter asked.

"I'm Number 148," Krissy said. "It'll be at least a couple of hours, but there's lots to do. They've got concessions, tons of vendors, plus agility, obedience, and rally obedience to watch."

Peter scanned the horse barn. "Food? Where's the food? I'm as hungry as a bird in a bush."

Krissy squinted in confusion and was unable to puzzle out this metaphor. Instead, she pointed east toward the main arena.

"Let's steal some grub." Dad moved toward the exit.

Krissy's stomach turned. The last thing she wanted was food. "I need to walk Aslan and spend some time with him. Y'all go ahead. I'll hang around the stall."

"I'll stay here with Krissy. We can grab something to eat later," Violet said.

Peter handed Aslan to Krissy. "Keep a good eye on Prince. He deserves extra care." Peter motioned at Team Aslan's circle of support. "Look at all of the people he's united. He's like the glue that sticks birds' feathers together."

"Birds of a feather stick together?" Krissy guessed.

"Sort of. More like birds get stuck together like glue."

Krissy pondered Peter's faulty metaphor as Mom, Dad, and Peter headed down the main aisle, chatting and laughing. Dad put a hand on Peter's shoulder and gave him a masculine shake—Dad's way of saying, "I love you."

Krissy's skin formed goosebumps as her family—her very happy family—walked away.

All her worries. All the attempts to fix everyone. All the times she'd stuffed her emotions inside to bring peace to the house. And here they were, brought together by a diminutive dog—the totally-wrong-for-agility runt. While Krissy had been plotting ways to feed her family happy, stress-free emotions, Aslan had been dispensing teddy-bear love.

Why had his love worked, but hers hadn't? She'd loved with her useless attempts to make everyone happy—hadn't she?

She looked at Aslan in her arms. He raised his head and snuffled her chin, his long whiskers tickling. His soft brown eyes gazed into hers with simple trust and love. Simple love. That was the difference. Aslan loved regardless. He didn't love in order to change people. He loved because he just did. Her love had failed because it was prompted by a desire to change her family into what she thought they should be. A selfish kind of love. And truly, was that really love? In the end, her dog's sincere love that asked for nothing in return had brought the family together.

He loved. Period. Whether change happened or not, he loved.

She kissed Aslan's silky head.

Apparently, that kind of love sticks birds together.

* * *

Violet checked the live electronic running order for Ring Four on the event app she'd downloaded to her cell phone. "They're only at dog sixty-two. Lots of time left."

Krissy's foot tapped a nervous rhythm on the metal floor of the bleachers. So far, she'd taken Aslan out to potty three times and herself to the bathroom four times. Could she be any more stressed?

"They're livestreaming this," Krissy said. "Anyone from any-where in the world can watch."

"That's cool." Violet looked at Krissy's wiggling foot. "But you're going to make yourself a nervous wreck before you even reach the ring."

Examining the handlers and dogs gathered in front of the ring below, Krissy spied Tango. He gazed with love at Basma as they went through their pre-run ritual. "Tango and Basma should be up soon," Krissy said.

"Maybe seventeen more dogs," Violet said, skimming the run-ning order on her phone.

Krissy yelled, "Go get 'em, Basma!"

Basma turned and waved, her dark curls bouncing. Her atten-tion had returned to Tango when Mia walked past the stadium seats to the adjacent ring where the twenty-inch dogs ran. Mia glanced into the stands and threw Krissy a nasty glare.

"Did you see that?" Violet sat upright and stared at Mia. "Who is that, and what does she think she's doing?"

"That's Mia, Charlotte's daughter," Krissy said. "Remember Charlotte from the trial we visited at Soccer City?"

Violet made a face and nodded.

"Mia is a long, sad story," Krissy said. She told Violet everything, ending with Mia playing and giggling with Cool in the empty exercise ring a few months ago. "I guess there's good and bad in everyone."

"She hit her dog. I don't care what pressure she's under. Unacceptable. And that evil look she gave you? She'd just better stay away." Violet kicked her foot lightly against the metal bleacher bench in front of her.

Krissy laughed. "Is that Mia's office desk? Did you dent it?"

Violet's grin turned wicked. "Her desk will never be the same. Friends protect friends."

Krissy's smile faded. "I'm glad you came."

Violet's grin fell, too. "You're my best friend. I wouldn't miss it."

"Yeah. You're my best friend, too. I just. . ." She probably shouldn't have said this, but the words were too close. "I mean. . .Evan doesn't seem to like you hanging around me."

Violet looked away. "Evan doesn't choose my friends. I do."

A border terrier popped out of the weaves in the ring below them. The handler gathered the dog for another attempt at the poles, but Krissy gave it scant attention. Why was Violet here? She said Krissy was her best friend, yet she'd also been pushing Krissy away.

*I'm going places you shouldn't go. . .*It all conflicted. What was the truth?

"I'm confused," Krissy said. "I mean, that day in the backyard you said you were going places I shouldn't go. Remember? And since then we've hardly talked at all. Yet, I'm your best friend? Don't best friends talk?"

Violet sat motionless for a moment, watching the border terrier take the last two jumps to cheers from the crowd. "It's complicated. I. . .I can't describe it, you know? You fit in one part of my life, but the other part. . .Well, you fit in the first part. And you are my best friend."

"Maybe, instead of slicing up your life to fit your friends, you should get friends who fit what you want to become. You know. Like what the Bible says about sharp iron."

Violet cocked her head and gave a bemused grin. "You're making as much sense as Peter. Is this metaphor problem hereditary?"

Krissy snorted. "In the Bible it says something like people make each other better like iron sharpens iron. Aslan's iron for me. He makes me a better person. So do you. But maybe Evan and his friends don't sharpen your iron? Maybe they dull it."

Violet shook her head. "Evan's a good guy. You just don't know him. He makes me a better person. When I'm with him, I feel wanted, ya know?"

Krissy didn't. Evil Elvis Evan gave her the willies. How could he make a girl feel anything but revolted? And making a person feel wanted didn't make that person better.

Violet continued. "Look, I'm happy the way I am. Everything's fine. And, I'm here, aren't I?"

Violet gestured at the ring and leaned forward as Basma and Tango entered. "She's up." It signaled the end of the conversation, but Krissy had more questions. What part of Violet's life did she fit into? And why had Violet been so distant since the scene in the backyard?

In the ring below, Basma unhooked Tango's leash and left him on a sit/stay in front of Jump One. She led out between Jumps Two and Three, released him, and ran. Tango moved with grace through the serpentine created by Jumps Three, Four, and Five. Basma nailed the cue for the wrap at Jump Eight, allowing Tango to turn insanely tight, which cut time off their run. They ran faster than normal with Tango bouncing through the weaves and over the next few jumps.

But Basma had gone too deep through the weaves and ran too far behind Tango as they turned for Jumps Fourteen and Fifteen. Krissy stood and entwined her fingers, as if praying. Basma attempted to cue the wrap to Jump Sixteen, but her body blocked Tango's line to it. With a valiant, athletic effort, he dodged around her to access the right third of the jump. In the small space, he was unable to gather his legs underneath him to properly elevate. The bar crashed to the dirt, and the crowd moaned. The judge raised both hands, calling a failure to perform.

Undaunted, the team finished the course, and Basma celebrated with Tango as if they'd won it all. Krissy and Violet cheered and clapped.

"Aw. She must not know the bar came down," Violet said watching Basma whooping and jumping up and down with Tango as they left the ring.

"She knows," Krissy said. "Basma's always super positive with her dogs. And Daniel says almost every mistake made on course is the handler's fault. The dogs rarely mess up, so she always cheers for her dog's hard work."

Basma and Tango walked past on the arena floor toward their treat bag. "That was spectacular!" Krissy yelled.

"He made me so proud!" Basma's eyes were watery. "He's wonderful. He gave me. . ." Her voice trailed off as she bent to kiss his head and walked away, wiping her eyes.

Krissy's heart ached for her. "So bittersweet. Tango's going into retirement after Nationals. This will be his last weekend of agility."

"That has to be hard." Violet rose from the bleachers.

"Back to the iron discussion," Krissy said tentatively, standing as well. "You know, if your friends aren't sharpening you—"

"They are." Violet emphasized each word. "I like hanging with them. They aren't bad, ya know. They just like to have a good time. I don't want to change my friends or myself. You're my friend on one hand, and on the other hand, I have Evan, Jessica, and the others as friends. You guys don't see things eye to eye, but it doesn't mean I can't be friends with all y'all." She gave Krissy an intense stare, and her voice got that sharp edge. "Look, I haven't tried to change you, asking you to party. In fact, I've intentionally kept you away from that. But it's not because you're not my bestie. It's because you *are* my bestie. I have a good time with Jessica and the rest. That stuff. . .It'd be sad if you got into that stuff." Violet rolled her eyes to the ceiling and gave an over-blown sigh. "I know it doesn't make sense to you, but it does to me. How about you don't try to change me by asking me to quit being friends with them?"

Change. Krissy was doing it again, seeking to change people into what she wanted them to be. Hadn't she learned anything from Aslan's simple love and how it created sticky birds?" But Violet wasn't making sense. She obviously knew that stuff was bad, or she wouldn't have told Krissy not to follow her. She wouldn't be protecting her from it.

Krissy opted for Aslan's simple love approach rather than more debate. "Okay. Just know, no matter what, you're my best friend. I'm here for you. For life."

"I know." Violet's voice calmed. "And that goes for me, too."

Violet headed down the bleachers. Krissy followed in uncomfortable silence.

* * *

Forty long minutes later, Aslan's head swayed as he tracked Krissy's hand and the treat it held. After a few seconds, he locked on and dove for the shaking target. With a snap, he nailed one of her fingers instead of the treat. "Ouch, buddy!" She couldn't blame him for the miss. Her hands were shaking. She reached into her jeans pocket and fumbled to pull out another treat. With focus, she steadied her hands, asked him for a sit, and delivered a less wobbly reward.

She took a deep breath in a fruitless attempt to control her nerves as they waited near the crowded, noisy ring gate. Feet away, a cattle dog mock-growled in a game of tug with his master. Aslan's head turned, and his eyes followed the pair with rapt attention. "Watch me, Aslan."

There was no response. His ears perked as the cattle dog's game became more animated. Raising her voice, she said, "Watch me, Aslan!" His head whipped back to her, and he stared into her face, waiting for her next command. He hadn't heard her first command. The ambient noise was too loud. They were in one of the more modest horse arenas at the Tulsa fairgrounds waiting to run in Ring Four, yet even with the smaller crowd, the din was deafening.

The gate steward called out the ring order, and Krissy barely heard their number over the buzz in the building. Two more dogs. How would Aslan, who was voice-controlled at distance, hear her in this thunderous environment? She hadn't prepared for that. Rubbing the back of her neck, her eyes darted across the white jumps clogging the ring. There were several sections on the course where Aslan would be working away from her and might not hear her. She'd be a good twenty to twenty-five feet laterally away from him for Jumps Fourteen and Fifteen. And the Third Vault Veto at the end? Oh man. She'd be twenty to twenty-five feet behind him and out of his peripheral vision at that point. Only voice would propel him over the last jump.

Her heart raced at the unexpected complication, and she stumbled to the start gate. This was so beyond them. Why had she come? Her family and friends were in the stands, people across the world were watching on livestream, and she was about to go in the ring with a verbally handled dog in a building practically rocking with decibels.

The team in front of them neared the end of their run, and the gate steward put a hand on Krissy's shoulder, nudging her toward the ring entrance. "You're next. Have fun."

Krissy's limbs went numb, and a petrifying panic froze her in place. How did the course go? Where was Jump One? She gasped for air, confusion stalling her mind. Shaking her head, she tried to swallow but couldn't. Her dry mouth had no saliva. A sob rose. She stuffed it. The dog in front of them hurdled the last jump. Krissy should be setting Aslan at the start line, but her feet would not move. She'd never known anesthetizing fear like this.

No. Wait. That wasn't true. She'd lived on dialysis for nine months. She'd gone through transplant surgery. She knew fear. Fear of pain. Fear of death.

This wasn't fear. It was simple stage fright. And stage fright didn't hurt. Stage fright didn't kill.

At her feet, Aslan pranced in place, eager to take his turn on the equipment. His eyes sparkled with life. She picked him up, and his quickened heartbeat pulsed under her hand. Feeding on his energy, her limbs thawed, and she walked into the ring.

Her sneakers crunched across the sandy dirt. This was Nationals soil. Aslan had brought her here. His joy, his iron, had undermined her fear. She'd overcome the fear that had driven her to sell Whickery, that dread of death left behind by her time on dialysis. Riding Aslan's joy, she would conquer the fear of him not hearing a command, the Third Vault Veto, and her inability to run. Because of her tiny dog, she stood on top of the mountainous rubble of her disease. They danced on Nationals soil. There would be no failure, regardless of the outcome. Shoot, just earning the right to stand on center stage was a win. Success.

The fear vanished.

Blinking away tears, Krissy kissed Aslan's silky head, set him in front of the first jump, and said, "Thank you for it all, Little Man. Sit. Stay."

She led out and pulled her mind back into focus, reviewing her handling for the first five obstacles. She must stay in the moment and yell her commands. She pivoted between Jumps Two and Three, held out her right hand, and stared back at her dog.

He quivered, every cell in his little body eager to be released to attack the course, yet he held his stay. In a clear, strong voice, she yelled, "Okay!"

And then, he flew.

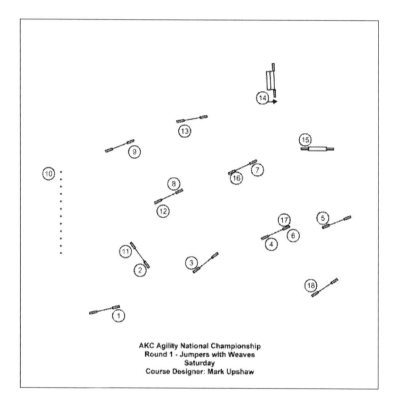

AKC Agility National Championship
Round 1 - Jumpers with Weaves
Saturday
Course Designer: Mark Upshaw

The first six jumps ran to plan. He heard her verbal commands, but she raised her voice anyway. A late cue caused him to go wide at Jump Seven and consider taking the off-course Jump Thirteen, but he turned in time. At Eight, she gave another late command. Perplexed, he slowed before taking the jump but managed a tight wrap to Jump Nine. Then, they hit their rhythm again. He whined through the weaves, frustrated to be slowed by the slalom motion the poles required. After the last pole, she turned him and signaled him over Eleven and Twelve. As he committed to Jump

Thirteen, she raised her voice and yelled, "Back out!" to change his direction toward Fourteen. He head-checked her as he sailed over Thirteen, looking back for physical cues. He hadn't heard her. Fortunately, he'd changed to the correct direction. "Out!" She screamed, every muscle in her body straining to indicate the far Jump Fifteen. He heard her amplified command and turboed for the jump. "Around!" Reading her body cues, he ran toward Jump Sixteen as she turned to maneuver herself for the wrap.

Upon turning, she gasped and faltered. Like Basma, she'd gone too far into the pocket and was out of position for Jump Sixteen. She darted to the side to try and pull Aslan over the jump, yelling "Dig, dig, dig!" for a left wrap. He understood in spite of her mixed signals and bent his body around her and the jump's stanchion, landed, and kicked out for Jump Seventeen. Still befuddled and now behind, her feet pounded the earth as she pushed the last line of jumps, yelling for the ending—the Third Vault Veto.

"Straight!" He ran at speed for Jump Seventeen. She was out of his peripheral vision, yet she ran the line as hard as she could.

"Straight!" He landed over Seventeen.

And spun.

He looked back at her, confusion in his eyes. He hadn't heard it. He didn't know where to go. The crowd moaned. Fearing he would take Jump Seventeen backward in an attempt to return to her, causing an off-course, she bounced a step to the right and called him to hand. He responded and trotted around Jump Seventeen, but he looked bewildered and unhappy. Using hand signals, she gathered him to her left side and sent him over the final jump.

The crowd remained silent waiting to see if the judge would call a refusal for the spin after Jump Seventeen. Krissy circled her arms and cheered for Aslan as he leaped into her embrace, but her cheers became lost in the crowd's roar. The judge's hand never raised.

It was clean.

Basma met Krissy as she exited the ring. Her eyes were moist again. It was a teary day for Basma. "Oh, my word! Oh, my word!" She hugged Krissy and Aslan, who was still in Krissy's arms.

"That was incredible!" Krissy yelled. The cheers subsided as the next dog began her run. "The judge never called it, did she?"

"No. It was a good non-call. Aslan wasn't close enough to the last jump." Basma beamed. "You got a clean run at your first Nationals! And it had a sort of Third Vault Veto, too!"

Krissy waved to her parents, Peter, and Violet standing in the bleachers. Dad pumped his fist. "That was beautiful!" he yelled. "Smokin' fast!"

Krissy gave Aslan one last hug and told him what a spectacular dog he was before putting him on the ground. He ran to the end of the leash and pulled her to the arena wall, where she'd left his bag of treats.

She hadn't let him down. Together, they'd conquered. This is what it was like to run joy.

* * *

That evening, Mom's phone vibrated on the hotel nightstand next to Krissy. A text from Abby.

Abby Weber:

Estelle did the math. Right now, Aslan and Cool are in the lead for the state cup. The other fifteen Oklahoma teams either incurred faults or are pretty far behind in times. Way to go, Team Aslan! 7:52 p.m.

Joyce Johnson:

It's Krissy. I'm using Mom's phone. Where are you and Jeeves in the standings? 7:54 p.m.

Abby Weber:

With that dropped bar in Standard, we're out of it. But he did post his fastest yards per second ever in JWW today. Did you see he came in 52nd out of 231 in JWW? 7:56 p.m.

Joyce Johnson:

I didn't! That's so awesome! 7:57 p.m.

Abby Weber:

You go get 'em in the morning. 7:58 p.m.

Joyce Johnson:

Cool is ahead in time, right? Aslan had that big bobble in JWW. 8:00 p.m.

Abby Weber:

Cool is slightly ahead, but it's anyone's game. Don't stress over that. As Judy says, enjoy the journey! 8:00 p.m.

Putting down Mom's phone, Krissy laid her head back on the hotel pillow. She was beyond exhausted. Her family and Violet had gone out to dinner, but she'd been too tired. They'd promised to bring her back something. Not that she would eat much with her stomach all knotted up.

Aslan had run clean in Round Two—the Standard round. According to Daniel, their bobble in Jumpers would keep them out of the highly competitive Finals Round. But to be running second in the whole state of Oklahoma!

She reached her hand across the bed and found the familiar warm, furry, bird-like body. Aslan, sleeping, sighed at her touch.

No matter what happened tomorrow, no one could ever take away the feeling of walking out on Nationals soil for the first time. She would always remember what it felt like to finally and forever stand on the mountain.

CHAPTER 28

A Rare Dog

March: Two Years Old

Aslan burrowed deeper into the warm pillows in his crate. It was chilly in the stall building. The place had a constant hum—dogs barking, stall doors clanging, people talking and laughing. His eyes remained shut as he tried to sleep. The day before had been so tiring. This agility trial was different from any other he'd known. Not only were there lots more dogs and people, but the atmosphere sparked. All the dogs felt it. He could see it in their eyes and body posture as they passed each other. They were all experiencing emotions to the extreme—some happy, some stressed, some over-the-top and ready to run.

Right now, he was over-the-top exhausted. Earlier, his Mistress had left the stall with her friend, Peter, and Mom. Dad remained, sitting in a bag chair and holding the paper he liked to stare at every day.

As Aslan began to doze, the stall door opened, and his Mistress and the others walked in. He rose, sensing anxiety. She grabbed his leash and treats from the training bag and talked to the family in excited tones. He knew this routine. It was time to run.

All weariness left his body, and he danced in his crate. Would they run a course of jumps with weaves, or would all of the agility equipment be included? Would they run fast? He liked it when his Mistress pushed him for speed. He liked to go fast with no confusion to slow them down.

His Mistress opened his crate door, and he bolted through, eager to play. He stood still long enough for her to slide the fleecy, braided slip leash over his head before pulling her toward the stall door.

"Wait, Little Man." His Mistress turned to the family, and there was more incomprehensible discussion. With impatience, he pulled toward the door again, and this time, she followed.

"Good boy, Aslan." Peter bent to pet his back as he passed. "Do a good job."

Good boy. Good job. Aslan knew those words. He was a good boy. His Mistress told him that a lot, and he believed her. He was a very good boy who knew how to play the game called agility, and he wanted to go play again. Now.

Seconds later, he tugged his Mistress along the aisle heading out of the building of stalls toward the agility rings. As he pulled, his ears flattened, his butt tucked, and he ran, barked, and hopped at the end of the leash. All of the energy of the hyped-up event flowed into him. He wanted to run. He wanted to fly.

When they entered the door to the big building with lots of seats up high and agility rings below, he stopped his on-lead butt-tuck zoomies to soak up the spectacle surrounding him. His Mistress smiled as he yapped in place, his drive leaking out through his voice. They walked through a mass of dogs and handlers who waited in loose groups in front of the rings. Gate stewards' voices yelling for teams due in the rings were dimmed by barking dogs and cheering spectators.

Aslan deftly wove his way through the sea of human legs and furry canines. The atmosphere was super charged, and he fed on it. Everyone wanted to play agility, and he couldn't wait for his turn on the equipment. His body thrummed with the energy. He bounced and high-stepped, glancing back every few strides to make sure his Mistress followed as he led her through the crowd. They stopped in front of the last of the three rings.

He peered through the ring's fencing at the agility equipment. He spun back to his Mistress and barked his joy. Opening the treat bag, she took out some of his favorite treats that kinda smelled like the silver animals that lived in the lake.

"Sit."

"Drop."

"Stay."

She steered him to one side where the crowd had thinned, and they trotted back and forth. His young muscles loosened, and he barked again. Then came more commands.

"Back."

"Easy."

"Stretch."

He snapped through the games and gobbled his rewards.

His Mistress was nervous; he could tell by her strained voice. This didn't bother him, though. She was often like that before they did agility.

As they worked some stays in their familiar pre-run warm-up, someone called his Mistress's name. She turned her head toward a girl walking to them. He recognized her from other agility trials. She was the one who'd hit that other dog.

Aslan quit barking and positioned himself between his Mistress and the newcomer, like a small canine shield.

* * *

Krissy was pleased. The pre-run warm-up had clipped along as planned. Five more dogs until their turn. Aslan gaited well, and her body wasn't as stiff and truculent as usual. With a smile, she guided him next to the cement wall that circled the arena floor, and she commanded, "Sit. Stay." He plopped his furry haunches on the ground and waited as she released the leash's slack and moved five feet from him, speaking nonsense words in an attempt to verbally pull him off his stay. "Blue. Red. Pizza. Sky." Aslan sat through all of the gibberish although he leaned forward in anticipation. She said, "Okay," and he released, running to her for his reward.

"Krissy!" She turned at the sound of her name to see Mia pushing her way through the crowd. Wonderful. As Mia approached, Aslan, quiet now, slipped between her and Mia like a small canine shield.

"I wanted to wish you good luck." Mia smiled with no trace of sarcasm.

Krissy, head tilted, was dumbfounded. Mia being a good sport? Had the world stopped spinning? "Thank you," she replied after a few seconds. "I hope you and Cool do well, too. And have fun out there."

"Oh, we did! We ran near to ten minutes ago. We was fast and clean!"

"Congratulations. You've had a great Nationals."

"We have! Mom thinks we got a real chance to make it into finals and win the Oklahoma Cup. You guys do good on your last Nats run!"

"Thanks," Krissy said.

Mia spun, ponytail flipping, and disappeared back into the masses.

A male voice above Krissy said, "Ignore that." Daniel leaned forward in one of the first-row stadium chairs above the arena's five-foot concrete wall. "She's trying to get to you. Dismiss any thoughts of the Oklahoma Cup. Focus on this moment and your time with your dog. This is precious. Go play and make a lifetime memory. I mean it. Stay in the game."

Stay in the game. It was true. Krissy was about to go in the ring. She couldn't—wouldn't—let Mia distract her. "I will."

"Aslan is a rare dog. Have fun." He climbed back into the stadium seats, where Krissy's pep squad sat. They waved and cheered her name. Mike and his wife had joined the other City Doggers. They were all there: Judy, Basma, Abby, Alonzo, Estelle, Violet, and Krissy's family. She flashed them a wide grin.

"16148. 16148." The gate steward's voice was barely audible over the cacophonous noise bouncing around the bowl of the arena.

She waved. "Here!"

"You're up in two," the gate steward said. Krissy grabbed a couple treats and headed to the ring. Her brain wanted to focus on what Mia had said, but she fought it. She could think about that later. Instead, she narrowed her focus on the course.

It was the third round of Nationals. Their last round. The hybrid course—a mixture of Standard and Jumpers With Weaves. It wasn't too challenging for a team with distance skills. Well, until the end. There, laid out like a pit viper, lurked the Third Vault Veto. She planned to keep Aslan on her right hand out of the weave poles and send him to Jump Fifteen. As long as he went to the jump on his own without her having to get too close to Fifteen, they would be okay. Then, she hoped to run the line of the last three jumps with enough lateral distance to stay in his peripheral vision. If she could do that, the chance he'd take the last jump was good. If she had to run with him all the way to Jump Fifteen, then she would be caught behind him and out of his peripheral vision for the run out to Eighteen—the perfect Third Vault Veto storm.

She shifted from foot to foot at the gate entrance and watched the team ahead of them rip through the course. Fear niggled in her stomach. No. She was done with that. Daniel's words floated through her mind. *Aslan is a rare dog.* Looking at his little face alight with excitement, she knew Daniel was right. Aslan *was* a rare dog. He deserved her all on this run—successful or not. She vowed to give it to him.

They had nothing to lose. They were already winners.

Focused.

Fearless.

The team in front of them headed for home. "Third Vault Veto or not, let's go rock this, Little Man." He barked as she picked him up, and they stepped onto Nationals soil for their last run. After kissing the top of his head, she placed him on the ground in front of the tire with the command to stay.

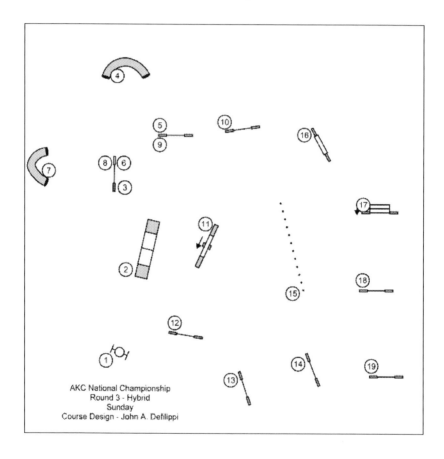

AKC National Championship
Round 3 - Hybrid
Sunday
Course Design - John A. Defilippi

Krissy led out beyond the up-ramp to the A-frame, her hands shaking with the thrill of the game. She looked back at Aslan now framed by the circle of the first obstacle—the tire jump. "Okay!" she called, releasing the tiny wheat-colored sheltie.

At her call, he flew. He jumped through the tire and raced toward the A-frame. She moved as soon as she released him, but only reached the bottom of the A-frame as he sailed over the obstacle's pointed apex. The instant his front feet hit the yellow contact zone at the bottom, she called, "Okay! Here!" quick-releasing him from their usual, slower two-feet-on, two-feet-off contact performance. He reacted with lightning reflexes to the little-used command and powered off the A-frame, running full speed toward Jump Three.

Her timing and line on the rear cross between Three and tunnel-entrance Four was flawless. A split second before he entered the tunnel, she yelled, "Here!" letting him know where to look for her when he exited the tunnel. Coming out rocket-fast, his turn was already sharp and angled toward her. He locked onto the jump on his line and ignored the off-course Eight Jump. He carried all of the speed retained from banking the tunnel over the jump and headed on a direct line into the second tunnel.

She gritted her teeth against familiar pain and an unwilling body and hobbled to position herself a few feet behind Jump Seven, giving him the perfect line to her as he left the tunnel. Upon his exit from the tunnel, they made eye contact, and he sped toward Seven as she turned to cue Jump Eight.

"Around!" she yelled as Aslan neared Eight. The command was muted in the noise, but it was enough. He obeyed. He saw the ninth jump set at a 180-degree angle from Eight. He sliced over Eight and stormed to Nine. Before he could wonder what obstacle was next, she yelled, "Here! Teeter!"

There was no hesitation on his part. No consideration of the weaves—a strong trap. He snapped to the teeter, not slowing until he crouched in the yellow contact zone at its end and rode it to the ground.

The teeter banged, but not before she called, "Straight!" He let it hit and bounced off in the direction of Jump Eleven. The next two jumps were easy—a distance team's dream. "Back out! Out!" she yelled, now standing a few feet to the left of the teeter. As he *neared Jump Thirteen, she called, "Turn! Weave!" and pulled her right shoulder hard toward the weaves. Impeccable timing allowed the sheltie to collect his body and wrap it around the stanchion of Jump Thirteen as he raced to the weaves.*

With a stiff-legged, short-stepped run, she pushed with everything she had to meet him at the end of the poles, but he beat her out of them by a foot. Not what she'd planned, but it was okay. She was prepared with Plan B. She yelled, "Back!" and he flipped away from her, dashing with confidence toward Jump Fifteen—the first obstacle in the Third Vault Veto.

With him now on her left and the weave poles on her right, she ran the ideal line, hugging the poles. This line should keep her in his peripheral view. It should keep him from spinning, wondering where she was. She pushed her body hard, forcing her reluctant, tired legs forward. "Straight!"

Without question, Aslan headed to Obstacle Sixteen.

"Straight!" His stride ate Jump Seventeen. One to go. The third jump of the Veto. "Straight!"

Her heart pounded in her ears. She gasped for air, attempting to feed her already taxed lungs. Aslan's fur streamed flat as his small, powerful body coiled and sprung open. There was no deceleration.

No doubt.

He soared over the final jump.

She screamed and fell to her knees, fists pumping. He spun and ran to her, barking his triumphant war cry. She gathered him into her trembling arms and hugged him as the tears began to fall.

* * *

Krissy, Aslan in tow, hobbled up the stairs to the stadium seats and her still-cheering family and friends. Daniel, grinning like a fool, wrapped her in a bear hug.

"It was the zone, wasn't it? Totality! From start to finish."

"It was. Everything. Like slo-mo on steroids. Like perfect freedom." She sobbed through laughter and hugged him back. "I want that again. And again. And again. I could feel his soul."

"I know," he whispered, pulling back and looking at her with moist eyes. "And now you know, too. The power of this sport. Of your dog. The beauty of it all."

Basma and Abby, standing at their seats, screamed. Abby waved her phone, and Basma pointed at the screen that displayed Krissy and Aslan's run time. "Aslan won! By a tenth of a second! Aslan won the Oklahoma Cup!"

* * *

Aslan sniffed. The sole of her shoe smelled like—cheese? Not like the white sticks of cheese his Mistress sometimes used for rewards, but like the kind of wet cheese Peter fed him once when the humans were watching the talking box and alternatively cheering and booing at it. That had been spicy cheese. Like this. He'd seen her step in the cheese moments ago as they'd walked past the place that handed humans food. Only now, though, did she quit walking so he could examine the unexpected treat. He licked the tip of her shoe. Yum.

She moved her foot and picked him up in her arms, away from the cheese remnants. They were high up in the building and overlooked the agility equipment below, which was empty of dogs. Only people remained in the rings, milling about, rearranging the equipment.

A woman with a big smile on her face came toward them carrying a silver cup that caught the arena's lights and reflected them out to the world. As she neared, his nose worked the air. The cup smelled so good. Like chicken. Chicken was much better than spicy cheese.

The lady held the cup in both hands and spoke to the gathered crowd. Then she handed it to his Mistress, and as they had earlier, everyone clapped and cheered. His Mistress held the cup high, a ridiculously wide smile on her face, and lowered it to him. He didn't need to look inside to know what was there. As soon as the cup's rim was within reach, he buried his nose in the pile of shredded chicken within.

This had been a really, really good day.

CHAPTER 29

Still Cool

May: Three Years Old

The strap slid off her rounded shoulder and landed painfully smack-dab on the fistula. Reacting instinctively, Krissy snapped her wrist straight and let the strap and bag attached to it slam to the ground to release the painful pressure. She raised her wrist to her ear, and the comforting *whoosh, whoosh* of her fistula buzzed. Assured it was safe, she picked up the bag, slung its strap back onto her shoulder, and continued across the parking lot to the car. Thirty feet later, the strap slipped once more, and the process repeated.

Rounded shoulders sucked when it came to loading and unloading trial gear. In this case, it was loading. Another weekend's trial was in the books. They were back at Soccer City for the Red Dirt Agility Club's Memorial Day trial, and the long, successful four-day show had left her spent but happy. Today, just two months after the Tulsa Nationals, Aslan had qualified for next year's Nationals to be held in Perry, Georgia. She needed to plan strategies to convince her parents to let her skip some school to attend.

As she readjusted the bag on her shoulder, Mia breezed by, little Cool at her side. "Hey, Mia," Krissy called.

Mia stopped and seemed to vacillate before turning. With a hand on her right hip, attitude steamed off her.

"You had a beautiful run with Cool in Standard," Krissy said.

"Thanks." Mia's tone fell flat as she stared at Aslan, who roamed as far from Krissy and her precarious load as his leash would allow. With a sniff, Mia dropped Cool's lead and ordered, "Heel." Cool jumped to her left side and trotted in perfect heel position, leash dragging, as she left.

Krissy's lips pressed into a line. Would Mia ever get over the results from Nationals? Cool was a great dog whether he won, placed, or lost. Krissy hunched up her right shoulder and continued her trek to the car, wondering how far she'd get before the bag slipped again.

After reaching the SUV, she allowed the strap to slide from her shoulder for the last time. It landed on the asphalt with a clatter. She dropped Aslan's leash to the ground by her feet and, stepping on it to keep him from wandering off, began loading the gear. From her vantage point, she could see Mia at the edge of the parking lot talking with a fellow competitor. Obedient, Cool sat by her side, eyes focused on something across the street.

Turning her attention to the car, Krissy began to tackle the Tetris-like puzzle of arranging the gear in the car's hatch. It was no small feat with the incredible amount of stuff required by one little dog, and Dad was bringing more. . .

An intense, eerie silence ripped the air an instant before tires squealed. A soft, sickening *thump* followed. A dog cried. A human screamed.

Krissy's eyes flew to her feet. Aslan, his leash trapped by her foot, looked with bewilderment toward the source of the noise. Krissy gasped and gathered him into her arms. For a moment, she stood there, eyes shut tight against the dread that had caused her mouth to taste of metal. With the initial burst of fear-based adrenaline past, she hugged Aslan tight and ran toward the accident.

Mia's hands covered her mouth and muted her sobs. The competitor she'd been talking to moments before tugged on her arm to pull her back, away from a car and the small white-and-tan body lying motionless on the ground.

"No. No. No." Krissy trotted to the scene.

Dad ran past Krissy and dropped the trial gear he'd been carrying onto the asphalt next to her in one deft move. "Stay here. Don't come any closer."

Calls for help echoed behind her. "Get Dr. Carley!"

"Dr. Carley!" someone yelled from within the open doors of the soccer facility, relaying the summons.

A loose crowd formed around the accident scene and stared in communal, grieved silence. A few circled Mia, holding her and crying with her. Some hovered over Cool, who lay too still on the concrete street. Dad reached the dog and bent over him, prodding the little injured body with gentle fingers, feeling for a pulse and looking overwhelmed. He was a human doctor, not a veterinarian.

Dr. Carley, a fellow competitor and veterinarian from Ardmore, ran past, her brunette ponytail streaming. She reached the street and knelt beside Dad, who gladly let her take over the examination. They talked in low tones and gave quiet orders to a few competitors who kneeled nearby in readiness.

Moments later, Charlotte arrived, breathless. "Is he okay?" she asked the huddled doctors. Her voice wavered. Dr. Carley held up a finger to ask for patience and silence.

Charlotte took in Cool's prone body and the car stopped in the street before wheeling on her daughter, who was being comforted by friends as she cried. "What did you do? How could you let this happen?"

"I didn't do anything," Mia whispered. Krissy's heart broke at the anguish in Mia's eyes.

"It was an accident," one of the ladies holding Mia said. "You can sort out the details later. This isn't the time—"

"My dog is lying in the middle of the street!" Charlotte pointed at Mia. "She isn't lying there with him, which means he was out there on his own. Why, Mia, was Cool in the middle of the street?"

"Stop it, Charlotte. I need to concentrate." In spite of the words, Dr. Carley's voice was soothing. She didn't look up as she took a colorful fleece blanket held out by one of Mia's friends and covered Cool.

Ignoring Dr. Carley's plea, Charlotte whirled to face an overweight younger man with a pale, drawn face who slouched against the car. "Is this your car? Were you driving? How fast were you going?"

"I—I'm sorry," the man stuttered. "I wasn't going fast, I swear. He came from nowhere. I didn't have time to stop."

"Someone call the police." Charlotte's arm shot out toward the man in accusation. "I want him arrested."

"Charlotte!" There was steel in Dr. Carley's voice this time. "Calm down. We need to keep our heads here. Cool is alive, but he's got to get to a vet. He's unconscious. I think there are broken bones and probably internal bleeding. You're a bit overwrought, so I'll need someone else to drive. What vet do you want to go to?"

Charlotte looked from the doctor to the dog. "Broken bones? Will he ever do agility again?"

"Seriously, Mom?" Mia's round tear-reddened eyes went wide with disbelief. "That's your concern? Will he ever compete again?"

Dr. Carley, with Dad's help, carefully bundled Cool and slid him onto a plastic crate floor tray someone had brought to support his injured body.

"We can take our car," Dad offered.

"Absolutely not!" Charlotte screeched. "I won't have Cool in your hands. My van is over there. Mia, go get my purse and make sure the keys are inside." Mia, gasping through sobs, ran toward the building, feet pounding the asphalt.

"I think I should drive," the competitor who had been holding Mia suggested in a wan voice. Charlotte gave a sharp nod of consent.

As the group neared her van, Cool carried on the makeshift stretcher, Charlotte asked Dr. Carley, "Well, will he ever do agility again or did Mia ruin him?"

"I can't say." Dr. Carley's voice held ice. "How about we just focus on getting to the vet as quickly as possible?"

"This is a nightmare," Charlotte said, her shrill voice still easily heard while she slid into the passenger seat. "A perfectly good dog. Ruined."

* * *

Colors blended together—pastel blues, greens, purples, and pinks. Soft images of dogs and cats sleeping by a fire or sitting beneath a tree fronted the cards displayed under a placard that read *Pet Sympathy*. The card in Krissy's hand was all wrong. A yellow lab stared out over a placid lake as ducks flew into the clouds. She needed a card with a terrier, not a retriever.

She opened it. *May fond memories of your beloved pet warm your heart always.* Krissy frowned. She needed a card with a Jack Russell tearing up an agility course or playing tug with his girl. And, the card needed to say *Get well, sweet puppy*, not *Sorry for your loss.*

She replaced the card with the lab and sighed. The only pet cards she'd found were under pet bereavement. There had to be a market for get-well cards for dogs. And yet, a bereavement card for Mia seemed appropriate, too.

After the accident, little Cool's right rear leg had been amputated, signaling the end of his agility days. As soon as she'd heard the prognosis, Charlotte had rushed to find him a new home. Like a broken toy, she'd paid his medical bills, chucked him out of the house, and waved adios. Poor Mia.

According to Abby, Charlotte had said she wouldn't have a dog in the house who couldn't earn its keep. "All dogs here compete. I teach agility. I can't afford to keep a useless young dog for years."

Cool had won the rehoming lottery, though. Mike had claimed him as a lapdog for his wife and a playmate for Honey. Upon his release from the vet's, Cool would go to rehab at his new home. He'd be loved and spoiled.

It was Mike and Honey's gain, but Mia's great loss. The image of Cool and Mia playing keep-away in the empty exercise arena drifted into Krissy's head. It had to feel like a death for her—and after she'd had him off-lead. How could she bear it?

On second thought, a get-well card made no sense. Cool would be getting well at Mike's. Mia needed a sympathy card, but her dog didn't die. There's no way they made *sorry your mom is a jerk and forced you to give up your dog* cards.

From the corner of her vision, Krissy watched Peter approach. Home from college for the summer, his construction job framing houses had turned his skin a dark bronze. He stood next to her and perused the selection.

"Who knew there were so many pet bereavement cards?" He pulled a card from the rack and read it aloud: "'In deepest sympathy. May you find peace and comfort in the sweet memories of your beloved pet.' That doesn't sound cliché or anything." He slid the card back in its slot.

"I can't find the right one. It needs to have a Jack Russell terrier on the front and say something about healing or moving on or. . .I don't know. Not death, though. Cool didn't die. He's just—" She didn't finish the sentence. What was he *just*? Just injured? Just a tripod? He wasn't just a just. He was still Cool—still cool. She chose another one and silently read it. More *sorry for your pet's passing* drivel. Fighting tears, she blinked, looked up at the fluorescent lights on Walgreen's ceiling, and tried to think of something besides Cool lying on the pavement.

"I know it sounds like hollow sentiment from one of these cards, but I'm sorry about Cool," Peter said quietly. "I'm sorry you were there. Dad said it was horrible hearing that girl sob. He said he thought the dog wouldn't live. It makes you think about how short dogs' lives are, ya know? I mean, Ruffis is already fourteen. I remember when he was young. And Aslan is already three. Do you remember when we sat in the backyard on the quilt trying to come up with silly names for him?"

She smiled, glad for the distraction brought by the happy memory. "I remember *you* picking silly names."

"Who knew how important he'd become in three short years." He selected a small card hidden behind a large envelope. "I never said this, but there have been times when I thought Aslan was the only person in this family who understood me. No, make that thing, not person, I guess. Living thing. Family member. You know what I mean. I was a bit jealous when you got him, but he's turned out to be my dog, too, I think." He waved at the pet cards. "For an animal that doesn't live long, these dogs burrow fast and deep into your heart, don't they?"

She nodded. He handed her the card he held. "I think your friend may like this one." She fingered the card as he walked away.

Cool's accident seemed so random. Empty.

One second, he's there heeling by Mia, and the next, there's a heart-stopping thud. No warning. No buildup. No sad musical soundtrack playing woefully in the background to prepare the audience.

Senseless.

On the front cover of Peter's card, a tan terrier-mix trotted along a path through green fields leading to an open, slightly curved horizon. On the front, it read, *Your dog may be gone from you.* Krissy opened the card. *But take comfort in the knowledge that your sweet pet is forever under the watchful eye of a just and loving Creator.*

Krissy's Grace

June: Three Years Old

A warm breeze tickled the soft, wispy hairs on the back of Krissy's neck. Aslan lay curled and sleeping in her lap. She'd taken her camp chair west of the City Dogs' training building to find some isolation from the party happening in the outdoor agility field to the east. After angling her chair, she'd sat to watch the sunset pinking the early June sky.

Judy rounded the corner of the metal building. Dressed in shorts and a tee for the picnic and fun run, she carried an iced tea and an old-fashioned webbed lawn chair which she opened next to Krissy. She took a seat and, without speaking, joined in the sunset surveillance. The flat Oklahoma horizon was dappled with white outbuildings and shadowed green trees that swayed in the warm evening breeze.

"It's a beautiful evening." Judy broke the silence.

"Yeah."

"Thinking about Cool?"

"Yeah."

After several minutes, Krissy said, "I feel so bad for Mia. I can't imagine that happening to Aslan. You know, no warning. All's fine one second, and he's on the ground the next. And then there Cool was, lying in the street, and Charlotte starts yelling at Mia, accusing her of the accident. Right there. Cool's body was feet away. What if it'd been Aslan, and Dad had run out and asked me why I wasn't lying in the street, too?

"Then, Charlotte strips Cool away from Mia, like he's no more than trash. How can Mia go forward? She had Cool off lead. I saw him off lead."

Judy nodded. "It was a tragic accident. It's a lot to process."

Krissy twined Aslan's fur with gentle fingers. "Sometimes Mia was mean to Cool. But I could tell she loved him. I don't know if Mia ever hit him after I caught her that time. And I don't understand the dichotomy of a person who can hit a dog and love a dog, or of a mom who can wonder why her daughter isn't lying in the street with her dog and yet also love her daughter."

Judy took a sip of her tea. "People don't always act consistently. A person can get angry, become abusive, and turn around an hour later and bestow hugs and kisses with affection. Look at Mia's role model. Her mom leads a life filled with bursts of anger followed by moments of great compassion. Maybe Charlotte's parents lived that in front of her, too. So, the echoes continue down to Mia. Does that make the abuse of Cool okay? No. It doesn't.

"I'm amazed by dogs," Judy continued. "We humans are so, so damaged and unreliable. One minute, we're telling them we love them. The next, we're yelling at them for some minor infraction. Yet, they continue to love. They remind me of God. Their love is unconditional."

Krissy nodded. "I've thought that before, too. But Mia has to live with it, you know? Being that person who failed her dog—hitting him, letting him off lead near a busy street. If I'd been in her shoes and Aslan had been hit, I couldn't live with myself. What if Aslan had gotten loose and died?"

"It hurts—both emotionally and physically—to lose a dog, but you go on," Judy said. "You find healing from family, friends, and other dogs."

"I don't know. If I were at fault, I just can't see it."

"Let me tell you a story," Judy said. "Daniel was in his last year of college, and he owned a border collie named Grace. A beautiful, fitting name, it turns out. He and Grace did agility together in Tennessee where he attended school. They went to an agility trial one weekend, and their last class on Saturday, a Standard course, was a 'zone of totality' run. Daniel was over the moon, as you can well understand." She smiled at Krissy. "On a super high, he couldn't fathom sitting around the hotel for the rest of the afternoon, so he gathered some agility friends from the trial and went hiking in the Great Smoky Mountains. Once they'd hiked far from the road, Daniel let Grace off lead as did the other handlers. The weather was perfect, the camaraderie pleasant, and the dogs were having a fantastic time checking out the trail.

"The group turned back as the sun dipped west, and soon they neared the main road. Daniel knew where they were, but Grace was having so much fun that he didn't call her in to be leashed. She was in sight and had an almost perfect recall. Then one of the guys in the group began telling an entertaining story, and Daniel became engrossed in the tale. Grace wandered toward the road."

The setting sun made the tears in Judy's eyes sparkle. "I don't need to tell you details. You can see where this is going. Grace died, and Daniel was devastated. He still suffers from the loss, and he always will. Even now, he sometimes blames himself, although I have told him over and over it was an accident. He didn't get distracted and lose track of Grace on purpose. He didn't kill her.

"He's told me he thinks God inspired the naming of Grace. He knows Grace would want him to find forgiveness, to find grace. Most of the time, Daniel lives in the understanding of this forgiveness and the understanding of the word *accident*. Occasionally, though, he goes to the dark place where blame lives."

With a sad half-smile, Judy continued, "Mia will have to travel the road Daniel traveled. I pray she can find grace there. We humans are full of good, and yet we also fail—sometimes spectacularly. When I fail—and believe me, I do—I think of the photos Daniel has of a beautiful border collie named Grace."

They sat in silence for a while as Krissy absorbed Judy's revelation. It explained a lot—Daniel's occasional moodiness and his tears after their hybrid run at Nationals when he asked if it had been a "zone of totality" run. He'd touched Grace's soul during their last run. Krissy bet he held fast to that bond to this day, finding peace in the memory.

"When I got Aslan, I didn't like him," Krissy confessed, looking at her sleeping pup in her lap. "I've never told anyone that. He wasn't what I wanted. He was so serious. He didn't play. He wasn't bold. He wasn't puppy-like. He kinda sniffed around and always seemed to be thinking. But here I am, three years later, and I love him to pieces. He's a part of me now—my heartdog. In three years, he's changed from serious to happy. In three years, he's changed my life from one of fear and loneliness to a life full of adventure and friendships."

She lifted her eyes to meet Judy's. "Dogs make us better people, don't they? They sharpen us."

Judy nodded. "Like iron sharpens iron. Yes. That's what best friends do."

Pins and needles pricked Krissy's leg from holding Aslan in her lap, but she didn't care. He lay so peacefully, in that state between wakefulness and sleep, listening to the voices of two people he adored—his body warm and limp.

"When I first saw Aslan, I almost walked out on the ugly, long-nosed, brown-spotted pig on stilts that masqueraded as a sheltie puppy," Krissy said. "If I had, I would never have found agility. I wouldn't be me. I'd be—less."

"God gives us the right dog at the right time." Judy's face broke into a wide smile. "I believe that with all my heart. Aslan is your Grace."

Aslan sat up, looked at Krissy with drowsy eyes, and leaned his body against hers in a doggie hug. She heard the laughter of her friends floating from the agility field and smelled hot dogs and hamburgers cooking on the grill. Mike's baritone voice soared above the others. He was in the middle of another Honey-meets-Cool story.

And above it all, a teeter banged.

Map Legend

A legend of the obstacles on the agility maps used throughout the book. All maps were produced using *Clean Run Course Designer 4.*

Map Legend

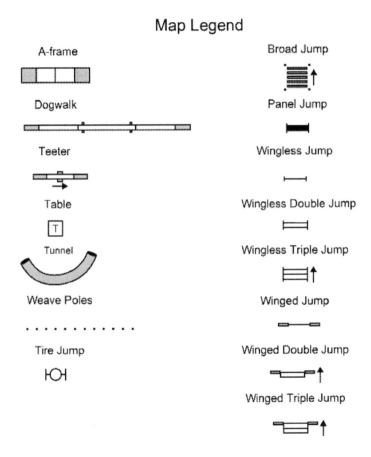

A-frame

Dogwalk

Teeter

Table

Tunnel

Weave Poles

Tire Jump

Broad Jump

Panel Jump

Wingless Jump

Wingless Double Jump

Wingless Triple Jump

Winged Jump

Winged Double Jump

Winged Triple Jump

Agility Equipment

A-Frame – Dog must run up one ramp and down the other. At least part of one paw must be in the yellow contact zone before the dog exits the obstacle.

Teeter – Dog must run up teeter, then tip teeter past the fulcrum until the teeter hits the ground. At least part of one paw must be in the yellow contact zone and the end of the teeter must hit the ground before the dog exits the teeter.

Dogwalk – Dog must run up the ramp, across the top, and down the other ramp. At least part of one paw must be in the yellow contact zone before the dog exits the dogwalk.

Pause Table – Dog jumps onto table and must remain there for five seconds before continuing the course.

Weave Poles – Dog weaves in a slalom motion through twelve poles. Dogs must enter the poles between Poles One and Two on the left shoulder and weave without skipping a pole.

Jump – Dog must jump over the obstacle without dropping a bar. There are several types of jumps including triple jumps, double jumps, jumps with wings, jumps without wings, wall jumps, and tire jumps.

Tunnel – Dog must enter one side of the tunnel and exit through the other.

Glossary

Agility Trial – An agility competition.

Back-Chaining – A learning process in which the end of a behavior is learned before the beginning of the behavior: for instance, learning the end of a piece of music before learning the beginning.

Blind Cross – A handling maneuver where the human teammate crosses in front of the dog to indicate a change of direction without spinning.

Clean Run – A run with no faults in time or accuracy.

Conformation – A breed show where the judge compares each purebred dog on how well they conform to the breed's type, often called the breed's *standard*.

Contact Equipment – The A-frame, dogwalk, and teeter are the pieces of contact equipment in agility.

Contact Zone – The yellow painted rectangle at the bottom of the ramps on the A-frame, teeter, and dogwalk. A dog must place at least part of one paw into the yellow before exiting the piece of contact equipment.

Excellent – The advanced/intermediate level in AKC agility. Qualifying on Excellent courses requires less speed than Master's but the same accuracy.

Front Cross – A handling maneuver in which the human team-mate, while in front of the dog, spins toward the dog to indicate a change of direction.

Hybrid Class – An agility class offered at the AKC National Championships that is a combination of Standard and Jumpers with Weaves classes.

Jumper with Weaves Class – An AKC agility class consisting of only jumps, weave poles, and sometimes tunnels.

MACH – Master Agility Champion title. AKC's highest agility title.

Master's – The advanced level in AKC agility. Qualifying on Master's courses requires no faults in time or accuracy.

Non-Qualifying Score (NQ) – Given when a dog does not pass an agility course. Requirements for passing vary based on the level in which the dog is competing.

Novice – The beginning level in agility. Qualifying on Novice courses requires less accuracy and speed.

Open – The intermediate level in AKC agility. Qualifying on Open courses requires more accuracy and speed than Novice courses, but less than Master's courses.

Performance Prospect Puppy – A puppy who shows the potential to do well in performance dog sports such as agility, obedience, fly ball, nose work, and others.

Pushback – Also called a backside or other names. This is a maneuver in which the dog is cued to run to the back side of the jump and jump it rather than jump the more obvious front side.

Qualifying Score (Q) – Earned when a dog passes an agility course. Requirements for passing vary based on the level in which the dog is competing.

Rear Cross – A handling maneuver in which the human teammate crosses behind the dog to indicate a change of direction.

Refusal – A fault incurred on course when a dog spins, halts, or turns away from an agility obstacle the dog is supposed to take.

Send – An agility behavior which occurs when the dog runs ahead of the handler to perform one or more obstacles.

Serpentine – Three or more jumps or other obstacles in which the dog's path makes an S pattern to properly complete.

Standard Class – An AKC agility class in which the dogs have to navigate all the various types of agility equipment, including the contact obstacles.

Title – Letters before or after a dog's name indicating achievements in the agility ring. Titles are earned by accumulating qualifying scores in agility trials and other canine sports.

Walk-through – A set amount of time given for agility handlers to familiarize themselves with an agility course by walking the course without their dogs. Walk-throughs are held for each agility class prior to the beginning of the class.

Wrong Course – A fault incurred when a dog takes an obstacle out of sequence.

Author Notes

When I was a little girl, I had an insatiable appetite for books about dogs and horses, and after each story, I would wonder if the dog or horse depicted in the book was based on a real animal. So, to answer that sense of wonder a reader may have in this case: yes, Aslan was real. He didn't live with Krissy, her family, or Ruffis, but he did cavort with Honey the beardie.

Aslan was born in 2001 in a suburb of Dallas, Texas, to a breeder very different from the one in the book. He came to live with me in Oklahoma City where together we learned agility and competed for about a decade. The real Aslan earned six AKC agility championships, qualified for the AKC Agility National Championships nine times, attended Nationals four times, and competed in the National's Challengers class in 2013.

But it wasn't his agility accomplishments that set him apart in my heart. It was his loyalty, spirit, and joy. I think I captured Aslan well in these pages, and the dog you see "sticking birds together" in the novel is very akin to the real-life one.

Aslan died a few days shy of his fifteenth birthday in 2016 from renal disease, and my heart has been a bit lost ever since.

Ruffis the collie was also real, although he lived and died years before Aslan was born. The two were never contemporaries except in the pages of this book. Ruffis served as my canine sidekick when I was in high school.

All the human characters (and most of the canine ones) in this book are fictional, and while Krissy's family has similarities to my real one, they are substantially products of my imagination.

Krissy is also fictional, although very heavily based upon myself. I gave my invented doppelgänger more backbone than I had at her age, which was fun to write.

I tried to make the depictions of agility as realistic as possible. I took a few liberties, but I wanted those involved in the sport to nod in understanding and agreement as they read. I hope that on the whole I achieved this.

For more on what is fact and fiction in *Aslan: Running Joy* and also for photos and videos of the real Aslan and Ruffis, check out my website at kristinkaldahl.com.

And thank you for choosing to spend your precious time with Aslan, Krissy, and their friends.

Thank you from CrossLink Publishing

We appreciate your support of quality faith-based books. If you enjoyed this book would you consider sharing it with others?

- Mention the book on Facebook Twitter, Pinterest, or your blog.
- Recommend this book to your small group, book club, or work colleagues.
- Pick up a copy for someone you know who would be encouraged by this book.
- Write a review on Amazon.com, Goodreads.com or BarnesandNoble.com.
- To learn about our latest releases, check out the Coming Soon section of our website: CrossLinkPublishing.com